broken boys can't love

Cover Design: Emily Wittig Designs
Editing: KM Editing
Formatting: Micalea Smeltzer

broken boys can't love

micalea smeltzer

For all the hopeless romantics.

I hope you have your own "book-worthy" romance.

one

Millie

I'M LIVING IN A HOUSEFUL OF DUDES.

Not just any dudes either, no, a bunch of jocks, one of which being my brother.

But I won't let that stop my sunshine.

I, Millicent Madison, am finally, blessedly, on my own. Well, for the most part. I love my parents, I really do, and I'm so lucky to have such great ones, but they can be overbearing. This is why I was so insistent on enrolling at Aldridge University. It's my brother's senior year, so that means he won't be around much longer. It gives me time with him before we fully transition to adulthood, while also getting to stand on my own two feet.

But as exciting as all of that is, there's one teeny tiny issue.

My brother's friend, and now my roommate, Jude.

Hot as fuck with tousled dark brown, nearly black hair, a constant 5 o'clock shadow, angry brows coupled with the most perfect pillowy lips I've ever seen. They don't make guys like him back home. No, those guys are preppy prep school little shits that just want to spend daddy's money and crash their expensive cars. I know from my brother, Cree, that Jude comes from a prominent family, but you wouldn't know it with the rugged handsomeness of him. He's just different.

And a total manwhore—at least, according to Cree.

The four of us—me, Cree, Jude, and their friend Daire—have only been settled in the off-campus home for a day. Classes don't start for a few more days and I'm already a nervous wreck over it.

Everything is so big here.

It's overwhelming.

My alarm goes off, jostling me from my thoughts and reminding me that I've spent the past ten minutes awake, staring at my ceiling, while thinking about Jude. The only reason I even have my alarm set is because I want to get used to getting up early again since I spent the summer sleeping in until noon unless I had to be at the dance studio. I've been doing ballet practically since I could walk. I know a lot of people, my family included, were shocked when I didn't accept an offer from an art school with a ballet program. But while I love ballet with my whole being, I don't want to be a professional ballerina. I want to continue appreciating it as a hobby.

Throwing my covers off, I swing my legs out of bed and open the bathroom door to the shared space between mine and Jude's room. I'm not paying attention, or I would've noticed the light on inside, the barest hint of yellow leaking from beneath the door.

Opening it, steam hits me in the face, and a moment later my jaw drops at the sight of a naked Jude getting out of the shower. He hasn't heard me yet, and I'm frozen, staring at his ... at his *penis*. Because it's right there, and it's huge, and it's just hanging *right in front of me*. I've never seen one in person. A penis. Cock. Dick. Whatever you want to call it. I mean, I've seen them in porn before, but not ... not like this.

Are they always so big?

A smattering of dark hair trails beneath his navel, leading down to well-trimmed hair, that frames his ... cock.

"Jesus, fuck," he curses, grabbing a towel and holding it front of his junk.

Why does he have to hide it? I wasn't done looking.

"I'm sorry," I cringe, slapping a hand over my eyes. "I-I opened the door and you and I and your—" I wave my hand in the vicinity of said cock was just moments ago.

Why didn't he lock the door to my room?

Why am I glad he didn't?

He blows out a breath, looking frustrated. Not with me, though, but with himself. "Don't tell your brother. He won't believe this was an accident." His tone is utterly perturbed.

I peak through my fingers and find that, sadly, the towel has been wrapped around his waist. Though, he certainly makes my pale pink towel look way better than it did on the shelves at the store.

"That's my towel," I state stupidly, because frankly I'm still in shock after seeing my first in-person penis. This is a monumental moment for me.

He looks down at the pale pink—my favorite color—towel and back at me. "Do you ... want it back?"

"Oh, um, no. You ... uh ... just keep it on."

His lips twitch with the threat of a smile, his hands on his trim waist. God, he has big hands. "Millicent?"

I wrinkle my nose at the use of my full first name since I prefer Millie. "Yes?"

"I need to finish up in here."

"Right!" I practically scream the word. I hustle back a few steps and slam the door closed, his laughter audible through the wood.

I smack my hand to my forehead. I hate myself.

I THOUGHT it would be genius to just move my stuff to Daire's bathroom and use that one since it would save me from more run-ins with Jude's penis.

Even if I kind of want to see it again.

But the idea of him walking in on *me* naked? That's terrifying. Not that I think he'd do anything about it, but... It would be embarrassing for me. Already in the few days we've all been living under the same roof I've heard Daire and my brother ribbing him about his exploits and the types of girls he likes.

They sound nothing like me.

Not with my petite frame. I have barely a B-cup, but my butt is pretty nice, I guess. Ballet keeps me toned, but it also makes me more muscular than other girls.

One of the girls at my high school sneered at my legs once when we were changing for gym. She told me guys don't like muscular girls and that not only stuck with me, but it hurt too. I don't know what makes people think they have any right to comment on anyone's body.

There's a knock on my bedroom door. I've mostly been hiding out in my room today since the guys have all commandeered the living room.

"Come in." I know more than likely it's my brother.

The door squeaks open and he leans against the open doorway with an amused smile. His wavy brown hair is pushed back from his forehead like he keeps shoving it out of his eyes. "I hear you have a ton of razors in the bathroom. A bathroom that isn't even yours."

My cheeks pinken. There's no way I can tell him *why*. Not only because I promised Jude I wouldn't say anything, but also because it was a total accident walking in on him and I know Cree wouldn't believe that. He'd probably twist it around and think Jude just came into my room, dick swinging, for funsies.

My brother, bless him, is a tad melodramatic.

Not that I would ever tell him that.

"Not a ton—there's like three. One for my legs, the backup for my legs, and the one for my lady bits." I count them off on my fingers, hoping the mention of *lady bits* is enough to send my brother running down the hall.

He gags, my words having their intended effect. "Ugh, Mills. I don't need to hear about your lady bits."

"Why *are* you asking me about my razors?" I ask curiously. I didn't think Daire would mind enough to say something to my brother.

"Because Daire cut his foot on one."

Oh.

"Aw." I tilt my head, pouting my lips. "Should I kiss it and make it better for the poor wittle baby?"

Cree's eyes narrow to slits. "Don't even joke about kissing my friends in any way. Just keep your razors picked up and hair from going down the drain. Oh and all in *your* bathroom." He points a forceful finger at the door that connects the Jack and Jill bathroom between my room and Jude's.

I love my brother, but his over-protectiveness is a bit much. It's so stereotypical.

"Ugh, but I hate sharing a bathroom with *him*." He glares at me. We both know who I'm talking about. It's not even that I actually hate it, it's just awkward. More awkward than Daire, but I'm not sure why that is.

You know exactly why it is, Millie.

Because I'm attracted to Jude, not Daire, but I'm sure to a guy like Jude I'm nothing more than a child. An annoyance. Perhaps he even potentially sees me as a kid sister

"All right, whatever, now go. You're getting on my nerves." I shoo my brother out of my room, not wanting to deal with any more of his questioning.

His color pales a bit and I know instantly what he's thinking. "Jude didn't do anything funny did he?"

"Oh, God. No! Nothing like that! He just annoys me. Tell Daire I'll move my crap back later." I cross my arms over my chest, annoyed. At my brother. At Daire. At Jude. Maybe living in the dorms would've been easier after all. But I look around my private bedroom and think about how I have a whole house and full kitchen to use and decide that I'm definitely better off here.

Cree shakes his head, easing out of my room and shutting the door behind him.

With my brother gone, I pick up my laptop and look over the map of the campus for the millionth time. I've already visited campus a few times, seeking out the buildings my classes are in, but my anxiety is still through the roof. I don't like feeling like a fish out of water, which is ironic, since I'm naturally a pretty bubbly person who lets things roll off my shoulders. But I guess at the end of the day, we all have different things that make us anxious.

There's another knock on my door not very long later. I groan, setting my laptop aside. Getting up, I swing the door open with a little more attitude than necessary, but *seriously* is it so difficult to get a moment of peace in this house? If it's about those stupid razors again, I'm going to scream.

"What?" I snap at my brother who stands on the other side.

"Whoa." He rears back, his hands flying up in front of his chest like he thinks he has to ward me off or something.

"I wanted to let you know the guys and I are headed to the bar."

"Of course, you are."

His brows furrow at my less than nice tone. "What's that for Millicent?"

"Nothing, I'm just in a bad mood." I know it's silly, I wouldn't want to go anyway, but he didn't think to ask me to go. There's food at bars. Let me stuff my face with tacos, what's the big deal? But since I'm the pesky little sister, I guess it's easier to leave me behind than even ask if I want to go.

"About what?"

"Nerves." It's not a total lie. I'm feeling a little raw over classes starting and feeling as if I don't have it completely sorted. I'm also a tad hangry, but I don't tell him that. The protein bar I scarfed down a few hours ago wasn't enough to fill my grumbling stomach.

"Aw, Mills." He pulls me into a hug. Cree understands how I get over new situations. After all, it was his lap I threw up into when I was eight and started at a new ballet school. "Don't be nervous."

"College is scary, Cree." And it *is*. It seems to be hitting me all at once now, that I'm an adult. This is what I wanted, independence, but that doesn't mean I can't be wary over what a big deal that is.

"You've got this. Besides, you have three awesome roommates to help you through it."

Jude's dick flashes unbidden through my mind.

Do not think about your brother's friend's penis in front of said brother. That's just weird.

But- now my brain just keeps ping-ponging the word around my skull.

"Ha. You guys are seniors. You'll forget all about my poor pathetic freshman self."

And it's true. It's to be expected.

"Not a chance." He ruffles my hair like I'm a tiny tot. "I gotta go but text me if you want me to bring you back something."

"I have a car, and I'm capable of using the kitchen," I remind him. My ability to get around a kitchen is something I'm proud of, considering neither of our parents are great cooks.

"Hey, it's just an offer. Take it or leave it."

I take a step back. "Have fun with the boys."

He smiles, tipping his head in a nod and then he's heading down the hall.

It feels like forever before the boys finally leave. I even made a trip down for a drink, expecting them to be gone, and they were still home. Eventually, though, I heard the Uber pull up and decided to use my alone time to my advantage by moving all my stuff back to the shared bathroom and taking the longest, hottest shower I've had in the past few days.

I blow dry my hair halfway and gather it up into a bun before changing into a pair of blue sleep shorts and a tank top. I don't bother with a bra, it's not like my boobs are that big anyway, and with no one home, I don't give a shit.

Padding down the stairs, I hum softly as I make my way to the refrigerator.

I eye what we have, trying to decide what I want to make. Thankfully, the fridge is fully stocked thanks to the guys and their need to keep a pretty strict diet with their sports.

There are a lot of greens, lots of chicken too, so the simplest answer seems to be to cook a chicken breast and put it on top of a salad. Besides, I don't see the point in making something that takes more time with no one else to eat it.

Sitting down at the table, I eat by myself. It's a bit strange, since I'm used to my parents being around, or my brother, or even friends. It's surprisingly nice, just myself and the quiet hum of the house.

Washing up my dishes when I'm finished, I pop a bag of popcorn then settle in the living room, putting on one of my favorite shows from the beginning. *Vampire Diaries* is a guilty pleasure for me. I can never get enough of Damon and Stefan. I refuse to choose between the two.

I'm only fifteen or so minutes into the first episode when I hear the hum of the garage door going up.

Why is it going up?

I freeze. The guys shouldn't be back yet. It's still pretty early for them to have finished up at the bar.

I sink down on the couch, practically hiding beneath the blanket.

The garage door into the house opens and closes, boots loud on the hardwood floor.

The light suddenly flips on in the living room and I shriek at the big form now highlighted in the archway. The popcorn bowl nearly tumbles to the floor, but by some miracle I manage to save it.

"What the fuck?" Jude curses, clearly just as surprised as I am.

"You jerk!" I toss a handful of popcorn at him. It bounces right off his muscular chest. "You scared me! I thought you were an intruder."

"Intruders know garage codes now?" He turns the light

back off, and moves through the living room, joining me on the couch.

Why oh why is he sitting on the couch with me?

"Do you know nothing?" I snap at him. "I watched this documentary one time about this murderer dude who used like a universal garage opener to get into people's homes."

He nods along with my rambling. "Okay."

"You could've texted me and told me you guys were coming back."

"I don't have your number, and it's just me."

I blink at him. "Just you?"

"That's what I said."

"Why?" From what Cree's told me about Jude I can't imagine him going to a bar and coming home without a companion for the evening. Not that I'm complaining. I'm not sure I want to hear him having sex practically right next to my room.

And it's definitely not because I have a teeny-tiny crush on the guy.

Sue me. He's hot. I think any female with a pulse would acknowledge he's good-looking whether he's their type or not.

"Wasn't feeling it tonight." He shoves his big hand in my bowl of popcorn, his knuckles dusted lightly with hair.

"Get your hand out of my popcorn." I try to yank the bowl away, but he grabs ahold of it, holding it steadfastly between us.

"It's our popcorn now."

"No, it's not. You're crashing my party."

"Party?" He repeats, looking around. "This place is rocking."

"It's a party of one," I retort, trying in vain to get my popcorn back. He still doesn't budge.

"What are we watching? This looks familiar."

"*We* are not watching anything. *I'm* watching *Vampire Diaries*."

His lips twitch with amusement. "Nah, I'm joining you."

I think my heart picks up speed. "Why?"

He shrugs. "It looks interesting."

I bite my tongue, holding back more words. "Fine." I cross my arms over my chest. His eyes follow the movement and I look down, realizing belatedly that I've unintentionally pushed up my cleavage and it's very obvious I'm not wearing a bra.

I let my arms drop, pulling the blanket up.

"You know," he begins, going in for more popcorn, "we should try to get along. We're roommates after all. It'd be nice if we could be friends."

I narrow my eyes on *my* popcorn in his big meaty hand. "I'm shocked you know how to be friends with someone who possesses a vagina." I have no idea where that comment came from. It sort of flew from my mouth.

For a second, he looks almost offended, but just as quickly the expression clears and he flashes a winning smile, show-casing perfect straight white teeth. "You haven't even had your first day on campus yet and you're already hearing rumors about me?"

"My brother."

"Ah," he nods, something almost sad in his eyes, "he's scared I'm going to corrupt you."

"I don't know about that."

Okay, so maybe it's exactly that.

He smiles again, but there's nothing genuine in it. "Nah, it's okay. He's already given me at least twenty long-winded speeches on leaving you alone and we haven't even lived under the same roof for a full week yet. It must be some sort of record."

"And clearly," I wave a hand around us, "it's working."

He kicks his shoes off, then rests his feet on the ottoman. "I'm watching a show with you. Not corrupting you. I *am* capable of keeping my hands to myself, contrary to popular belief."

"So … what? You want to be my friend?"

His eyes drift lazily over to me, meeting my gaze steadily. "I could do with another friend. What about you?"

My heart skips a beat. "I … yeah."

It's not like I have any friends on campus yet. Only my brother.

"Good. But Millie?"

"Mhmm?" I hum around a mouthful of popcorn.

His tongue slides out the slightest bit, gliding over his top lip. "Friends don't look at my cock like you did."

My jaw drops, popcorn falling out, and Jude?

He just laughs.

IT'S the first day of classes and campus is a colossal maze, one I'm hopelessly lost in.

Sure, I took a tour last year with my parents, and I know some things from visiting my brother. But visiting and actually attending are two vastly different things.

Panic seizes my chest, my information packet with my schedule and building information clutched in my fist.

Where the frick is the science building?

My lower lip wobbles, and I spin in a circle.

I will not cry. I will not cry. Not on my first day.

I blow out a breath.

Come on, Millie. Be sensible. You have a brother who goes here. Text him.

Right. Okay. That makes total sense. I push my hair back off my sweaty forehead.

Wait, why am I sweating?

Stop getting distracted! You're going to be late!

I quickly type out a text.

Me: This campus is HUGE

Me: <GIF Attachment>

Me: I think I'm lost.

I wait for the appropriate brotherly response, but none comes.

Me: How hard can it possibly be to find the science department?

Surely, that'll prod him to help me.

Me: Dude, help me.

No response from Cree. *Ugh.*

Me: I bet you have your phone off in class. You goody two shoes.

I don't have Daire or Jude's phone numbers yet, and I'm not sure either would respond to me, even if Jude kind of is my friend.

"Hey," I call out to a passing student who looks like they're probably a junior. "Where's the science building?"

The girl looks at me like I've lost my mind. I touch my damp forehead again. Do I look like a sweat-drenched swamp monster or something?

She points. "You're right beside it."

My mouth falls open, blinking at the bronze plaque on the building that says *Science Department.* Wow, in my panic I totally missed that.

"So sorry for bothering you. Thank you."

I dash for the entrance of the building, immediately inhaling the familiar fumes of formaldehyde and cleaner.

I type out another message to my brother.

Me: Never mind, I was in the right place all along. Tata.

Aldridge is an old school, and that means most of the buildings don't have elevators.

I run up the stairs as fast I can, my bag banging into my

hip. I've already learned my lesson today—the messenger bag has got to go and I'm buying a regular backpack. My shoulder is *killing* me.

I find the right room and burst inside.

Despite being in good shape from hours and hours of ballet, I sound like I'm dying as I gasp for air.

All eyes in the room shoot to me.

I hold up a hand. "Don't worry. I'm okay."

Gathering myself, I spot an empty chair at one of the lab tables and take it.

At the front of the room my professor clears his throat. "Shall we begin?"

two

Jude

AS I WALK ACROSS CAMPUS TO THE ATHLETIC center, the last thing I should be thinking about is the look on Millie's face when I caught her looking at my cock. There was innocence in her sweet wide-eyed gaze, her plump lips parted in awe.

Yeah, she was fucking *awed* by my cock.

It puts a smirk on my face, one I instantly wipe away because Millicent Madison is off-limits to the likes of me.

Not only is she Cree's sister, but she has virgin written

all over her. In fact, I'd almost bet on the fact that she's never been kissed.

I'm not going down that path.

Virgin pussy gets attached, and I don't do relationships.

Not anymore at least.

Besides, that was days ago so I'm not sure why I'm even still thinking about it.

I open the door to the building and bump fists with Carter Compton, one of my teammates, who comes in behind me.

"Hey," I pop out one of my Air Pods, "what's up with you?"

"Nothing much, man. First day back jitters and all that."

"I wouldn't know about those," I joke.

But truly, I don't get nervous.

Nerves aren't good in any situation. Not at school, not at work, and not on a football field.

"I'm sure you wouldn't. You're always so solid."

I'm not sure many people would describe me that way.

Playboy.

Manwhore.

Pussy Chaser.

Those are terms I'm used to hearing when it comes to me.

It wasn't always that way, but those days are in the past.

I follow Carter into the state-of-the-art gym. It's shared amongst the athletes, the whole building is, between the

Olympic size swimming pool as well as all the coaches' offices.

I say goodbye to Carter as he heads off to work with the D-men and I head over to my offensive guys.

Playing wide-receiver means I have to not only be quick physically, but my mind has to be in sharp focus. I like that the position takes more than brute force. It forces me to stay on top of my game.

The thing I hate is that our team's quarterback, Keaton Haas, is dating my ex.

She shattered my heart. Completely obliterated it and moved right on to him.

The worst part is, he's not even an asshole so I can't even hate the dude.

According to my ex-Macy, and Keaton himself, we were broken up when they got together.

It's in the past now, so it's not like it even matters.

Then why are you still so fucking hung up on it?

I shove that thought out of my brain and get to work. It doesn't serve anyone well to dwell on the past.

IT'S LATE when I finally make it to the dining hall on campus. I'm meeting my little brother. It's his first day of his freshman year and I haven't seen him since we rolled into the small Tennessee town that's home to the university.

Grabbing my food, I scan the massive space searching in the area he told me he was.

I finally spot him, impossible to miss with his wide shoulders.

I always tried to get him to play football, but he never had any interest in the sport. Instead, he chose swimming.

Swimming.

Of all things.

Swim caps, and speedos, and goggles.

It's what earned him his nickname.

"Hey, Bug," I say in greeting, setting down my tray and plopping into the chair across from him. Girls at the next table size us both up, but Jonah is absolutely clueless of their perusal. He's always ignored attention from the ladies. Unlike me.

"I wish you'd stop calling me that," he grumbles. "It's such a stupid nickname. We're in college now. Besides, my goggles don't make me look like a—"

"Bug," I finish for him. "Hate to break it to you, but the nickname goes nowhere." He groans, shaking his head. Reaching over, I ruffle his shaggy head. "When are you going to cut this mop?"

He shoves me off. "Not any time soon."

"Are you trying to grow a man-bun?" I arch a brow in curiosity.

"No. I kept it buzzed for years." He shrugs his shoulders up to his ears. "I like the change."

"Have you talked to mom?" I ask, biting into my dinner of salmon, cooked spinach, and sweet potato.

Jonah groans, wiping his mouth with the back of his hand. "No less than twenty times in the past twenty-four hours alone. What about you?"

I chuckle, pushing spinach around with my fork. "A few less than that. Maybe fifteen times."

"She's so over-protective. God love her. What's she going to do when it's Jade's turn?" He refers to our youngest sister.

All J names in our family.

Jude, Jonah, and Jade.

"Poor Jade isn't going to be able to catch a break."

Jonah pinches his brow. "That's for sure."

We finish up with our dinner and I walk with Jonah back to his dorm before I head to where I parked my truck. I crank the engine, and I'm about to back out when I see them.

Macy and Keaton walking hand in hand toward one of the coffee shops on campus.

She's smiling up at him, her long chestnut hair spiraling down her back. He says something to her, and she laughs. I used to make her laugh like that until...

Well, until.

They reach the door and Keaton's hand goes to the small of her waist, his other to do the door.

I finally back out, the rumble of my truck catching their attention, but I don't look back.

THE SOUND of the running shower hits my ears the second I walk into my room. I drop my bag on the floor, kicking off my shoes and changing into a pair of sweats and a wife-beater.

Wife-beater, such a stupid name for a guy's tank.

I check my phone, going through texts, some with names attached, others just a string of numbers. Most of them asking if I want to meet up.

Is this all you are? The guy who's only known for sex?

My momma would beat me to within an inch of my life if she knew what I'd become. She always adored Macy and she's never understood why things ended. Not that I've told her the truth. That's a complicated, painful discussion I've never wanted to have with my mom.

Turning around, I spy Millie's pink towel hanging on the back of my bedroom door. I should wash it and give it back, but for some stupid reason I haven't. I actually have my own towels, but when she caught me off guard one of her pink ones was the first thing my hands landed on.

I should forget about it, but I've replayed the look on her face when she caught me naked roughly five-hundred thousand times in the days since. Might've jacked off to the visual once. Or twice.

It's no secret my love life has been … scandalous, to put it lightly since my long-term relationship with Macy ended. I got my heartbroken and for some reason I've convinced myself screwing my way through campus is the way to fix it, even if that hasn't worked yet. But even with all of those experiences, no chick has ever looked at my dick as eager as Millie did.

I press my fists to my eyes, trying to block out the image of the surprised O of her mouth, but nope, it's still there.

The shower cuts off, the curtain squeaking when it's pulled back.

Do not picture her naked, Jude. Don't do it.

Too late.

I cross the room to where I left my phone, flick through them to a random one and send a reply.

This is exactly what I need.

three

Millie

It's official, I love this campus.

It's gorgeous, the school so rich in history. Not to mention the old buildings with creeping vines of ivy and wisteria makes me feel like I've been transported to a European country. I find myself practically floating on the way to all my classes. There's something so magical here.

Breezing into the dining hall, I get into line and grab a salad with grilled chicken. After swiping a bottle of water, I sit down at an empty table. I haven't made any friends yet, but it's only the end of the first week, so I'm not feeling too worried.

While I eat, I check my text messages, replying back to my mom, and my brother asking if pizza's okay for dinner.

Finishing my lunch, I toss my trash and head to my final class of the day. I'm glad we've made it to the weekend. My schedule is packed, not leaving much breathing room, and I want nothing more than to veg on the couch and continue my binge-watching sesh.

Psychology is my last course of the day. It's my third time having this class, and I think it might be my favorite. I expected to hate it, but so far the professor is engaging and the content intrigues me.

Slipping into the large room, I take a seat in the middle row. I'm not a front of the classroom kind of girl, never have been, but I don't want to sulk in the back either.

Students trickle into the auditorium for the lecture. Setting down my backpack, I dig out my laptop for notes.

I know it's stupidly ridiculous, but I feel like such a grownup sitting in these lecture halls, typing out notes on a computer. I'm sure soon this feeling will wear off, but for now I'm going to enjoy it.

The room fills up and our professor starts the lesson. Time passes in a blur, and soon class is over. But before he dismisses us, Professor Grant says, "One last thing."

Movement halts, many students pausing in the middle of packing up their bags.

"Next week I'm going to be discussing a semester long

project. I'll be partnering you up with one of your classmates and each of you will be expected to analyze the other over the coming weeks. But," he holds up a finger, "you'll be doing this from the perspective of famous psychologists which I will also assign. You are to be yourself through this project and will be expected to turn in a paper at the end of the semester on your final analysis of your partner through the lens of whoever you're assigned. Got it?" Lots of nods and murmurs fill the hall. "Good. You're dismissed."

I finish stuffing everything in my bag and swing my backpack onto my shoulders, pulling my hair out when it gets caught. My eyes catch with a guy across the aisle, a blush stealing up my cheeks. He ducks his head almost shyly. He's cute, really cute.

Stop thinking about guys, Millie. You need to focus.

With that thought, I stand up a little straighter and head out of the hall and across campus to where I parked my car. There's a ballet studio in town that I want to check out. Even though I don't want to pursue dance as a career, it is something I love, and I want to continue to do in some shape or form.

Opening the back passenger door of my car, I toss my backpack onto the seat and climb in the driver's seat. Blasting the AC, I gather my hair up into a loose messy bun on top of my head.

I put the address for the dance studio into the GPS and let it guide me from campus to the center of nearby downtown. When the GPS chirps at me that I've reached my destination I'm outside a small brick two-story building flanked on either side by restaurants. I find a parking spot on the street and head up the concrete steps to the entrance.

The inside smells of old wood, copious amounts of hairspray, and a mixture of different perfumes. There's a door straight back, and another immediately to my right, with a narrow staircase winding up to the left. That's where the sound of music trickles from—the second floor. I hesitate only a moment before climbing the staircase slowly, my fingers gliding along the railing.

My eyes close as I continue up the stairs, the music filling my body. I can already visualize the movements I would make.

I reach the landing and follow the music down to the end of the hall to the studio room.

Watching from the doorway, a woman, who seems to be around ten years older than me, instructs a class of young girls and one boy. I give a soft knock on the side of the wall, not wanting her to turn around and spot me and think I'm creeping.

Her head jerks in my direction and she claps her hands. "Give me a second guys." Her ballet slippers tap lightly against the wooden floor as she crosses the room. "Hi," she gives me a questioning look. "Can I help you?"

"Um..." I rub my lips together. "Maybe. I hope so?" It comes out as a question. "I'm sorry." I push an errant hair out of my face, since the stupid strand refuses to stay in my bun. "I'm new here. New in town." *Oh, God I'm rambling like a lunatic. She's going to think I'm insane.* "I just started at Aldridge," I explain, tossing my thumb over my shoulder like I'm pointing out the school that's miles away. I don't even know if that's the proper direction. Her brows rise, probably questioning where this tirade is going, so she can get back to work. "I'm a dancer," I explain, gesticulating wildly with my hands. I suddenly wish my mom had followed through with her threat to tie my hands together when I was a child. "I've been dancing my whole life. Ballet is ... it's like oxygen to me. I wanted to know if I could maybe rent out a room from time to time to just come and dance, or if there are advanced classes, or maybe—"

"We could use another instructor."

It's not the female in front of me who answers. Instead, it's a smooth male voice with a slight accent. I turn around to find a man in probably his early thirties. Dark hair is smoothed back, his brows arch above the lightest blue eyes I've ever seen. These aren't ocean eyes. Pure ice is more like it.

"Oh. Hi." I thrust my hand out between us. "I'm Millie. Millicent, but I prefer Millie." Behind me I hear the sound of the teacher walking away to go back to her class. Can't say I blame her for not wanting to listen to my word vomit.

The man takes my hand, giving it a firm shake. "Aleksander. My parents own the studio," he explains. "Would you be interested in teaching?"

I press my lips together. No, it's not what I had in mind.

I've never taught anyone anything, but suddenly, when I think about it, the idea doesn't sound half bad.

"What age?"

"The youngest ones." He crosses his arms over his chest, leaning against the wall behind him. "Anywhere from three to six in age, I'd say."

I do love kids, and I can't help but smile at the image in my mind of making young children fall in love with dance like I have.

"I'm a college student," I explain.

"That's fine. We're wanting to open up classes three nights a week. Probably from around five to six in the evenings for an hour. Would that work for you?"

"Yes!" I practically jump up and down. "That would be amazing."

He clears his throat, nodding his head down the hall. "This isn't a very proper interview, but we'll have to make do." I follow him into an empty studio. He flicks the light on, illuminating our reflections in the wall of mirrors with the barre. Turning to me, he says, "Pretend I'm a child and teach me."

"Teach you?" I sputter. "Uh … okay."

Obviously, it makes sense that he'd want to see that I can actually dance and not only perform the moves myself but teach them too. Not everyone has the ability to impart what they know onto others.

Aleksander turns on some music. Squaring my shoulders, I take a deep breath, and start talking. About dance, ballet, jazz, tap, hip-hop. I speak as if I'm talking to a group of children since I know that's what he wants me to pretend. Then I launch into explaining and demonstrating some of the most simple and basic moves in ballet.

After about fifteen minutes I stop, clasping my hands in front of me. "Well?"

Aleksander smiles slowly, clapping his hands. "Welcome to our humble little company, Millie. We're happy to have you."

I take his hand and it's a done deal.

I WALK INTO THE HOUSE, vibrating with excitement over the fact that I have my first job.

It smells like pizza as I move from the garage back to the kitchen, expecting to run into my brother, or Daire, or even Jude, but there's no one.

Not a single person to share my excitement with.

Dejection settles in the pit of my stomach.

I just ... I guess I feel proud over this endeavor and wanted someone, anyone, to celebrate with me.

"Good job, Millie," I mutter to myself, grabbing a plate. "Good for you. A job. Wow. So awesome." I put two slices onto the plate and pop it into the microwave. "I'm so proud of you."

The last part comes out with a wobbly smile.

I will not cry.

It's silly, to feel bad right now. In the big scheme of things, this isn't important.

The microwave dings, forcing me to grab my plate. I start up the stairs, freezing halfway up them.

"Oh my God! Yes! Yes!" The porn star level screams are very obviously coming from Jude's room, along with the squeaking of his mattress. I hear him groan and hate, absolutely hate, that my core tightens from that pure masculine sound.

But more than anything, I'm pissed.

"Right there, baby. Don't stop. Oh, you feel so good. I love your cock."

I storm up the rest of the stairs, my pizza nearly falling off the plate in the process, but luckily, I'm able to make a quick save of it.

Banging my open hand against the door, I yell, "Other people live here, you know!" The sounds continue, her screams getting louder. "You're not in a porno!" I bang again and again, but she doesn't shut the fuck up. Jude's sounds are much softer. Grunts and groans, but just as annoying. "Did you remember to take your medicine? I think herpes is contagious."

The bed stops squeaking, the girl gets quiet, and I smile to myself.

Satisfied, I move down the hall to my room.

Slamming the door behind me, I sit down on the edge of the bed. I take a bite of pizza. It tastes like freaking cardboard.

four

Jude

"HERPES, REALLY?"

Millie stands silhouetted in her doorway, looking irritated at my disruption. *I'm* the one who should be put out with her antics. Even after I told Livy it was a lie, she didn't believe me, promptly rolling off the bed and putting her clothes on so fast I'm pretty sure she could give firemen a run for their money.

Millie's little stunt will get around and there will be girls who believe it. Granted, there will always be the ones who don't. Thank God for that. I get tested often. I like sex, not diseases, and even though I always wear a condom it's better safe than sorry.

"It's plausible." She crosses her arms over her chest, pushing up the pitiful excuse for breasts she has. Her tiny pert nose sticks up in the air along with her chin.

"Listen," I point a finger at her like she's an unruly child and she glares at the digit like she'd love to rip it off, "I don't know who pissed you off today, but I live here too, and I'm allowed to have sex."

She rolls her eyes, and if I had half a mind, I'd toss her over my shoulder and spank her ass.

You cannot be thinking that kind of shit about Cree's sister. She's untouchable.

"You'll get over it." She moves to shut her door, but I stick my foot in the way, blocking her from shutting it.

"What's wrong?" I demand, my voice deeper than normal. My eyes scan the room behind her, my brain jumping to the conclusion that there's a guy there she's trying to get away from.

Yeah, that's why she's shutting the door on you. *Imbecile.*

"Nothing." But the way she says that one word, the slight wobble to her voice and quiver in her lip tells me that my hunch is correct.

"Don't give me that bullshit, Little Madison. If I ask you what's wrong and there's something wrong, that means you fucking tell me."

She crosses her arms over her chest, looking so small

and in need of protection. "It's stupid," she mumbles so low it's like she doesn't want me to hear.

"Try me."

Big doe eyes dart up to mine. "I got a job, okay? I was excited to tell someone. My brother, Daire, or even you, and—"

"And you got home and they were gone and I was…"

"Fucking someone," she finishes for me.

I rub my hand over my head. "Right."

"Like I said, it was silly." She rolls her eyes, not at me but at herself. "Anyway, you can go now." She tries to shut the door again, but my foot is still there. We both know she's not the kind of girl to slam my foot in the door so we're at an impasse.

"What kind of job?"

She frowns, a sigh rattling her chest. "You don't have to pretend to care."

I cross my arms over my chest, brows furrowed. "Who says I'm pretending?"

"You just knocked on my door to yell at me, I highly doubt you want to hear about this." Her shoulders fall. It's like her body is caving in on itself. It's a strange sight to see, because even in the short time we've been living together, it's obvious to see that Millie is a bright and bubbly person. She's not this meek, insecure version I'm seeing right now.

Keeping my foot where it is, just in case she decides—yet again—to close the door on me, I brace my arms on top of the frame, staring down at her. Her eyes flicker over my arms, taking in the muscles, and I can't help but smile. I didn't do it on purpose, but I might as well have.

She clears her throat, forcing her eyes to mine. I try to hide my smirk, but know I fail when her eyes turn to slits. I can see the sassy retort forming on her tongue, but she swallows it back. With a sigh, she says, "I'm going to be a ballet instructor."

"You dance?"

"Since I could walk." There's a glow in her eyes now. They're a deep blue color with flecks of gold. I lean a little closer, noticing that the ring around her eyes is a green shade. Interesting. I've never seen eyes like hers before. "Dancing is like breathing for me. I can't live without it."

"And you're going to be teaching?"

"Yeah, the little kids." Impossibly she glows brighter.

"Kids, huh?" I rub my jaw, stubble rough against my fingers after I just shaved this morning.

"Mhmm," she hums. "I think it'll be fun."

I narrow my eyes behind her, spotting a plate with two slices of pizza. There's a bite taken out of one and that's it. "Not hungry?"

She looks over her shoulder at where I'm staring. "It tasted like shit."

I chuckle. "That's because your brother always orders from the crappiest pizza place. I won't touch that kind. Want me to order more?" She gives me a puzzled look. "What?" I blink back at her. "I can be nice."

"Do *you* want pizza? I won't let you order it just for me."

"I've gotta eat."

She wets her lips with a swipe of her tongue. "Okay."

"Cool." I back away from her and head to my room, placing the order. Since the pizza won't arrive for at least forty-five minutes I jump in the shower, making sure to lock both doors.

By the time I'm out of the shower, the food should be arriving any minute. I swipe a pair of sweatpants from the drawer and yank them on along with an old football shirt.

Swiping some cash from my wallet, I head downstairs just in time for the doorbell to ring. I hand the delivery driver the cash and take the pie.

As soon as the door's closed, I yell, "Millie! Food's here!"

"I'm literally right here."

My eyes fly back in the direction of the kitchen to find her sitting at the table with an open book beside her and her laptop across from her. A pair of round glasses sits on her pert nose. Her hair is pulled into a bun, showing off the elegant slope of her neck.

Elegant slope of her neck? What the fuck, dude? Who describes a neck as elegant?

But the fact is, Millie's neck checks the box for that descriptor even if I sound ridiculous to my own self.

Clearing my throat, she gives me a funny look. Closing her laptop, she takes her glasses off, setting them on top. I put the pizza on the island, swiping a beer from the fridge. "What do you want to drink?"

"Grab one of my La Croix's please."

I grab one for her, setting it on the counter before I get the plates. Turning around, I nearly collide with Millie.

"Whoa." I step to the side.

"Sorry." There's a faint blush stealing up her cheeks. "I was going to grab those, but then you got them."

"S'okay," I mutter, passing her one. "Let's eat. I'm starving."

"I bet." I arch a brow, her face growing redder.

I decide to mess with her. "Why?"

"Y-You know, because you must've worked up an appetite. You um ... in there ... it sounded very ... uh ... vigorous," she finishes with, scratching the side of her nose nervously.

"Vigorous, huh?" I inch into her space. It's the last thing I should do. If I was smart, I'd back away, eat my pizza, and ignore her comment. But I'm not very smart when it comes to Cree's little sister it seems. "Tell me, Little Madison, what *do* you know about sex?"

Her cheeks burn a violent red, confirming my suspicion that she's a virgin. There's nothing wrong with that, it just reaffirms my need to stay away from her.

"Plenty," she argues, jutting out her chin and sticking her nose in the air.

I take a bite of pizza. Around a mouthful, I say, "Do tell."

Straight white teeth dig into her bottom lip. "I-I don't have anything to prove to you."

"Sure, you don't." I take another bite. "It's okay to tell me the truth."

Her nose goes impossibly higher into the air. If she keeps this up, I'll be able to see straight to her brain. "I don't know what truth you think that is."

Lowering my head, my lips brush the shell of her ear. Total accident. I think. "That you're a virgin." She stands up straighter and there's something like … shame in her eyes, which is strange to me. I'm not making fun of her, at least I don't mean to be. "Nothing to be ashamed of here." I swipe my beer from the counter and take a swig.

"Nothing to be ashamed of, right?" She laughs humorlessly, looking away from me.

I arch a brow, the beer bottle held loosely in my grip. "I feel like there's a story here."

"It's stupid."

When she doesn't elaborate, I prompt with, "I'm waiting."

She sighs, finally digging into a slice of pizza. She chews and swallows before she speaks. "It's really not that deep. It just seemed like all my friends from high school were losing their virginities left and right, then there was me." She shrugs her slender shoulders. "My parents didn't want me dating. It wasn't expressly forbidden, but I knew they wanted me out of high school before I got serious with a guy. I guess to know myself first." She pauses, chewing another bite. "And honestly, between school and my extra curriculars I didn't have time to date. I know you don't have to date for sex, but I'm not the kind of person who could lose my virginity to a practical stranger. It's not that I view it as this sacred thing or anything like that, but sharing your body with someone is intimate no matter what."

"What extra curriculars did you do?"

She seems thrown off by my inquiry, probably wondering why I didn't probe on the dating thing. But I did that. Macy and I were high school sweethearts. I thought we were in it for the long haul, but when the going got tough we couldn't handle it. I used to blame her for all of it, but now I see I was an equal player in our demise.

"Oh, well, obviously ballet and I was student body president."

I smile. "Of course, you were."

Her nose crinkles. "What's that supposed to mean?"

I shrug. "Just that I'm not surprised. You're talkative, bubbly, nice to everyone from what I've seen so far, so it makes sense."

"Oh." She seems surprised by the compliment. "Thanks. I think."

"You're welcome. I think." I can't help but wink at her. Popping open the box, I pile more slices on the plate, I nod toward the family room. "Wanna watch *Vampire Diaries* again?"

She looks shocked I asked. "You want to watch it with me?"

"That's why I asked."

"That's cool, I guess. Sure." She grabs her drink and follows me out of the room with her plate.

Settling on the couch, she brings up Netflix and puts the

show on. I'm careful to keep a full couch cushion between us, which she doesn't miss. I'm not going to feel bad about it. I have no idea when Cree might return, and I don't need him getting the wrong idea about me with his sister. Contrary to popular belief, I can control my dick. It doesn't just fall into unsuspecting vaginas.

It's funny, though, sitting here with Millie just eating pizza and watching a show. It reminds me of when I lived in the dorms last year with Teddy; and his girlfriend Vanessa would come over and we'd all hang out. It was ... nice. It was the first time I'd hung out with a female, other than my sister, with no expectation of sex, in a long time.

"What are you thinking about?" Millie obviously notices I've zoned out, not paying much, if any, attention to the show.

"My friend Teddy."

"Teddy?"

"He was my roommate in the dorms and he's a good friend. He graduated last year."

"Why were you thinking about him?"

I can't help but smile. Millie is always so full of questions.

"No reason."

She gives me a doubtful look. "Are you really interested in this show or are you just trying to appease me?"

"Nah." I take a swig of beer. "I kind of got into it last time. I want to keep going. Don't be watching without me, Little Madison."

Her lips purse with a challenge. "And what are you going to do about it?"

Arching a brow, I lean over and set my beer down. "I'm not sure yet, but I'll figure something out."

"I'm shaking in my boots." Her words drip with sarcasm.

Shaking my head, I cluck my tongue. "You really shouldn't have said that."

She looks mystified for about one-point-five seconds before I launch across the empty space between us, fingers attacking her stomach.

She shrieks, her shrill laughter filling the air. "Stop! Please, stop! Have mercy!"

I relent, returning to my spot once more. "That's what you'll get if you watch without me."

"Fine, fine." She straightens herself, trying to recover her poise. "I'll never watch *Vampire Diaries* without you. Cross my heart." She makes some kind of gesture with her fingers over her chest. Then she sticks out her pinky to me. "Promise."

Reluctantly, I wrap my much larger pinky around hers, echoing the sentiment. "Promise."

Why do I feel like somehow, I just made a deal with the devil?

five

Millie

MY PULSE BUZZES WITH EXCITEMENT WHEN I WALK into the ballet studio for my first ever class. I didn't expect to be this enthusiastic over teaching, but I think this might be a good fit for me.

I met with Aleksander over the weekend, going over music and what I thought should be included in the first lesson. He tweaked some things that I had planned, but for the most part he said he was impressed with what I came up with.

Flicking the light on in the studio, I set my bag down

and change out of my sneakers into ballet slippers. I'm already wearing a leo with a pair of pink spandex shorts over top. There are a few chairs inside the room for parents that want to stay and watch. The studio is in an older building so there's no space for a separate viewing room for parents which I kind of like. The less people watching takes some pressure off of my shoulders.

When I told my parents I'd be teaching ballet classes they seemed happy for me, but disappointed at the same time. I know they're both still wondering why I didn't pursue an art school.

There's a light tap on the open doorway and I look up to see Aleksander standing there with a smile. "I wanted to stop by and wish you good luck with your first class."

I smile. "Thanks. I'm excited. And thank you again for giving me this chance."

He waves a dismissive hand. "I'll leave you to finish getting ready. Students should be arriving in the next few minutes."

"Thanks." I give him a shaky smile.

He shoots me a thumbs up, his steps echoing down the stairs to where I learned there's a larger waiting space and an office.

Letting my hair down from the sloppy ponytail I tossed it into on my drive over, I walk over to the wall of mirrors and do my best to smooth the strands on either side of my head and tie it back into as much of a sleek bun as I can get.

A few pieces refuse to lie flat, but I deem it good

enough. I figure by the time the hour's up it'll be a mess anyway.

Minutes later, children and their parents filter into the room. My first class has only eight girls.

I introduce myself to the parents and the girls, taking my time with introductions.

"All right, girls," I clap my hands together to get their attention, "line up over here."

Dutifully, the little girls do as I say. We run through some stretches before we start with some basic dance moves. One of the girls, a tiny ball of energy with bright red hair named Vivian, struggles with her hand placement so I'm quick to help her.

All of them are such a blast, and quick learners too.

By the time the class is over, I'm tired but happy as I help them grab their bags and get with their parents.

I realize, as I sling my own bag over my shoulder and head downstairs, that I didn't stop smiling once through the whole lesson. Huh. Maybe I've inadvertently found my calling. I know becoming a ballet teacher wouldn't be what my parents want for me, but tonight has me thinking it's something I should consider if I continue to enjoy it.

Poking my head in the office, I lift my hand to wave at Aleksander. "I'm heading out. The class went great."

He smiles over the top of a laptop. "Great. So happy to hear that. We'll see you Wednesday."

"Thank you again for this opportunity."

He waves a dismissive hand. "I think it's us that's lucky

to have you. Here," he pushes back his chair to stand, "let me walk you out. It's late."

"You don't have to do that."

"It's not a problem."

He walks me outside and down the street to my parked car. It's almost fully dark out. My stomach chooses that moment to rumble loudly, reminding me I was too nervous to eat before the class.

Aleksander doesn't miss the grumbling sound. "Hungry?"

"Yeah, I'll grab something on my way home."

He smiles, his eyes sparkling with amusement. "Drive safe, Millie." My name sounds so unique on his softly accented tongue.

He waits for me to get in my car and drive away before he heads back to the studio.

I swing by a drive-thru and pick up the greasiest cheeseburger I can find and fries. After the stress I endured today, this is exactly what I want.

It doesn't take me long to get back home.

"Hey," my brother says in greeting, getting up from the couch. "How'd it go?"

Jude turns his head, watching me over the back of the couch like he's curious to know the answer to this too.

"It was great." I can't help the beaming smile that returns to my face. "I had a blast and can't wait for the next class. The kids are fun."

Cree trails behind me as I head for the kitchen, plopping

down at the table so I can dig into my food. My stomach rumbles, desperate to be fed.

Unwrapping my burger, I moan on the first bite. "Ah, sweet sustenance," I mutter with my mouth full.

Cree chuckles, shaking his head at me. "Mom and Dad can't figure out why you're teaching classes instead of taking them."

I sigh, swiping a fry and popping it into my mouth. "This is something I want to do, why can't that be good enough?"

It's a rhetorical question, but my brother answers anyway. "Because they're parents."

"True." I lift my shoulders in a shrug.

Jude saunters into the kitchen, an empty glass held loosely in his fingers. I don't mean to, but I can't help but look him over. Jude is easily one of the best-looking guys I've ever seen. Between his wavy dark hair, brown eyes, five o' clock shadow, toned body, and the utter intensity that radiates off of him, he's pure kryptonite. But he's not the kind of guy I should be lusting after. He's older, a player, and one of Cree's friends.

I shoved another handful of fries into my mouth, only half-listening to my brother while watching Jude fill the glass with ice and then top it off with water.

He turns around, his eyes meeting mine for a beat. He looks like he wants to say something, but eyes my brother and walks away instead.

Cree chats with me about classes and other randomness

while I eat and clean up. He ends up going back to the living room with the guys while I head up to shower and go to bed. It feels like I've been running on adrenaline and now I'm crashing. I want to fall face first into my bed, but a shower is a must first.

I've just gotten out of the shower, with a towel wrapped around my body, when there's a soft knock on Jude's side of the door.

I hesitate for a second before cracking the door open. "I'm almost done here."

Jude clears his throat. "I ... uh ... I just wanted to see how it went today with the class?"

I knew he heard what I said when I first got home, but I answer anyway. "It went really great. Honestly, I loved it."

"Good." He clears his throat, tilting his chin back to stare at the ceiling.

I realize he's trying to avoid looking at me in my towel. Rolling my eyes, I huff, "Need I remind you, *you're* the one who knocked on the door after I got out of the shower. Besides, this towel covers way more than a bikini. Don't be such a wuss."

Slowly, oh so slowly, he lowers his head. His eyes meeting mine. My breath catches and I silently curse myself for that fact, because there's no way he didn't miss my slight intake of air.

"And need I remind *you*, you're the one who stared at my dick. I'm trying to respect you a little more than that."

My eyes narrow on him. "Why'd you really knock on the door?"

He sighs, running his hands through his hair. "Because I wanted you to tell me how it went, not just overhear it."

"That ... that makes no sense."

He sighs, his tongue wetting his lips. His head lowers, shaking lightly. "No," he replies, looking confused, "it doesn't."

He tugs the door closed, leaving me alone in the bathroom wondering what the hell that was about.

six

Jude

SWEAT IS DRIPPING OFF MY BODY AS I ENTER THE locker room. Literally pinging off the tile floors. All the guys are equally as sweaty. Coach put us through the fucking ringer today. I'm pretty sure I pulled my groin—talk about embarrassing. I shower as quickly as possible, wincing as I dress, and then get the hell out of there before Coach comes up with some other form of torture.

There's no way in hell I'm doing anything tonight besides going home and covering myself in ice packs.

Shuffling out of the locker room with my duffel tossed

over my shoulder, I head for the exit. The door whooshes when I push it open, my eyes on my truck in the distance. I'm not paying attention and that's why the quiet, "Hi, Jude," takes me by surprise.

Her voice is sweet like honey. It reminds me of summers driving around listening to country radio and kisses under bleachers.

My gaze collides with Macy, and I grit my teeth so I don't wince at the sympathetic smile she sends my way. She opens her mouth to say something more.

"I don't want to hear it," I snap, walking away, but not before I see the hurt on her face.

That stings. I never wanted to hurt Macy. She's the one who broke *my* heart. She's with Keaton now, and that pisses me the fuck off, but I can't do anything about it. Besides, while it was reluctant, I've accepted she's a part of my past. I don't need to rehash shit with her.

Sliding behind the wheel of my truck, I spot Keaton coming out of the building. He walks up to Macy, putting his arms around her shoulders and leans in for a kiss. She says something to him and his eyes go to my truck, narrowing on it.

Putting my truck in reverse, I back out and drive away.

I've successfully avoided confrontation with them for the most part all these years. There was that one time I ran my mouth and Keaton punched me so hard there's a scar on my cheek from the indent of his ring. I didn't even hit him back. I fucking deserved it and still regret some of the things I've said. Not that I apologized. Guess that makes me a pussy.

Heading straight home, I park my truck in the driveway. Opening the garage I find that Millie's sporty little car is the only one in there. Cree's Bronco is gone and Daire's vehicle too so that means once again I'm alone with the forbidden fruit. You know, you'd think if Cree was so fucking dead set on keeping me away from his sister, he'd keep a better eye on her.

As soon as I open the door, I hear her singing. Not well. In fact, she's pretty fucking awful. Something smells amazing coming from the kitchen though.

I round the corner, watching her at the stove cooking. Her hair is up in a messy knot, strands curling around her slender neck, and she's wearing a pair of jean shorts and some kind of cropped t-shirt. It looks like maybe she took scissors to the bottom of the shirt herself and sheared it off.

"Nice song." I have to shout to be heard above the music.

She shrieks, turning around with her hands clutching her heart.

"You dickface! You scared me!" She looks like she wants to smack me upside the head with the tongs in her right hand.

I throw up my hands innocently. "Not my fault you're blasting One Direction so loud that you didn't hear me come in."

She turns the volume down on the Bluetooth speaker.

"Warn a girl next time. Jeesh. And you know what," she sticks a hand on her hip, "since you scared to the shit out of me, now you've volunteered yourself to help. Thanks so much. You can get the sauce started." She points out a set of ingredients on the counter and then motions to the saucepan. "Start mixing, Maestro."

I don't argue with her, because frankly I don't mind. All four of us have been trying to take turns making dinners so that we eat proper meals, and it doesn't all fall on one person to do it.

Washing my hands, I get to work doing what she tells me. Her music continues to play in the background. A part of me wants to poke fun at her for her obvious love of boybands, but something keeps my mouth shut. Maybe it's the way she softly sings the music under her breath now that I've joined her and she's no longer belting it out, or maybe it's the way she gently sways her body. I can't help but watch her, my eyes drawn away from the simmering pot of sauce to her. Attraction wars inside me, but I tamp it down.

Not her, not her, not her, I chant.

I might've been serious about a girl once, but that's not who I am now, and Millie isn't the kind of girl to fuck around with, even if she wasn't Cree's sister.

I'm smarter than that. Besides, I did tell her I wanted us to be friends, and for some strange reason I find myself not wanting to fuck that up.

With a smile, Millie bumps my hip out of the way,

taking the spoon from me to sample a taste of the sauce. She adds a bit of garlic, samples it again, and smiles approvingly.

“I need you to do the garlic bread next.”

“Is it in the freezer?”

I think it’s an innocent enough question, but the way her eyes bug out and shoot daggers apparently, it’s not.

“No, no, no,” she chants vehemently. “None of that fake artificial garlic bread bullshit is ruining my dinner. I’m talking about the real deal.” She pushes her hand into my back, steering me around the kitchen. “Get to cutting.” She hands me a long slab of bread. “And then you’re going to chop up fresh garlic and stir it into butter, put it on each slice and pop it in the oven.” She rattles off the amount of time it needs to be in there, telling me she’s already preheated it.

With a flip of her hair, she’s off to fill up a pot with water for the pasta.

As soon as I’ve popped the bread in the oven, she asks, “Can you cut up the chicken into strips? It should’ve rested enough by now.” She points me over the cutting board where the chicken steams the air.

I have no idea what *rested enough* means, but I’ll trust her judgment.

“Yeah, no problem.” I move around her, my arm brushing against her back. I don’t miss the way she shivers.

I’ve barely started cutting into the chicken when the door opens and Daire calls out, “Who’s cooking?”

Millie smiles brightly, calling out, "I thought I'd make dinner!"

Daire enters the room, Cree trailing him and heading straight to the fridge for a bottle of water.

"How'd you get this one to help?" It's Daire that asks.

"I told him to get off his lazy ass and help me, that this isn't the 1950s and he's just as capable being in the kitchen as I am." There's humor in Millie's tone but I can tell it goes right over top of Daire's head.

Daire tries to hold back laughter. "That true?" He addresses the question to me.

"Unfortunately." I try to sound as irritated as possible since Cree is in the room. I don't want him to think I'm actually enjoying cooking with his sister, because I know he'll read more into it than there is. God knows my dick-head friends think I'm incapable of being friends with a female. Millie points for me to add the chicken into the sauce so I do. "She wouldn't even let me use frozen garlic bread—no, I had to make actual garlic butter, slather it on some kind of fancy bread, and now it's in the oven, so you better fucking love it and if it tastes like shit, I don't want to hear it."

Millie gasps at my comment, swatting me with the spoon in her hand, only I'm positive from the look of pure shock on her face she forgot it was coated in sauce. Said sauce is all over me now. On my shirt, in my hair, on my face, and I'm pretty sure there's even some sticking to my eyelashes.

The room is silent. I'm not sure anyone is even breathing, waiting to see what I'll do.

I stare down the wide-eyed she-devil in front of me. Her shoulders hunch, her top teeth digging into her bottom lip in a sheepish expression.

Daire snorts. Cree's laughter follows behind.

But Millie and I never break eye contact.

Her hands come up to cover her face. "I am so, so sorry."

I breathe steadily. "Who's gonna clean this mess up, Little Madison?"

"Um..." She bites her lip and I know she doesn't mean for it to be a seductive move, but I feel my dick stir to life the longer I stare at her. "You?" Her eyes don't waver from their lock on mine, so she doesn't notice when I dip my finger into the simmering sauce. Shock transforms her face when I flick my finger and the white sauce splatters into her hair and across her face. For a split second my brain thinks about how it almost looks like cum. "I know you did *not* just get sauce in my hair?" Her shriek is supernaturally high —I'm pretty sure it conjures demons from another dimension.

Millie swipes a rag off the counter, lunging at me.

I turn, running out of the kitchen while she chases, swatting at me with the dish towel.

"I just washed this hair! Do you know what that means? I shouldn't have to wash it for three more days, but thanks to you, I have to wash it again!" Her voice is loud behind me as I take the stairs two at a time, bursting into my room with her hot on my heels. She's so close that I don't have a chance to close the door on her. "You're insufferable!"

She tries to shove past me into the bathroom. My fingers loop around her wrist. "Not so fast, Little Madison. You got me dirty first."

She whirls around, fire in her eyes. If my dick wasn't hard before, it definitely is now.

Not her, not her, not her, I chant silently. *She's Cree's sister. She's off-limits.*

It's not working. My cock is still hard as a rock.

Her eyes move down to where my hand is locked around her wrist. I should let go. I don't.

"I'm getting this shower first."

I smirk down at her. "You're cute when you try to be bossy."

Her face flames with indignation. Little Madison doesn't like being told she's cute. Interesting.

"I have to wash my hair," she argues, her cheeks puffing out like an adorable little chipmunk. I choose to keep that statement to myself. Something tells me if I said that thought out loud, I might earn myself a smack across the face.

"And I have to wash my body." With my free hand I motion to the sauce all over me. "My hair too." Now I point at my head.

"I'm a girl."

"That's not a sound argument, Little Madison, and you

know it." I reach back, turning on the water. "I'm showering first. Or," I draw out the word, "we could shower together."

She pulls her wrist from mine. "Ugh, you pig." She pushes at my chest. "Not a chance in hell. I can't believe you'd even present that to me as a viable option."

"Viable," I parrot back. "Look at you using big words, Little Madison."

Her eyes roll and she prepares to launch into another tirade, but I silence her when I yank my pants off, leaving me in nothing but my boxer-briefs. Her eyes drop to my crotch, her breath catching. I can't help but smirk.

I shouldn't play with her and I need to stop pushing her buttons, but I can't seem to help myself. Inching my boxers down, her eyes widen, lips parted. Stopping short of exposing my dick, I point to the door that leads back to her room.

"Run along and play now," I taunt.

Air hisses between her teeth. "You absolute, asshole."

With a dramatic flip of her hair, she shoves past me and into her room.

I shouldn't love messing with her so much, but I find myself smiling—a real smile—for the first time in a long time.

seven

Millie

I WALK INTO THE LECTURE HALL, MORE THAN A little excited for Professor Grant's class since we're going to be discussing the project. Sitting down in a seat, I arrange my laptop and notebook, ready for whatever is to come. Across the aisle, I spot the cute guy I noticed last week. His eyes meet mine briefly, a small smile curving his lips. He's hot, but somehow sweet looking at the same time. His arms are on display in a tight white shirt, and it's obvious he works out a lot. Maybe he even plays a sport for the school. I shoot him a shy smile back and he drops his gaze.

Well, then.

The room fills up and Professor Grant enters. He paces to the front, setting down his stuff before leaning his butt against the desk.

"Like we spoke about last week, we're going to begin a semester long assignment. Some of our classes will be allotted to time to work on it, but for the most part this is something you'll need to handle outside the classroom." He rubs his salt and pepper stubbled jaw as there are some groans around the room. "Take this as part of the experiment—stepping out of your comfort zone and not only putting yourself into the mindset of a psychologist, but being encouraged to get to know your fellow classmate outside of this room in a way you wouldn't normally." There are still some groans, to which he smiles, drumming his fingers against his desk. "I'm going to be passing out folders with everything you'll need for this project. If you have any further questions, please schedule a meeting with me and we can discuss it further. After I pass these out," he points to the stack of manila envelopes, "I'm going to call out names to partner you up. Don't open these yet." He taps the stack. "I'll let you know when you can."

The class seems to hold their breath as he hands out the envelopes. He hands a stack to the person on the end of each aisle, letting them pass them down through the row.

I finally get mine, setting it in front of me.

When Professor Grant is back at his desk, he picks up a piece of paper and begins rattling off names. He finally gets to mine, saying, "Millicent Madison and Jonah Cartwright." I look around, searching for this Jonah person, surprised when my eyes lock with the cute guy I've been noticing. I raise my hand in an awkward wave that he mirrors.

After the professor has finished calling out all the names, he encourages us to find our partners and move to sit together.

Jonah gets up and heads my way since there's an empty space beside me. He slides into the seat, bringing the scent of salt and earth with him.

"Hi." His voice is deep, really deep. It's at odds with his boyishly handsome face. "I'm Jonah." He holds out a large, tanned hand.

"Millie." I slip my hand in his. "It's nice to meet you."

He ducks his head timidly. "Likewise. Should we…" He trails off, pointing a finger at the unopened folder in front of him.

"Oh, right." I feel my cheeks heat. I open mine up, reading the first couple of lines. "I got Mary Ainsworth. What about you?"

"John B. Watson," he replies, flicking through the papers. "It says here he's considered to be the father of behaviorism."

"That's interesting."

He flicks a dark wave out of his eyes. "What does it say about yours?"

"Apparently she's famous for something called the attachment theory."

"I've never heard of either one of these people before," he admits, eyes scanning the paper in front of him. "I suppose that's better in a way."

"I think so too." I flip through my own packet, scanning through it, reading sample questions. "It sounds to me like we should do some reading on these people first before we even try to tackle these."

Jonah studies his own paper, clearing his throat when he nods. "Agreed. Do you want to meet up at the library tonight and start on it together? I mean, I know it's sort of separate studying but I thought maybe … I don't know." The tops of his ears have turned a bright red.

For someone so gorgeous he's incredibly introverted. It's cute and endearing. Most guys who have looks like this are incredibly cocky and full of themselves.

With a wince, I say, "I'm so sorry but I have work tonight. Maybe we could meet up tomorrow evening?"

He blows out a breath. "Tomorrow works for me."

"Cool."

"What do you do for work?"

I sit up straighter, brightening. "I'm a ballet instructor at a local place in town. It's a recent thing. I don't really need the job for money." I blush at that, but the majority of attendees at Aldridge comes from the upper crust of society and don't need to work a menial job. Not with our parents padding our bank accounts.

"Ballet, huh?" His lips turn up at the corners. "My brother did ballet when he was younger."

"That's neat. How long did he do it for?"

He shrugs. "I can't really remember. A few years I think."

"But not anymore?"

He snorts, shaking his head. "Definitely not. He probably wouldn't even admit to it now."

I frown. "Ballet isn't something to be ashamed of."

"I know," he hastens to add, "but my brother is kind of a guys' guy, I guess you'd say."

"Ah. One of those types."

He ducks his head. "Yeah."

I decide to change the subject. "What time do you want to meet tomorrow at the library?"

He thinks for a moment. "Would five or six work?"

"Six would be great."

Class comes to an end, and I walk out with Jonah, heading our separate ways once we get outside. I can't help but pause and watch him walk away. I definitely feel attracted to him, but...

Unbidden, my brain conjures an image of Jude.

Not him, not him, not him—I chant to myself as I head to my next class.

With my inexperience he's the last person I should be thinking of.

eight

Jude

I NEED TO GET MY HEAD ON STRAIGHT AND STAY FAR away from Millie.

She's Cree's sister, I remind myself over and over again, all the way through practice. Coach picks up on my distraction, calling me over at the end of practice while the rest of the guys go inside to shower up.

Holding onto my shoulder pads, I lower my head. I don't want to meet his eyes and see the disappointment in them. Sure, this is only a practice and it doesn't count, but I was a fucking newb on the field today. It's like I'd never played the sport a day in my life.

"What the fuck was that?" Coach Hawkins gestures wildly to the field. "You looked like a newborn baby deer out there." He shakes his head roughly, his body language bleeding disappointment. "Keep playing like that and I'll stick a rookie in your place for the first game." Ice fills my veins. I know he's serious. Coach doesn't spew empty threats. "Whatever's on your mind, let it go."

I nod once. "I will."

No more thinking about Millie.

He jerks his head, turning to gather his stuff up. "Good. You're one of my best players."

He waves me away, with my head lowered and my helmet in my hand I head inside to the locker room. I shower off the sweat and grime, changing into my clothes on autopilot.

Checking my phone, there's a text from Daire.

Daire: Wanna meet at Harvey's for some drinks?

I reply back quickly. **Be there in ten.**

PULLING into the parking lot of the bar, it's packed like usual. Harvey's is the local favorite with Aldridge students.

Striding inside, my eyes scan the room.

Not for Daire.

I know he'll be at our usual table.

But I need a distraction, one of the female variety. I know I should be better than this, stronger than to need this kind of distraction. But it's been my go-to for years, and I'm not sure if I know any other way to be anymore. That probably makes me a complete asshole, but sex is the only distraction that's worked. Besides, the women I hook up with always know it's not going to lead to more.

My eyes catch with a dark-haired beauty. She's gorgeous. Nice tits. Curvy body. I head toward her, then past, feeling her eyes trail me.

I lean up against the bar, a few spots down from her. "Hey, Donny." I slap my hand on the bar. "Coors, please." The bartender tips his head in my direction, swinging around to grab a beer. By the time he's slid it across the bar, and I've slapped some bills on the table, I feel the presence of her body sliding into the chair beside me. Tilting my chin down, my eyes collide with dark brown ones framed by thick lashes. "Hi."

"Hi, yourself." Her tongue slides out the tiniest bit, my eyes watching it disappear back into her mouth.

Yeah, I definitely need to get laid tonight.

"I'm Jude." I hold a hand out to her.

"Hannah." She takes my hand, lashes fluttering against her cheeks.

"Dude!" Daire's hand slaps down on my shoulder. "There you are. Hurry up."

Ignoring Daire, I ask Hannah, "You want to join me and my friends?"

She makes a show of looking me up and down. "Sure."

I grin, taking her hand and pulling her along through the bar behind Daire. The massive U-shaped booth in the back of the bar isn't as full as usual but there's still some of the usual crowd. There are the noticeable absences of Mascen, Cole, and Teddy who graduated last year. Even though Teddy could be a massive pain in my ass as my former roommate, I do miss his booming laughter and ability to make everyone else smile. He was always the life of the party. Rory, Mascen's girlfriend who's a junior this year sits with a couple of her friends, the three of them sharing an appetizer of mini tacos.

Scooting into the booth I pull Hannah down beside me. Her leg is plastered against mine. I rest my hand on her knee, testing her reaction. Her answering smile is flirtatious.

In the back of my mind, though, I feel a level of guilt I haven't felt in a long time. But I refuse to puzzle it out. Not right now, at least.

Later, though, when I disappear into the bathroom with Hannah that guilt only grows. And that night, I wake up in a cold sweat, throwing up in the bathroom, and I know it has nothing to do with how much I drank and everything to do with my attraction to the girl in the room beside me.

nine

Millie

I NEVER CONSIDERED MYSELF MUCH OF A LIBRARY girl before, but the one on campus has me changing my mind. With its old-world architecture, ivy growing all along the outside of the building, and the warm dark woods of the shelves and tables on the inside it's incredibly charming.

Navigating my way through the shelves, back to the area where Jonah said I would find him, my stomach decides to rumble reminding me I forgot to eat dinner. I got busy studying and it slipped my mind to grab a bite to eat.

Eventually I make it around to the back of the library to

the study room Jonah reserved. We figured that would be easier than being out in the open since we will have to be discussing things out loud and don't want to disturb anyone who's there for the quiet.

Tucking a strand of hair behind my ear, I reach for the door and step inside. Jonah looks up from his computer, his eyes wide and startled like he forgot I was coming. He quickly shakes his head, a slow smile upturning his lips.

"Hi," I say breathlessly, letting my bag down onto the table. "Sorry I'm late."

"Not by much."

"Fifteen minutes feels like a lot to me," I mumble, ducking my head to set out my stuff. I glance back over at Jonah, noticing he has a thick black case on his computer covered in stickers with things like Pokémon, a game controller, and even one that says, "I don't swim. I fly." Below the quote is a picture of a swimmer.

"You swim?" I open my laptop and take a seat across from him.

I swear the tops of his cheeks turn pink. Jonah is so different than most guys I've been around—granted because of my brother I've mostly always been around cocky hockey players, so it's not like I have too much to base things on.

"Yeah. I'm on the team."

"Wow, that's so cool. I've never known a swimmer before."

His physique makes even more sense now—how his

arms and chest are rather bulky but his torso and the rest of him is on the leaner side.

He sits up a little straighter. “Now you do. This is for you.” He slides a coffee over to me. It’s iced, slightly melted since I was late, but I grab onto it like my life depends on it. He chuckles at my enthusiasm. “I wasn’t sure what you’d like, but I was getting myself something and didn’t want to come empty handed. It’s a vanilla iced coffee.”

“You, dear Jonah, are a saint.” I take a sip, letting the caffeine hit my veins. He bends over and digs in a bag, holding up something wrapped in paper. He passes it to me, and I gently open it. “A chocolate croissant? Did I say saint? I meant you’re a god.”

He laughs at this, his chuckle warm and comforting. Clearing his throat, he says, “I guess we better get to work, then?”

With a sigh, I nod. “Yep.”

TWO HOURS LATER, Jonah and I call it quits.

Standing up, I stretch my arms and legs, stiff from the uncomfortable wooden chairs. Jonah watches me from the corner of his eyes.

“You could’ve told me you needed a break.”

I finish stretching, beginning to gather my stuff into my backpack. “I know, but I wanted to get as much work done as possible.”

"We have plenty of time," he reminds me, shouldering his bag.

I bite my lip. "I know, but... I want to do good on this project. This is my favorite class. I would be majorly disappointed in myself if I let this flop."

"You won't."

"How are you so sure?"

"Simple. I won't let you." He shoots a devastating grin my way, quickly ducking his head.

Holy hell if Jonah released that smile on campus, I'm pretty sure most of the female population would combust on the spot.

"You won't let me, huh?" I jest, bumping his shoulder playfully on our way out.

The library is mostly subdued as we make our way through to the exit. It's after eight, so this is probably the last place most people want to be.

Stepping outside, I inhale the cool crisp scent of the approaching fall air. Don't get me wrong, the heat of summer will hang around a few more weeks, but autumn is almost here, and I'm thrilled. It's my favorite time of year. Layered sweaters, apple cider, football games.

"Where's your dorm? I'll walk you there," Jonah offers.

"That's okay. I live off campus, actually, with my brother."

"That's cool. I could walk you to your car?"

"Sure, that would be great."

My stomach chooses that moment to rumble again,

reminding me that the croissant might've helped stave off my appetite, but it wasn't enough to fill me up.

Jonah chuckles, lips curled in amusement. "I'm hungry too and we're not too far from the dining hall if you'd like to grab something?"

I bite my lip, hesitating. A part of me wants to go home and dive headfirst into bed, but I know that's not the best choice.

"Let's get something."

Jonah slows his long-legged stride, so he stays in sync with my shorter ones. I glance over at him, taking in the shape of his sharp jaw, narrowing to a dimpled chin, with brownish-blond hair sweeping over his forehead. For a moment, I let myself think about what it might be like to have a boyfriend to go places and do things with, just like how we're headed to get something to eat. It's a strange picture for me since I've never been in a relationship before, but not entirely unpleasant.

"I can feel you staring at me."

I jump like I've been electrocuted. "Sorry!" I scream way too loud.

He doesn't say anything, reaching for the door into the dining hall, but I can practically see the amusement bleeding from his pores. Ugh.

We get in line together for a sandwich, my stomach growling loudly again. He arches a brow. "I think your stomach is mad at you."

"Mhm," I hum, still embarrassed.

"For the record," he follows behind me as the line moves, "I don't mind you staring."

My breath catches, my eyes darting up to his. He looks away quickly, his shyness returning.

I quickly grab a sandwich and he does the same, both of us swiping our student IDs before finding a table.

I'm worried it'll be awkward after he caught me staring at him, but apparently Jonah's not the type to dwell.

"Besides dance, what else is there to know about you?"

I twist my lips, trying to think. I hate being put on the spot with these kinds of questions. My brain always goes completely blank, then I feel like a complete idiot for not knowing such a basic answer about myself. "I like music?" For some annoying reason it comes out like a question.

He finishes chewing a bite of sandwich, clearly trying not to smile at my weirdness. "Are you asking or telling me?"

"Telling. Definitely telling." I sit a little straighter.

"What kind of music then?"

I shrug, hiding my mouth behind my hand as I chew. "A little bit of everything. This week has been a steady rotation of ABBA, Dolly Parton, and One Direction."

"Interesting," he muses.

"What about you? What do you love other than swimming?"

He grins, lighting up. He looks perhaps the most animated I've ever seen him. "I love all things water related. Boating, just hanging on the beach, fishing."

"Don't tell me you're one of those guys on a dating app holding up a dead fish?"

He looks mildly horrified. "Definitely not. I've never actually been on a dating app before." He shudders like the very idea gives him a skeevy feeling.

"Me either," I admit, looking down at the table. "It feels like you're setting yourself up for judgment."

"I guess call me old-fashioned but in an ideal world I'd meet someone in person."

"Agreed." I take a sip of water. We exchange smiles and finish eating our sandwiches with plans to meet up again this weekend to work on the project.

Jonah walks me to my car, watching until I drive away.

He's sweet, kind, smart, and good-looking on top of it—I think maybe I could see myself with him. If only I get the courage to make a move.

ten

Jude

IT NEVER CEASES TO AMAZE ME HOW QUICKLY I FALL into the routine once school starts back up. Letting myself into the house, it's mostly dark, but I notice the blinds on the deck door open and can see Daire and Cree through them. My eyes roam up the stairs, wondering if Millie's up there in her room or … out.

The idea of her going out shouldn't fill me with such a possessive rage, but it does.

I catch Cree through the door again, gesturing wildly

with his hands. Just seeing him is like a bucket of ice-cold water being poured over the top of my head.

Whatever I do, I can't go after his sister.

Swiping a beer from the fridge, I step out onto the deck. "What are you two bitches gossiping about?" I hop up on the deck railing, staring the two down. I know they're closer than I am with them, but based on their postures and facial expressions it seems like they're arguing.

Daire pipes up first. "Cree's got it bad for some chick."

My brows furrow, not seeing the issue.

Cree looks like he wants to rip Daire's head off. I don't think I've ever seen Cree with anything other than an easy smile and his eyes right now are spelling murder. "She's not some chick."

Daire implores me with, "He's only met her twice. *Twice*." He holds up two fingers, shaking them.

"So?" I respond, still not seeing the big deal.

I knew the first time I saw Macy she was the girl for me. Granted, it didn't work out, but I can relate to the feeling.

"So?" Daire repeats like something tastes bad on his tongue. "It's fucking weird, that's what."

His antagonistic behavior strikes me as odd. The Daire I know is typically easy going.

I'm already shaking my head as I say, "Nah. I've had the same thing happen before." I think of Macy, of those early days in our relationship. We were so in love, but insanely young and naive. "Just because you haven't experienced it, doesn't mean it doesn't happen. Don't be such a judgmental asshole."

I can tell he's affronted since he expected me to be on his side. "Yeah, but look how that shit turned out for you."

I glare at Daire. Macy and I might be long over, but I wouldn't wish away being with her. "It went to fucking hell. I know. I was there. I lived it. It fucking hurt losing her, but that doesn't mean just because things ended badly that I would trade all the good times we had."

Daire looks flabbergasted. He definitely expected me to be on his side. I have no idea who Cree's even talking about, but if he's into someone then he shouldn't have his so-called best friend shitting on him.

"What the fuck is in your drinks?" Daire looks at the bottle clasped in my hand, then to Cree's. "Both of y'all are fucking crazy. Insane. Off your mother-fucking rockers."

He shakes his head roughly, letting himself into the house. Apparently, he can't handle being wrong.

Silence descends upon the deck. I sip at my beer, waiting for Cree to say something. When he doesn't, I decide to speak up.

"Don't let him drag you down. He's in a shit mood today."

Cree's eyes shoot to mine, curious. "Why?"

"Apparently, Rosie chewed him out real good in the dining hall. Wish I could've seen it." I shake my head, amused. I heard some of the guys talking about it at practice today. Rosie's a girl that's known for chasing after athletes. Particularly the hockey guys like Daire and Cree. If I'm not mistaken she grew up with Daire. "I have my own shit to work through when it comes to women after what happened with Macy. But I know not all women are like that. Bro, if a girl makes you happy then see where it goes."

Cree winces, leaning forward. "Daire's right. I've only met her twice. It's crazy to feel this way. I'm not in love or anything, that's stupid, but there's just this feeling like I'm supposed to get to know her."

I get up, my ass having had enough of sitting on the thin railing. Cracking my neck, I say, "Then do that and see where it goes. Not everything needs a label and not everyone has to understand."

He looks at me with hope in his eyes. "You don't think I'm crazy?"

"No, I don't." I pat him on the shoulder as I walk by him, heading for the door. "But girls can make you get that way."

Especially the one living upstairs.

Closing the door behind me, I empty out the last of my beer and toss the bottle in the recycling bin. Upstairs, I undress and dive for my bed, scrolling through the endless stream of text messages.

The hookup at Harvey's wasn't enough and I *have* to get Millie out of my head.

Where there's a will there's a way, or however the fuck the saying goes.

eleven

Millie

I LEFT the library to come straight home after another study sesh with Jonah. The only vehicle at the house is Jude's truck, so I figure my brother and Daire are out at the bar.

Letting myself into the house, my stomach rumbles with the need for food and my body aches, begging for a long hot shower. I wouldn't mind sitting down and watching TV for a little while too. I would ask Jude if he wants to join me, since he kind of pushed himself into my rewatch marathon of 'Vampire Diaries' but he's been distant and cold for the last week. There's no way in hell I'm asking him and if he gets pissy about it, then that's on him and his sensitive male feelings. I swear, guys act like women are the overly emotional ones, when in actuality it's them.

Pausing on my way to the kitchen, I stop and listen.

Bed creaking.

Moaning.

A cry of pleasure.

My eyes squeeze shut.

Not a-fucking-gain.

My heart squeezes with pain, which only makes me annoyed. This stupid tiny flame of a crush I have for Jude needs to be snuffed out, because he's the last guy on the planet I should be giving any of my attention to. I think of Jonah, and how he sweetly brought coffee and donuts today. *That's* the kind of guy I should want.

Trying not to let Jude's sexcapades get to me, I carry on my merry way into the kitchen and whip up a quick dinner, scarfing it down quickly enough that I burn my tongue. You'd think I would've learned my lesson by now to wait for my food to cool down, but that little lesson has never quite sunk into my brain.

Heading upstairs, I hum under my breath in an effort to drown out the breathy moans. Stupidly, I feel … aroused. My core clenches with desire, some part of me wishing it was me making those sounds. That fact only makes my temper flare more.

Slamming my door shut behind me in an effort to remind Jude that other people live in this house besides him, I gather up my stuff to go shower. I can only pray that once that's finished, so will Jude, because I desperately want to get some studying in before I crash.

Turning the shower on, I wait for it to warm up before stepping inside. The sigh of relief that comes out of me when the hot water touches my tightly coiled muscles should be downright embarrassing.

I wash my hair, taking extra care to massage my scalp. I might have to forget studying all together and head straight to bed.

When I get out of the shower, I'm horrified to find a chick sitting on the toilet. At least she's wearing a t-shirt, big enough that it's probably Jude's, but she's *peeing* and I'm standing here buck-ass naked.

I scream, slapping my hands over my bits. Stupid, I know, she's already seen them. I scramble to grab my towel, holding it in front of me.

"What are you doing in here?" I scream at her. *Fuck me for forgetting to lock the stupid adjoining door!*

She grabs some toilet paper. "Peeing, obviously. Didn't anyone ever tell you to pee after sex?"

"But I was in the shower!"

"So?" She shrugs, letting the paper drop into the toilet. She flushes it and goes to wash her hands, her bare butt peeking out from beneath the shirt. It's a nice butt, I'll give her that. "I needed to pee, and the door was unlocked. That's on you, hun."

She sends me a not very nice smile, opens the door to

Jude's room and slips inside. I swipe the door locked before Jude can barge in next.

Fury sends my blood pressure spiking.

I.

Can't.

Do.

This.

I should feel comfortable to shower in my own fucking house. *My* parents bought this place, not Jude's.

I brush my hair with fury, slapping my glasses on my face. I wear contacts most of the time, but in the evenings, I like to let my eyes rest. My hair ends up in a wild nest on top of my head and I put on my comfiest pjs, because if I ever needed comfort, it's right now.

When I hear the garage door open, I barrel downstairs because Jude and his fuck buddy are at it again. I left the door from his room locked, so if she has to pee again, she can pop a squat on his floor for all I care.

Cree's eyes widen when I practically knock him down and I know he can read the fury written plainly on my face.

"He has to go!" I point upstairs with a forceful finger. I'd like to poke Jude in the eye with this finger.

"Who?" He asks dumbly and I've never wanted to punch my brother in the face more than this moment. What an asinine question. Sure, Daire can be a dick, but at least he doesn't bring girls around constantly and share a bathroom with me.

"The football playing, womanizing, annoying, dick-headed, motherfucker upstairs!" Surely *that* will spell out who I'm referring to, if not my brother is the densest person I know.

He finally shuts the door, since he forgot to when I ambushed him. "Language, Mills!" I can't believe he's scolding me about language right now. He brushes past me, heading for the kitchen. Does he think I'm letting him off this easy? No way. Jude is his friend that he invited to live here. He can deal with him.

"Don't fucking reprimand me when Casanova over here is running a brothel! I share a bathroom with him." I'm ranting and raging at this point. Well, I guess I already was, but I'm just that mad. He opens the fridge, poking his head inside. "I got out of the shower to some chick *peeing!* I was naked, Cree! Sure, we share all the same bits, but I don't need some stranger seeing all of them!"

That gets his attention.

He eases out of the fridge with a deadly calm, slamming the door closed. "What?"

I'm on a roll now and can't seem to stop. "I know, I should've remembered to lock his side of the door, but in my defense who expects a strange girl to be there peeing when they know someone is in the shower? Besides, there's a hall bath too!"

He holds up a hand, trying to silence me. "I'm not mad at you, Millie."

My shoulders sag, realizing I don't have to keep trying to prove my point. "Oh."

"Is the girl still here?"

I roll my eyes. "Yes. They've been going at it for hours now. Honestly, I would be impressed with his stamina if it wasn't so fucking annoying." Hours might be a tad of an exaggeration, but since they were having sex already when I got here then hours seems like a safe bet.

Cree pinches the bridge of his nose, his mouth twisting back and forth as he seems to think over whatever it is he's going to do next. He holds up both hands, gesturing for me to stay put before he even utters the words, "Wait here."

Wait here my ass!

"Don't tell me what to do," I seethe from behind him. The headboard bangs against the wall, probably leaving a permanent dent in the plaster.

"Millicent," he spins back around, giving me a look identical to one our dad gives me when I've done something to piss him off, "again, I'm not mad at you, but I am asking you to stay down here and respect that. Okay?"

"Fine, I'm just upset. This isn't cool. If you can't get him to stop, then I'm going back to Daire's bathroom."

Cree winces. "That won't be necessary."

Jesus, is Daire that pressed over sharing a bathroom with a girl? He better get over it, because I'm sure one day he'll be married and dealing with hair clogging the drain.

Since Cree wants to handle this on his own, so be it. I make myself comfortable on the couch where it's impossible not to hear them yelling at each other. I hear a punch and hope to God that Cree decked Jude, but the silence that follows worries me.

I creep out from my position on the couch and up the stairs, only to find my brother flat on the floor, knocked out cold, and Jude standing there shaking out his fist.

"What did you do?" I shove Jude's bare chest. There's only a blanket wrapped around his trim waist. "Did you punch my brother because he called you on your bullshit?"

The girl from the bathroom scuttles past us, half-dressed with her hair sex-mussed. "This is too much drama for me."

Same girl, same.

"Don't you have anything to say for yourself?" My hands go to my hips.

His eyes narrow on me, jaw taut. "Stay the fuck out of my business, Millicent."

My jaw drops when he turns into his room, closing the door behind him. The lock clicks a second later, leaving me alone to deal with my brother.

He starts to stir, pressing a hand to his, no doubt, aching cheek. "What happened?"

I throw my hands up, exasperated.

Stupid boys.

twelve

Jude

I LET SOME TIME PASS BEFORE I BURST THROUGH THE adjoining doors into Millie's bedroom.

She sits straight up in bed, a book falling to her lap. Her hair is a massive clump on top of her head, glasses perched delicately on her nose. The tank top she wears to sleep in hugs her small chest.

Her astonished eyes dart from the doors to me. I know what she's thinking.

I hold up the long, thin end of the paperclip.

"I had to get into the bathroom somehow." She really

thought on top of everything else she could lock my door too and I'd be fine with it. Her lips open and close, gaping like a fish. "I don't know what other way to say this to you, except don't meddle in my sex life. You wanna bring a guy here and bang his brains out? Go for it." Except, my stomach sours at the thought of that happening. God, I'm fucked up. "You know, before this year your brother threw all these parties." I spread my arms wide. "Why did he stop? Is it because you're a fucking prude?"

I'm being mean. On purpose. But it doesn't make it feel any better when her eyes turn sad, troubled. Quickly, her gaze changes, becoming fiery, and steel straightens her spine.

"Don't be so cheap and bring your dates to a hotel. I shouldn't come home and have to listen to that shit. It's ridiculous."

I try not to smirk. "It's only sex." She sucks her cheeks in. "That's right, you wouldn't know."

She sits up on her knees, revealing the tiny pair of shorts she's wearing. *Fuck me.* I divert my eyes to a shelf on my right with decorative fairies in ballet shoes. Slippers. Whatever they're called.

"Don't shove my virginity in my face like it's something to hold over me." Her words force my gaze back to her. "You think you can hurt me talking shit? You're the one who's stupid. In my opinion, virginity needs to stop being talked about like it's this ... this monumental thing." She juts her chin into the air. "Do people make it out to be that way for guys? No," she answers her own question. "I'll have sex when I'm good and ready, and you sir, aren't going to judge me for it."

She ends this statement with her hands on her hips. I don't think she realizes the gesture makes her tits look bigger. For a second, I think about what it would be like to kiss her. To wrap my hand around the back of her neck, pull her lips to mine.

I wonder how she'd taste.

What the fuck!

Shaking my head roughly, I remind myself this is exactly why I've been trying to avoid her.

"You don't have to be such an asshole to me," she goes on, oblivious to my inner turmoil, "I know you're not attracted to me that way." I have to stifle the urge to snort. Millie's beautiful, any straight guy with a pulse is going to be attracted to her. "And *you* were the one who broached the topic of being friends. Not me." She shoves a finger in her own chest. "So maybe remember that before you treat me like shit? All I want is to be able to come home, study, and crash. Oh, and not get out of the shower to some chick I don't know peeing in the toilet."

I sigh heavily, running my fingers through my hair. She's right. Sure, I still think she overreacted, but I could've handled things better too.

"Fine." I shove my hand out to her. "Truce?"

She eyes my hand, hesitant, lips twisting back and forth. "Truce." We shake on it and she drops from her knees back onto her butt. "Get outta here. I have more pages to read before I go to sleep."

I hesitate for a second longer, I'm not even sure why. She raises a brow, silently asking why I'm still standing there.

Flashing her a smile, it's impossible not to miss her intake of breath before I'm passing through the bathroom and back into my bedroom.

What are you doing, man? I ask myself.

I don't know.

I don't know.

I WATCH Jonah arc through the water. I've never told my brother, but I've always been fascinated by how easy he makes it look. His body cuts through the pool like he was born to do this. I love football, I'm good at football, maybe even better than good, but nothing I do on the field compares to Jonah's talent for swimming. I told him once I could see him in the Olympics. He laughed, I guess thinking I was being sarcastic or something, but I was serious.

He climbs out of the pool, swiping his goggles off. He reaches for a towel and that's when he spots me, surprise evident on his face.

"What are you doing here?" He starts drying off his body.

"I could ask you the same thing. You don't have practice

today and we were supposed to meet for breakfast." When he didn't show up or answer his phone, I knew this is where I'd find him. Whenever Jonah has something on his mind, good or bad, he seeks out the nearest body of water.

Jonah winces, rubbing the towel over his hair. "Sorry, I forgot."

"You forgot?" I repeat, brow arching in surprise. "That's not like you."

And it's really not. My brother is the kind of person who can remember something you said ten years ago. Him forgetting anything is shocking.

"Just got a lot on my mind." He grabs his bag, heading toward the locker room. "You mind waiting and getting something now?"

"That's fine."

While he's gone to change, I stand up stretching my arms above my head. Metal bleachers have to be one of the most uncomfortable things to ever exist. I check my phone, finding a string of texts, some from my friends, others from girls, and one from my mom. I reply back to my mom first, then my friends, laughing at the photo Teddy sent me of some guy in New York City walking an iguana, and ignore the texts from the girls. It's not like I'll be getting laid anytime soon unless I want to treat them to a night in a hotel, and frankly, I'm not about to do that shit. It sounds stupid, but doing that almost feels like I'm paying for the sex.

Jonah walks out of the locker room, motioning with his head for me to follow.

Pulling my keys out of my pocket, I twirl the ring around my finger.

"Should we go somewhere off-campus for breakfast?"

He raises one shoulder. "Sure. I don't care."

I end up taking him to the diner I went to a lot last year with Teddy since his girlfriend Vanessa worked there. The food's decent and it's a little off the beaten path where we're not likely to run into many people from campus. Jonah hardly speaks on the drive over, only to ask if I've spoken to our parents.

I let him remain quiet until after we've placed our orders, and both have some soda in front of us.

"What's up with you, Bug? And don't give me some bullshit about being fine. You're quieter than normal."

"Nothing," he replies, gulping down half his Coke. "I just don't have a lot to say."

"You can't bullshit a bullshitter."

He sighs, wrinkling his nose when his fingers encounter something sticky on the table. Frowning, he holds his hands up. "I have to wash my hands."

"You're not getting out of this conversation." I'm speaking to his back, but I might as well be talking to a wall.

Leaning back into the booth, I wait for him to return. There are four girls in a booth diagonal to ours. They look young enough to be high school students, but are clearly checking me out, all while nudging at one girl. I watch as she gets up and strolls over to me.

"Hi." She sways back and forth, tugging on the bottom of her shirt.

Picking up my glass of soda, I take a hearty sip. "No."

Her face falls. "What?"

"Whatever you're about to say, the answer is no."

"Oh." She bites her bottom lip, tugging on a strand of blonde hair. "But what if—?"

"No," I repeat, my tone icy and mean. Even if I didn't suspect that these girls are barely seventeen, I wouldn't be in the mood to deal with this shit.

I'm starting to realize that all girls see when they look at me is a pretty face and good fuck and for the first time since I started sleeping around, that feels incredibly hollow. There's more to me than that.

Shoulders slumped, the girl retreats back to the table with her friends. A small part of me feels bad for being an asshole, since it did take some guts for her to come over here, but I'm tired of this shit.

My brother returns, sliding into the booth.

"Now spill it, Bug. I'm not messing around."

His eyes go to the ceiling, like maybe he's saying a prayer that I'll get off his back. Not happening. I know when something is up with my little brother.

"It's a girl, okay?" He blurts defensively, like he assumes I'll be pissed by this news.

"A girl?" I repeat questioningly, wondering what the big fucking deal is.

"She's in my psychology class and we're partners on a project now."

"Okay," I drawl out slowly, hesitantly. "And what's the issue?"

"I'm just not good at the whole girl thing." He shrugs, not meeting my eyes. "I'm not you."

I snort, wiping condensation from the red plastic cup. "Trust me, you don't want to be me."

Jonah eyes me warily. "What changed after Macy?"

I can't meet my little brother's eyes. I don't talk about what happened, not with anyone. I'm sure a therapist would tell me I need to get it off my chest.

"Life," I answer simply, and it's true. After all the shit that happened with us, I went in one direction, and she went in another.

"You've never been the same." His tone is hesitant, like he's almost scared to voice that aloud.

I lower my head, staring at the top of the table. "I know."

I pictured it all with Macy. We'd go to college together. I'd play football. She'd cheer me on from the sidelines. I'd propose our senior year. We'd get a house. Married. Have kids. The whole shebang. But that's not what happened.

"You gonna talk about it?"

Sitting up straighter, I clear my throat. "No."

He chuckles, leaning out of the way for the waitress to set down our food. “Maybe you should.”

“Or maybe,” I steal one of his fries, “I should help you get this girl.”

He eyes me for a moment, debating the merits of dropping the subject. “Deal.”

thirteen

Millie

IT'S POURING OUTSIDE. I'M TALKING THE KIND OF rain that sends people into the nearest shelter.

Not me. I love the rain. I love driving in it, blasting my music, and letting my thoughts wander. Deciding I've studied enough, I close my laptop, grab a sweatshirt and yank up the hood.

I have no idea who is home, but as I make my way downstairs I begin to suspect it's only me. But not for long.

My hand is on the doorknob, ready to go into the garage

when a gruff voice comes out of nowhere with a growly, "What are you doing?"

I jump, hand flying to my chest. "Don't do that!"

"Do what?" Jude gives me an innocent look, all while holding a mixing bowl full of cereal. Yes, a literal mixing bowl.

"Sneak up on people." I'm still waiting for my heart rate to slow.

"I wasn't sneaking, you just weren't paying close enough attention. If anyone is sneaking, it's you."

"I'm going for a drive."

His lip curls, looking at me like I've lost my mind. "In this weather?"

I stare back like he's the crazy one. "Obviously."

His eyes narrow, lips pursed. "I'm taking you."

"No, you aren't. This is my me time. It's where I blast my music and relax."

He sets the mixing bowl on the side table, crossing muscular arms over his chest. "Driving in a storm relaxes you?"

"There's no thunder and lightning, therefore not a storm."

"Whatever you say, Little Madison, but I'm still driving."

I very nearly stomp my foot in defiance but catch myself at the last second, thankfully before I can look like a petulant child. "I didn't invite you."

"That's okay." A slow smirk transforms his face. "I'm inviting myself."

Grinding my teeth together, I debate my options. Forget my drive and sulk upstairs, or deal with Jude.

"Fine," I spit out, "but I'm playing my music and if I want to stop for snacks, you do what I say."

His lips press together, and I know, I just know, he's trying not to laugh at me. "You're awfully bossy."

"You're the one high-jacking my rainy-day drive."

"Touché." He pats his pockets, cursing under his breath. "Don't even think of escaping. I have to grab my keys."

He takes off, leaving his mixing bowl of cereal behind. I'm not about to remind him to clean up his mess. He can figure that out on his own. He returns less than a minute later, spinning his keyring around his finger.

"Let's go."

I put up my hood, and he does the same as we dash out of the garage to his truck parked in the driveway. The rain quickly tries to soak through my clothes as I clamor into the truck. It's so tall for my little legs I practically need a step ladder. Somehow, I manage to make it. Jude cranks the engine, and it rumbles to life.

"Where's the AUX cord?" I demand with eager grabby hands.

He passes it over and I plug my phone in, quickly bringing up the playlist I curated for these drives. 'Cigarette Daydreams' by Cage The Elephant begins to play.

Jude looks at me with surprise as he backs out. "This is one of my favorite songs."

"Really?" I smile, gathering my hair on top of my head and securing it with an elastic.

He nods, starting to sing along. My voice joins his and we sing together as rain beats against the windshield, the wipers on the highest setting.

Jude drives toward town as the song changes to 'Somewhere Only We Know' by Keane, which he also knows word for word, so our sing-a-thon continues. Not that I'm going to admit it to him, but so far this is way more fun having him along.

He presses the pause button before the next song starts. "Is there anywhere in particular you go on these drives?"

"No, this is my first one since moving here. Back home I would drive backroads and then get something to eat."

"No plan. Got it. I like it." He presses play again, but he doesn't know the song this time. It's Halsey's 'New Americana'. He doesn't ask me to skip it, he lets me sing my little heart out.

We end up on the backroads of Tennessee, reminiscent of the ones I'd drive back home. He keeps his left hand on the wheel, his right arm resting on the console. We pass rolling green hills that lead to farmland. The stormy dark sky doesn't show a hint of the rain lessening. After an hour Jude asks if I'm hungry.

"Starving."

"What are you in the mood for?" He turns off the road we're currently on, heading toward the nearest town.

I smile slowly. "Tacos."

"Tacos," he repeats with a nod. "I could go for that too."

He doesn't have to drive too far before we come across a small Mexican restaurant. He pulls into the muddy gravel lot, his truck easily overtaking potholes that would've swallowed my small car whole.

"You wanna go in and eat or get it to go?"

I hesitate. "Do you mind if we eat in your truck? I know it's silly, but I love eating in the car. I'll take grabbing food to-go and eating in the car over a five-star restaurant any day.

His warm brown eyes take me in. "All right." He brings up the restaurant on his phone, letting me see the menu as well, and after we've decided what we want he calls it in. "It'll be ten minutes." He leans his seat back, crossing his arms over his chest. "I gotta admit, I didn't take you for this kind of girl." He waves his fingers lazily, like that slow moving graze of fingers through the air provides the definition for *this kind of girl.*

"And what kind is that?"

He shrugs his wide shoulders. "I don't know, the simple kind, I guess."

I throw my head back with laughter. "And here I thought you were supposed to be some suave ladies' man. I've been fooled."

His forehead wrinkles, lips downturned. "Why are you laughing?"

"Because," I wipe tears of laughter from beneath my eyes, "you guys are all the same, thinking you *know* women just because you have sex, but you're literally clueless."

His frown deepens. "What do you mean?"

"Do you have any idea how many women fake orgasms?"

"No one's ever faked it with me."

"Aw," I mock, patting his arm, "that's what all the guys think."

"What would you even know about faking orgasms?"

I roll my eyes at him. "I read, obviously, and lots of women are open about it. So, all I'm saying is, at some point in your sexual exploits, a woman has faked it."

His lips part and the poor guy looks stunned by this revelation. "I refuse to accept this information."

"Refusal or not, the average is not on your side my friend."

He mutters something under his breath, pulling his hood up. "Gonna go see if the food is ready."

"Men are so sensitive," I mutter to myself, watching him duck into the building.

The rain hasn't slowed, and if anything it has gotten worse. Jude emerges a few minutes later, having to duck severely through the doorway so he doesn't bump his head. I swear the guy is seven feet tall, but in actuality is probably around six-four.

He opens the door just as lightning strikes in the distance. "Fuck," he curses, slamming the door closed. "We really shouldn't be out in this. I doubt it's safe."

"Actually," I reach for the bag of food, rifling through it so I can divvy up our orders, "it's one of the safest places during a storm."

His face crinkles with doubt. "How would you know that?"

"Google, my dude. Google." I pass him a foil wrapped plate of food. "That's yours."

Digging into our food, my playlist continues to play in the background. We're quiet as we eat our food, but it's a comfortable silence. Surprisingly, I can't say I've shared much of the sort with others in the past.

"This might be the best taco I've ever had," I say after polishing off my second one.

Jude shoves a spoonful of rice in his mouth. "I think you might be onto something with these rainy-day drives."

I beam proudly. "They're something special."

"What made you start them?" He sorts through the takeout bag, pulling out a container of tortilla chips and salsa. I snag one before he can. He swats at my hand with a growing smile.

"The drives?" He nods. I press my lips into a flat line, not sure how much I want to divulge. Ultimately, I decide that Jude is someone I trust with this information. "Back home I went to an all-girls school and girls can be catty." I look away with a shrug, like it's no big deal even though it was absolutely devastating for me at the time. "I don't know why a lot of the girls didn't like me." I swallow thickly, thinking about how I literally have basically zero friends.

Already, the ones I did have from back home barely reply to my text messages. My brother doesn't count as a friend. He's family and forced to like me. Jonah's my study partner and my budding crush on him doesn't bode well for friendship. And Jude? I don't know what he is. He's more than an acquaintance, but a friend? I don't know. "Anyway, it became a distraction, I guess, getting out and driving. It was a boarding school, so when it rained everyone stayed inside and I didn't want to be where I wasn't wanted."

Jude's staring at me. His steady gaze feels like a weighted blanket around my shoulders. "I have a hard time believing you don't have friends, but I do, believe you that is, because I know you wouldn't lie. I'm sorry those girls were mean to you. It's their loss for not getting to know you."

My breath holds in my lungs for two, four, six full seconds. "And you think you know me?"

"Not fully," he admits, going in for another chip. There's a bit of salsa on the corner of his lip and the urge to wipe it away is strong but I keep my hands firmly to themselves. "But I'm starting to."

I duck my head, letting my hair hide my face. We don't talk much as we finish up, cleaning the trash from his truck. I won't admit it, but this was actually nice. Jude's not so bad after all.

He turns the music up and we head home.

fourteen

Jude

I WAS AT HOME ON A FRIDAY NIGHT.

This should be a complete and utter crime.

Me? Staying *home* on the biggest party night of the week? It didn't seem possible, but here I was. I knew I had only sworn off bringing my hook-ups *here*, nothing forbade me from doing it elsewhere, but surprisingly I wasn't in the mood.

For once, my dick didn't care.

I looked down at my lap, muttering to my dick, "What's wrong with you?"

"Me?" Millie blurts suddenly from somewhere behind me. The door to the garage closes a second later. "I didn't do anything. Did I? Is there something wrong with my leo?" She plucks at the tight garment, me watching her over the back of the couch.

"Nothing's wrong with your… whatever that is." I wave my hand at her get-up. Her hair is pulled back in a tight bun, a duffel bag tossed over her shoulder. "I was talking to myself."

She sets her bag down, bending to pull off her shoes. Somehow, she still manages to give me a speculative look. "You were asking yourself what's wrong with you? Huh. I'm impressed that you're so self-aware."

"Self-aware?" I parrot, too busy watching her every movement.

"Yeah," she straightens, letting her hair down, "to realize there's something wrong with you."

My mouth curls, since that's not what I meant, but I'm not about to give her more ammunition against me by admitting I was talking to my dick. It's weird enough admitting it to myself.

"Where is everyone?" She stifles a yawn as soon as the question is out of her mouth.

"Daire's … no idea. And your brother? No idea there either."

"Great," she drawls in a sarcastic tone, heading for the kitchen.

I don't know what makes me get up and join her, but I

follow her to the kitchen. She opens the fridge, eyeing what's inside.

Leaning against the counter, I tell her, "You can have what's in that bowl with the orange lid."

She pulls it out, taking off the lid so she can give it a sniff. "What is it?"

"It's chicken with a honey glaze, broccoli, and rice."

She shrugs, turning around to pop it in the microwave. "If everyone else is out, why are you home?"

"Ah," I open the fridge, grabbing a beer, "isn't that the age-old question? What in fact, am I doing home?" I pop the cap off, taking a swig. "Short answer; I don't know. Long answer: just didn't feel like it."

"Your long answer is only two words more than the short one, so I'm not quite sure it counts." The microwave stops and she pulls out the bowl, swiping a fork from the drawer. She stirs it all up together as best she can, taking a bite. "Hot! Hot!"

I try not to laugh. "What exactly did you think would happen?"

"I'm hungry," she defends, grabbing a water bottle to gulp down the cold liquid.

"How did your class go with the kids?"

Millie's whole face lights up with my question. She's clearly in her element teaching those kids to dance.

"Amazing! They're learning so fast. Bea was so nervous her first class, but she's doing so much better."

I wonder if she's aware of the way she glows talking

about it. Millie's found where she belongs, at that dance studio as a teacher. As much as I love football, I'm not sure I have the same sort of glow about me when I talk about the sport. The passion bleeds from her, and it's obvious how much she's already grown to love the kids.

"I love watching the way their face lights up when a move finally clicks. And Aleksander told me all my classes will be participating in the winter showcase come December so I can't wait to tell the kids about it. I think they'll be really excited."

"Who's Aleksander?" I bark out with more bite to my tone than I intend. Millie doesn't miss it, not with the way her brows curve inward.

"His parents own the studio. He's a dancer too." I grunt in acknowledgement. I don't know the dude, but I already don't like him. "What's that face for?" She sounds like she's trying not to laugh. I didn't even know I was making a face.

I don't know how to get myself out of this one, not easily anyway. "Aleksander," I repeat the name the same way she said it with a slight accent. Russian, perhaps

She arches a brow, chewing her chicken. Swallowing, she prompts, "And?"

"He sounds like an asshole." I cross my arms over my chest defensively.

Throwing her head back, she exposes the smooth column of her throat as she laughs. And laughs. And laughs some more at my expense.

When she sobers, she says, "You don't even know him."

"I don't have to," I grumble, looking away from her.

"Guys are so weird." I know she means for the words not to meet my ears, but they do anyway in the small space.

"No, we're not."

"Anyway, thanks for the food." She lifts the half-eaten leftover bowl like she's cheers-ing me and turns to leave.

"Where do you think you're going?"

"Upstairs?" She frames it as a question.

"Nope. We're watching that show."

"That show? You know the name."

"I do," I agree, "but that doesn't matter."

She rolls her eyes at me, but does as I say, taking her food and a bottle of water to the living room. She settles in the corner of the couch, and I sit at the opposite end far away from the temptation of touching distance.

I put the show on, picking up where we last left off. I didn't mean to get sucked into the show, but here we are.

When Millie finishes her dinner, she leans over to set the empty bowl on the table before pulling a blanket over her shoulders and wrapping up. I'm sure she wants to shower and change into something comfortable, but I'm a selfish prick because I don't suggest it. I'm enjoying her company too much.

We watch two episodes before I look over and notice Millie's eyes are getting heavy. Daire and Cree will probably return at any time and frankly, I don't want either one of them finding the two of us like this, even if an ocean practically separates us. My reputation doesn't bode well for what they might read into the situation.

I pause the show before turning the TV off. She jolts into a sitting position.

"I'm awake!"

Chuckling, I ease off the couch and hold out a hand to her. "Come on, Little Madison. Time for bed."

Something flares in her eyes but it's there and gone before I can decipher it. Carefully, she places her hand in mine so I can help her up.

Together, we go upstairs, brushing our teeth side by side in the bathroom before she takes a shower. I close the bathroom door behind me, and lie down on my bed with my arms crossed behind my head.

Friends, I remind myself. I can be friends with Millie.

But nothing more.

fifteen

Millie

HURRYING INTO THE COFFEE SHOP, WITH A STACK OF books clutched to my chest I nearly collide with the girl getting into line in front of me.

"I'm so sorry!" I cry, and then because my luck is shit today, I end up dropping my books right on my toes. "Son of a bitch!"

The girls wide brown eyes look at me with shock before she starts laughing. Bending down, she helps me gather up my books. "Rough day?"

"You have no idea."

First, I overslept which made me late to my first class. Then that professor was an asshole and called me out on it in front of the whole class. I've never been more embarrassed in my whole life *until* my stomach rumbled in the middle of class, and he said something about that too. I wanted to burrow in a hole and die. Then, to make matters worse, the minute I stood up at the end of class I knew I'd started my period *three days late.* I mean, at least that erased my worry that I might be carrying the next coming of Jesus.

To say it's been a bad day is an understatement. Now, I just want a coffee and some food to make it better.

"I'm Zara," the girl introduces herself. "You want me to hold some of those?" She points at the books in my arms—oh yeah, let me add that to the list, my backpack broke so I've been forced to carry half of my things.

"You don't need to do that."

"Give them here." She takes more than half of the stack as we move up in line.

"Thank you. I really am sorry about bumping into you and then, you know, cursing in your ear when I dropped my books."

She laughs, long wavy black hair swishing around her shoulders. "It's no big deal. I've had bad days too. I'm guessing you're a freshman?"

"Yeah." I frown. "Is it written all over me? Oh, and I'm Millie by the way."

"You look too frazzled to be anything but a freshman."

"What are you then?"

"Sophomore," she answers, taking another step forward in line. "This all gets easier, I promise. I know right now it might not feel like it, but you'll get there." She has a slight accent that gives her words this musical quality to them.

"I'm feeling pretty exhausted," I admit. "But strangely, happy too?" I don't know why it comes out as a question.

"That's college for you." She reaches the counter for her turn to place an order. After she's finished, she points at me. "And whatever she wants?"

"Oh, no." I shake my head rapidly back and forth. "I'm getting food and a drink."

"Like I said, get up here."

Reluctantly, I step forward and give the barista my order. I try to slide my card across, but Zara isn't having it. I settle for tossing some cash in the tip jar.

"Let's grab a table," Zara says, grabbing ahold of my shirt sleeve and somehow managing to tug me along with her.

She finds an empty table, quickly claiming it by tossing my books on the surface.

I settle into a chair across from her, watching her skeptically. After my experiences at my all-girls school, I've become wary of other females.

"Why are you being nice to me?" I blurt out.

Zara cocks her head to the side, giving me a funny look. "Because I want to? You're having a shitty day and look like you need a friend."

I do need a friend. It's never really bothered me all that

much, my lack of female friendships and friendships in general, but I guess getting older and seeing other friend groups has made me feel a bit sad that I don't have the same. I'll never have a lifelong friend that I grew up with. I know lots of people don't, but I think that would be so nice to have.

"I think I do. Need a friend that is."

Zara offers me a soft smile. "Today's your lucky day then. I'm not easily deterred."

"How'd you find yourself at Aldridge?" I try to make small talk. I've never been good at it, but it's the thought that counts.

"Like we all do ... I applied." She winks, pushing my books to the other end of the table. "I guess this seemed like the best fit. When I toured the campus, I could picture myself here. I didn't feel that way with the other schools I looked at. It also had the added bonus of being the school my dad didn't want me to pick."

"Daddy issues?" I wince at my question since I didn't mean for it to sound like that.

Zara laughs heartily. "No. I actually have a good relationship with my parents, but I love doing the opposite of what they tell me. You'd think my dad would've learned by now. But seriously, this is the place that felt the most right. I wouldn't make myself miserable just to spite my dad. What about you? What made you choose Aldridge?"

"My brother goes here."

She grabs some ChapStick from her purse, swiping it

over her lips like she expects me to say more. "Oh, that's it? That's the only reason?"

I sigh, resting my elbow on the table and my head in my hand. "My parents expected me to go to an arts school for dance, but I wasn't interested. Don't get me wrong, I love to dance, but I don't want to do it as a career. I want to keep it as my hobby."

"That's—" She starts to say, but her name is called. "Hold that thought." She slips from her seat, grabbing our stuff and returning in a blink. She passes me my iced coffee and the paper bag containing my coconut bar. "I was going to say that's understandable. Sure, some people want to turn their hobby into a career, but others want to keep it as something they enjoy and there's nothing wrong with that. I think it's commendable, especially if you're good enough that you could've gotten into a school for dance."

"Thanks. And thanks for this too." I hold up my coconut bar. "I was late this morning and didn't get breakfast so I'm starving."

"No problem, girl. Eat up and drink up." She lifts her own cup in a cheers. "I have to get to class but it was really nice getting to know you. Where's your phone? I'll give you my number."

I pull it from my pocket, sliding it across the table. "Here you go."

She types her information into my phone and says, "I sent a text to myself so I have your number too." She stands, tapping her fingers on the table. "I hope your day gets better."

I force a smile. "Me too. Thank you again."

"See you around, Millie."

With that, Zara is gone, her long hair swishing around her shoulders as she goes.

Finishing off my bar, I gather up my books in one arm, my drink in my free hand and head to my next class determined to make the most of this day.

THE DAY from hell won't quit.

My fucking car won't start.

It's not even an old car, so why is it failing me now?

Grabbing my phone, I call my brother.

It rings once. *Once.* Before he sends me to voicemail.

I ring again. Same deal.

I try one more time. When he denies my call, I send him a 'fuck you' text.

I'm on the verge of tears outside the dance studio. At least tonight's class went great, unlike the rest of my day. I want today to be over.

Searching through my contacts, I stop at Jude's name. I hesitate for only a second, not giving myself enough time to second guess myself.

"Hello?" He answers curiously, and because I'm so relieved to hear a familiar person's voice I promptly burst into tears. "Whoa, are you okay?" He sounds instantly on alert like he thinks I'm under attack. "Who hurt you?"

"N-No one," I stutter around my tears. "My stupid car won't start." I bang my fist against the steering wheel. "A-And I'm t-tired and hungry and grumpy and this is the worst day *ever*."

I know today could've been even worse than it was, but I feel justified in the fact that my period is making me extra sensitive and weepy.

"Where are you?" I hear voices in the background and he tells someone he has to go.

"Oh, God, are you with your friends? A girl? Don't worry about me. I'll get an Uber."

"Relax, Little Madison. I'm with my brother. He'll be happy to see my ugly mug leave."

I let out a sigh of relief. "I'm at the dance studio. I'll text you the address."

"I'm getting in my truck. I'll be there as fast as I can."

I wipe my nose with the back of my hand. "Jude?"

"Mhmm?"

"Thank you."

Somehow, I know he's smiling. "You're welcome."

I hang up, text him the address, and settle in the driver's seat reading a book on my phone to keep me entertained.

When there's a knock on my window, I let out a shrill scream. I expect it to be Jude, but it's Aleksander leaning over. He waves when I notice him.

Opening my door, I say, "Hi, um, my car won't start. I

have a friend coming to get me and I guess I'll have my car towed." I cringe, because I didn't even take towing into consideration and should've called somewhere by now.

"I wondered if everything was okay when I saw your car still out here."

"Yeah," I draw out the word with a grimace. "Today has not been my day."

"Don't worry about leaving your car here overnight. No one here will mind. You can have it picked up tomorrow."

I bite my lip, hesitating. "Are you sure?"

"It's no problem."

"Get the hell away from her!"

Aleksander jolts away from my car. No, not jolts, he's *shoved.*

"Jude!" I cry, scurrying out of the vehicle, nearly tripping over my own feet in the process. "It's okay! That's Aleksander!"

Jude is thunderous. He has Aleksander pressed up against the brick exterior of the building, the side of his arm pressed to the throat of my boss.

"Jude!" I tug on his arm. "Let him go!"

Somehow, my words reach him this time and he lets Aleksander drop. The tendons in Jude's neck stand out with each heaving breath he takes. "I thought—"

"I'm fine. Apologize to him."

Poor Aleksander is red-faced, struggling to regain control of his breath.

Jude runs his fingers through his hair. "Apologize?" He

sounds completely affronted that I would suggest such a thing. "He was—"

"Speaking to me because he was worried about my car still being here. That's it."

Hands on his hips, jaw twitching, Jude glares around the lot before uttering a completely insincere, "Sorry."

It'll have to be good enough because I know there's no chance of getting anything more from him.

Aleksander clears his throat, straightening. "You're clearly in good hands with your boyfriend. I'll see you soon, Millie."

He heads back toward the entrance of the studio.

"He's not my boyfriend," I mumble, but I know he's out of ear shot.

Jude looks me over like he's searching for injury. "You can't be so trusting."

"He's my boss!" I protest, reaching inside my car for my stuff. Jude's truck idles on the street, the flashers on.

He ignores me. "Give me that." He takes my books and bag from me.

"God, you're such an asshole."

"An asshole who's rescuing you." He opens the back door of his truck, placing my stuff inside. He then opens the passenger, waiting for me.

A part of me wants to refuse his help after he acted like an insane person, but he did leave wherever he was at to come get me. It's more than I can say for my MIA brother.

I climb into the truck, nearly falling, but big hands grip

around my waist and lift me easily inside. "Thanks," I mumble as he closes the door.

Pulling back onto the street, Jude drives toward home. We're almost there when he pulls into the McDonald's drive-thru.

"What are you doing?"

"I know you're hungry, and I am too since I had to leave dinner with my brother."

"I'm really sorry about that."

He smirks in my direction, sitting up slightly to pull his wallet out of his back pocket. "Admit it, you missed me and wanted to see me."

"Yeah." I snort—so very ladylike of me. "That's exactly it."

"What do you want?" He nods toward the menu board up ahead.

I want to be stubborn, to refuse his offer of food, but I *am* hungry, and this has been the day from hell. "Chicken nuggets. With ranch. Fries too."

"That it? Maybe a kid's toy, too?"

"What kind do they have?"

He squints, peering up ahead. "Hot Wheels and Barbie."

"Hot Wheels!" I cry.

He shakes his head, rubbing his fingers over his lips in an attempt to hide his amusement.

When it's finally our turn to order he gets a Happy Meal for himself too, but with a cheeseburger instead of chicken nuggets.

Moving forward, he pays for the meal and takes our boxes. He pulls the truck into a parking space, sliding his seat back. "You good with eating in the truck?"

"Absolutely." I check each box and pass him the one with the burger. Digging into mine for the toy I frown when I come up with nothing. "I was gypped!"

"Huh?" He's already stuffed half the burger in his mouth. The kid's meal will hardly be enough to feed the guy, but I appreciate his attempt at solidarity.

"There's no car." I know it's not the end of the world, I shouldn't have even gotten a kid's meal in the first place, but dammit I really wanted that little toy car.

Jude rifles through his own box and pulls out a plastic wrapped car. "Take mine."

"Are you sure?"

"I'm sure." He wiggles the car for me to grab.

I take it, removing it from the plastic. It's purple with gold flames. I drive it over the console making vroom-vroom noises with the goal of making Jude laugh, which I succeed at.

"You're such a dork, Millie."

"I know." I put the car down so I can dig into my nuggets and ranch. "Thanks for this. And the rescue."

"You don't have to constantly thank me for every little thing."

"I know, but I want *you* to know that I appreciate it."

"Noted." His burger has already been wolfed down and he only has a handful of fries left.

"You can go back through the drive-thru if you want."

He wipes his greasy fingers on a napkin. "I'm good."

I dip another chicken nugget, eyeing my companion. His hair falls lazily over his forehead and there's a treacherous part of me that itches to run my fingers through it. I want desperately not to like him, but then he's constantly doing things that prove he really has a heart.

He's not safe—not for you, my conscience whispers desperately to that aching kernel of lust.

There are so many other guys that would be better suited for me. Take Jonah for example. He's sweet and kind and seems like a good guy. I'm sure he's not as inexperienced as I am, but he's not a womanizer like Jude, at least not from what I've seen.

But still, pursuing anything with my lack of romantic knowledge is a tad frightening. I've kissed a few guys, but barely more than a peck, and with being away at an all-girls school it made dating impossible. But if I had someone to show me the ropes, what I should do and say…

"Teach me," I blurt the words out loud, instantly regretting them the second they're out.

Jude looks around, confused about my question since the entire conversation was taking place in my head. "Teach you?" He repeats. "Teach you what? Who are you talking to?"

"You." My voice is small, squeaky.

He throws his hands up. "I'm so confused."

I internally cringe, hating my own self for getting myself

in this situation. I need to learn how to keep my mouth shut.

"I just … I mean, you have lots of experience with girls, so I was thinking maybe you could teach me."

He blinks at me, face frozen. I think he's doing a factory reset. "You want me to teach you how to get girls?"

"No, I want you to teach me how to get a guy's interest."

"Trust me, you really just have to stand there. Guys are simple creatures."

I sigh. "You're impossible. I just … I'm not good at this."

"Good at what?"

"I don't even know." My hands flounder through the air and he grabs them, setting them back in my lap. He's probably afraid I'm going to send a chicken nugget flying through his truck. "You know I'm inexperienced and I just … I want some guidance. Please?"

"Guidance on what exactly." His jaw works back and forth with tension.

"Kissing. Sex. What to say and do and—"

"Whoa, whoa, whoa." He slashes his hands through the air. "I'm not having sex with you."

"I didn't ask you to have sex with me, just … I don't know, give me information. What to expect or do."

Jude looks like he wants to crawl in a hole and die. Frankly, *I* want to crawl in a hole and die.

"Don't say anything right now. Think about it, that's all I ask."

He looks like he wants to protest some more, but reluctantly keeps his mouth shut and nods instead.

If he says no, it's not the end of the world.

But if he says yes?

Oh God.

sixteen

Jude

Do I look like the relationship whisperer or some shit?

Between helping my brother out with his crush and Millie asking me to teach her about intimacy, I'm beginning to question my own sanity. Do I look like some self-help guru? Sure, I offered to help Jonah but this thing with Millie? I want to say no. I *should* say no. But I don't think I can. And that makes me all the angrier, because I should be stronger than this.

I pace back and forth in my bedroom, probably damn

near to wearing a hole in the floor. It's been three days since Millie asked me, and I haven't missed her side glances —her silent question on whether or not I've made a decision.

Yanking open the door to the bathroom, I find her at the sink brushing her teeth. She lets out a muffled scream at the intrusion, toothpaste dribbling onto her tank.

Pulling her toothbrush from her mouth, she spits in the sink, and uses the brush to point at me. "You have got to stop doing that."

"Doing what?"

"Barging in here."

"You could've locked the door," I argue, leaning against the sink counter with my arms crossed over my chest.

"I was only brushing my teeth. Besides, I mean about the way you yank the door open and stomp in all surly-like."

"I just wanted to inform you I've made a decision."

She pales a little, looking a tad green around the edges. If she's sick over this whole thing, then why'd she even ask? "Oh?"

"I'll do it. I don't know exactly *how* I'm going to accomplish this, but I'll do my best to teach you about intimacy."

"Intimacy?" She repeats it as a question.

"The kissing and sex stuff."

"Mhmm," she hums. "Okay. So, um, when do we start?"

Shit. Fuck. Mother-fucking-shit.

I didn't think about this part of the equation. "I'll come up with a game plan and get back to you." I'm hedging, that much is obvious, and from the tilt of her brow she knows it too.

"What if while you're coming up with a game plan you weasel out of it?"

I scoff at the absurdity. "I'm a man—I don't weasel."

She matches my pose—hip against the counter, arms over her chest. "Men are the definition of weasels."

I tug on the strands of my hair. "I ... fuck, I haven't thought about this part, okay? You're just lucky I even said yes."

"You didn't *have* to say yes."

"Then I take it back."

I turn to flee the bathroom, but her small hand wraps around my arm. "Nope, not so fast, sir. You agreed, this is a binding contract now."

My teeth grind together. "Fine." The words are bitten through my clenched teeth. "You tell me then, what do you want to know about first?"

She releases my arm, and I stupidly miss her touch as soon as it's gone.

Not her, not her, not her. I chant to myself. *Anyone but her.*

There's no telling that to my dick, though, who stirs to life in my pants. I say a silent prayer that she doesn't look down. It's probably a pointless wish, because I almost always have a boner around Millie and at some point, she's going to notice if she hasn't already.

She rubs her lips together, clearly nervous. "I don't

know, tell me what guys like? Should I be more forward? How do I flirt? Should I try to touch him in some way? What about—"

"Okay, slow down, that's a lot of questions with vague answers." She frowns at my response, sighing like she's already incredibly stressed by this whole thing. *If it freaks her out, why did she even ask me?* "First off, all guys are different and that means what they're into will be different too. Does it seem like he likes you?"

Her brows furrow, lips twisting to the side in thought. "I-I think so. I mean, I catch him looking at me and blushing."

Jealousy simmers in my veins. It's completely irrational. The last person I should be jealous of is this guy I don't even know—but he's checking out Millie and she clearly returns the sentiment.

"Step one is complete then," I reluctantly say the words. "He's interested, so now we go from there. What are things he likes?"

She bites her lip, thinking. "He's a swimmer, I know that much, and he talks about his family a lot. I can tell he really loves them, and I think that's cute, especially since I'm close with my family." She lifts her hair off her shoulders, putting it in a ponytail. "He's mentioned video games before, and he reads fantasy books. He brought me one the other day that he thought I'd like."

It sounds like this guy is already sunk for her and it would take no effort on her part to secure him, but it doesn't seem like that's her issue. Millie doesn't seem embarrassed by her lack of experience, but I think I know her well enough at this point to deduce that it's more about she doesn't like to be lacking in power. If this guy is more experienced than her, then she wants to be on an even playing field. Which I get, but *why* did she have to ask me. I'm the worst person to ask. Macy was the only girl I was with until she wasn't anymore, and after that I haven't kept a tally. I have a feeling I'd be appalled if I knew the actual number of women I've slept with.

Millie mentioned he's a swimmer, my brain immediately thinking of my brother. It makes me feel sick, because I can see it. Millie and Jonah together would be that quintessential couple and God knows my parents would fucking love her.

Running a hand over my jaw, I say, "Okay, so he likes to swim, why don't you hint at going to the pool together or something."

She thinks it over. "Maybe."

"Maybe?" I scoff. "This is free advice, Little Madison, don't dismiss it."

She rolls her eyes at me, and I want nothing more than to toss her over my shoulder so I can spank her ass.

"So, what, I just ask if we can go to the pool sometime?"

"Yep. Just like that."

"And then what?"

I look away from her, hating myself so much for

agreeing to this. "Then you come back to me, and we go from there."

"Okay." She nods her head, resolute. "I'll keep you posted."

I step away from the counter, turning toward the door. "You do that."

Jude, what have you done?

Something tells me I haven't even reached the tip of the iceberg of what a colossal fuck up this is.

"CARTWRIGHT!" Coach hollers my name at the end of practice, waving me over with his clipboard flapping through the air.

I remove my helmet, my hair soaked with sweat. "Yeah, Coach?" I'm thirsty and in desperate need of a shower.

"You're doing better out there, but still not quite on top of your game. I'm not pulling you from the game this weekend." Relief floods me at that news. "But don't make me regret that choice." He points a finger at me in warning. "We need you on top of your game."

I nod my head up and down like a puppet. "I promise. I've got this."

He pounds his hand on my shoulder pad. "I believe you."

He dismisses me and I run inside to shower. Some of the guys are headed to Harvey's and normally I'd agree, but I say no to all the offers. I'm not interested in a beer or a hookup.

"You're different lately," Keaton comments, snapping his watch onto his wrist. For once, the sound of his voice doesn't grate on my nerves. I guess I'm making progress—healing and all that shit.

"No, I'm not." I don't feel any different.

"Whatever you say, man. See you later." He holds his fist out for a bump and looks as surprised as me when I bump mine against it.

I finish up and head out to the mostly empty lot. Something makes me pause and look around, realization settling on my shoulders. This is my last year here and soon, all of this, will be a distant memory.

Ducking my head, I climb in my truck and leave.

seventeen

Millie

"WHAT ARE YOU WEARING?" MY BROTHER STARES AT me, spoon hovering almost, but not quite, to his mouth.

"Um." I look down at my outfit. "Shorts and a jersey." I pluck at the shirt.

"That's Jude's number."

The accusation in his tone makes me mad. "Yeah? So what? I'm going to the game with Zara and I wanted a jersey. It made the most sense to get Jude's since, you know, he lives here." I leave out the part about him kinda-sorta being my friend because God knows my idiotic brother will read way more into that than is necessary.

"You didn't tell me you were going to the game. *Fuck*."

Daire smirks at him from across the table and it doesn't take a rocket scientist to figure out that he kicked my brother in the shin. I'd thank him for his service, but he's been weird lately, so I keep my mouth shut.

I grab a La Croix, popping the tab on the can. "I didn't know I needed to fill you in on every detail of my life. It's a football game, not an orgy."

He cringes but ignores that comment. "You have ribbons in your hair."

"Thank you, Captain Obvious." I twist one of the ribbons I added to my ponytail in our school's colors of blue and orange. "There's paint on my face too in case you missed that." I point at my cheeks.

"Maybe I should go to the game," he grumbles, stirring cereal around the bowl.

"If there are tickets left you should," I say in a sickly-sweet voice, "but you won't be sitting with me."

Daire laughs, clearly enjoying Cree's pain. I love my brother, I do, but he's been a bit of a dick to me lately—ignoring me and then badgering me about Jude, as if my relationship with him, or lack thereof, is any of his business.

"I'll tell you what, if you're a good boy, I'll bring you back a souvenir or something. Perhaps a nice teddy bear? Would you like that?"

His lips twitch with a smile. "Smart ass."

"I learned from the best. I'll see you guys later. I'm meeting Zara at her dorm."

"Fine. Check in when you get there."

"Sure, Dad," I call over my shoulder.

I head over to campus, and I know I shouldn't be surprised, but I am anyway by the number of students dressed for the game and headed toward the stadium. It's the first home game of the season, so naturally people are excited.

Parking my car, which thankfully only needed a new battery, I shoot Zara a text. She responds quickly that she's on her way out.

Slipping from my car, I lock it behind me heading over to the dorm's entrance to wait for her.

I was surprised when I got her text out of the blue asking if I'd want to go with her, but I was happy to hear from her, so I said yes. There was no way I could pass up the opportunity and yes, I might've gone through the extra trouble of Googling Jude's jersey number so I could buy one that matched, just because I knew it would drive Cree insane. Getting under my brother's skin is number one on my job description as little sister.

Zara steps out of the building, dressed similarly in ripped high-waisted shorts with a cropped shirt bearing the school's logo. Her hair is pulled into a ponytail with a baseball cap.

"Hi!" She hurries over to me, throwing her arms around

my shoulders. I hug her back. "I'm so happy you said yes. I *love* football, but it's no fun going to games by myself."

"I'm happy you asked."

"You're in for a treat with this game. It's against—" She launches into a whole explanation of another college that is apparently one of our rivals and how there's bad blood, along with a lot of other football jargon that means absolutely nothing to me.

We make our way to the stadium, grab some drinks and popcorn, then make our way through the stands to our seats.

"Do you know anyone on the team?" I ask.

"Eh," she says in a dismissive tone, grabbing a handful of popcorn. "I had a situation-ship with one of the guys on the team for a while."

I arch a brow, intrigued. "A situation-ship?"

She rolls her eyes. "Well, basically we were just hooking up but it was supposed to be an exclusive hookup, you know? Aka don't dip your stick in other people's vaginas for however long we're having sex. Derek fucked some girl at a party, I heard about it, and put a kibosh on the whole thing. I'm fine with casual, but if we agree not to fuck other people, I expect the guy to uphold his end of the deal."

"Wow." I take a sip of soda. "That was way more than I expected."

Zara laughs, some popcorn flying out of her mouth. "My mom always tells me I'm an over-sharer. You'd think I'd learn, but I haven't. What about you? Do you know anyone on the team?"

"Yeah, one guy."

She blinks at me, waiting. "Do tell, girl. Don't withhold information. I'm too nosy for that."

"Jude. He's my roommate."

Her jaw drops. "You're roommates with *him*. Oh my God, Millie! He's so hot!"

It's on the tip of my tongue to say that I know, but somehow, I manage to keep those two words to myself. "He's all right," I say instead.

"Wait, how is he your roommate? Details, Millie. I need details."

"I live off-campus with my brother and a few of his friends. He's one of them."

"Wow." She fans herself. "This is a juicy tidbit of information. Do you need another roommate? Just kidding," she adds before I can answer. "He's so hot. I'm jealous. You're living every girl on campus's dream."

"I don't know about that," I mumble.

Zara goes on, "I'm pretty sure every girl wants to hook up with him."

Myself included, unfortunately. "And I'm pretty sure he's slept with most of them."

"I have heard he's quite the manwhore," she admits, digging in for more popcorn. "But you know what? He's hot enough I'd still do it. Are you into him?"

"No!" I blurt so loud that more than a few heads turn in

our direction. My cheeks warm with embarrassment, but I hope I can pass it off as the heat of the sun.

"Oh my God." She grips my arm, nearly causing me to spill our entire popcorn bag. Thankfully, I manage to save it. "You're totally into him."

"Am not." I hope I don't sound as defensive to her ears as I do to mine.

She grabs at a stray flyaway hair, trying to smooth it down with the rest of her ponytail. "You *like* him, Millie." She rubs her hands together. "Oh, this is so interesting. And you *live* with him."

"And my brother," I mumble under my breath.

She grins. "The drama of that situation is beyond juicy."

"It's *awful.*" I lower my head, wishing I could bury my entire body in the popcorn bag so I could disappear. "And I shouldn't like him. As we've established, he's a manwhore."

"So?" She argues, arching a perfectly plucked brow. My brows are always on the bushy side. For the life of me I can't make them look decent. "If you wanna do him, then do him."

"He's my friend," I argue, and the fact of the matter is, somehow, he really is my friend. I *like* Jude. I don't just want to have sex with him. And to make matters worse, I do have a crush on Jonah too.

Somehow, I went from liking zero guys to being interested in two. Not one. Two. Plural. I hate myself.

"You're friends with him?" She kicks her feet giddily. "This keeps getting better and better."

"Worse, you mean."

She swats playfully at my arm. "You're no fun. If you're into him, just go for it."

I press my lips together, wishing it was that easy. Stuffing a handful of popcorn into my mouth, I say a prayer that she'll drop the subject.

She doesn't.

"You're gorgeous, Millie. *He'd* be lucky for you to be into him."

I snort, hunkering down in my seat. "Yeah, right."

I'm the opposite of what Jude hooks up with. I'm not saying I'm ugly. I'm happy with how I look, but I'm ... plain. I'm not going to coat my face in layers of makeup, most of the time I barely put on mascara. My freckles across my nose always show up no matter what I do. I'm petite, with barely a B-cup for breasts. And yeah, I'm muscular from ballet, but a lot of guys don't like that. And, personally, I'm not interested in changing myself for any guy.

Lips parted, surprise fills her eyes. "I'm serious, Millie! You're so pretty and cute, and you have a great personality."

"I'm pretty sure the great personality part is an instant boner deflator for guys like him."

Zara rolls her dark brown eyes. "If that's the case, then fuck him." She wrinkles her nose. "Well, not literally fuck him, but fuck him, you know?"

I laugh, amused at her rambling. "I got you."

When the game finally starts, my eyes scan the field for

Jude. While most of the guys run onto the field, he walks, like this is no big deal and something he does every day. He looks even taller and more intimidating than usual with his gear on. Even from this far away I can sense the intensity around him, and my treacherous body is turned on by that. I gulp, silently cursing myself. Asking Jude to teach me about intimacy was the dumbest choice I could've ever made.

I'm screwed.

Figuratively. Definitely not literally, because I can't go there. Not with him.

MY FIRST COLLEGE football game was beautiful to watch. Probably a strange descriptor, but it's true. Or maybe it was only Jude that was so beautiful out there.

Regardless, football has a new fan.

After the game, Zara and I walk back to her dorm, and she drives us over to a bar named Harvey's. I know my brother and his friends go there a lot.

"I'm underage," I remind her as she turns into the lot, the tires of her car bumping over the gravel.

"So am I." She waggles her brows. "That doesn't matter here. They're pretty lax. Besides, there are always cute guys to buy you drinks too."

"That doesn't seem very safe."

She frowns, thinking it over. "Ugh, you're right. I never

really thought about it. I was only thinking about the free drinks. Why do you have to be so smart?"

Inside, we find a small high-top table with only enough room for us and maybe one other person if they stand and squeeze in tight to us. The place is packed already, and she says it's only going to get worse because most of the team will come here after the game.

"I'll see if I can get us some drinks." I eye her. "Not accepting any from strangers, of course."

Zara's not gone long when a waitress swings by the table. "Hi, I'm Chasity." She chews on her gum. "Can I get ya anything?"

"Um, maybe some waters." I have a feeling Zara will not be asking for those. "And some nachos."

I'm not sure my body can handle the nachos on top of the popcorn I already scarfed down at the game, but they sound pretty good right now.

"Sure. I'll get that in." She taps her pen against the pad. "Just holler if you need something."

I sit tight, waiting for Zara to return while watching even more people pile into the building. Everyone is in a joyful mood after the winning game, and a lot of people seem like they're already slightly drunk.

Zara shimmies her way back to the table with two margaritas in hand. "This is Harvey's signature drink—at least with the ladies," she explains, setting one in front of me. "There's not a lot of alcohol in them which makes them especially dangerous."

"How's that?"

"Because they're so good you keep drinking more until you're plastered." She takes a sip of hers. "Damn that's good." Holding her glass up to mine, she says, "Here's to excellent margaritas, a great game, and the potential for some good dicking."

"I ... um ... you know what, cheers."

We clink our glasses together and that's that.

eighteen

Jude

THE ENERGY IN HARVEY'S IS FUCKING INSANE. WHEN I walk in with some of my teammates we're instantly swamped with pats on the back, cheers, and free drinks shoved in our hands.

"I'm heading to the back," I say to my friend Daniel.

I'm not sure he even hears me.

Navigating my way through the swell of bodies, I move in the direction of the giant U-shaped booth my friends are usually at.

Something stops me.

Maybe it's some sort of freakish sixth sense, but I find my eyes moving toward the dancefloor, and there in the middle, eyes closed and arms thrown above her head is Millie. Her hair is in pigtails, fucking pigtails, and dammit if my treacherous mind doesn't picture her on her hands and knees in front of me, while I pound into her from behind with those two pigtails wrapped in my fist.

My eyes scan the rest of her, my dick immediately at attention when I realize she's wearing my jersey number.

Fuck, fuck, fuck.

I know Cree's not here. I sent him and Daire a text earlier asking if they were coming to the bar. Daire said yes, but Cree said he had plans.

My feet ignore my brain's protests, carrying me toward where Millie is on the dancefloor. I see other guys eyeing her, and with one look I tell them all to back off.

I wish I could say it was for unselfish reasons, like trying to protect her, but this is purely selfish.

I haven't wanted a woman the way I want Millie since Macy and that scares me to fucking death. I swore up and down I'd never be weak enough to fall in love again and for the last few years that's been an easy promise to keep. Then Cree's sister shows up and all my plans and rules are ready to go flying out the fucking window.

When I'm in front of her, her eyes open like maybe she senses me in the same way I'm always aware of her.

"Little Madison," I grin, placing a hand on her waist. "What do you think you're doing?"

Her eyes are more dilated than normal when her gaze meets mine.

"Dancing," she replies, still swaying. "What does it look like I'm doing?"

"Dancing," I reply and she smiles. "But I'd rather you dance with me."

What the fuck are you doing?

When it comes to this girl, I have absolutely no fucking clue what I'm doing. I should put her at arm's length, but for some reason I just fucking can't.

She puts her arms around my shoulders, her small body pressing closer. "You wanna dance with me, Jude?"

"Yes," I practically groan. "I shouldn't, but I want to so fucking bad."

"Hmm," she hums, sliding a hand down my chest. Her palm settles over my heart. I wonder if she can feel how fast it's beating. I'm not sure my heart was pumping this hard out on the field today. "Interesting."

I bend my lips to her ear. She shivers at the intimate touch. "What's interesting?"

She smiles, her tongue slipping out to moisten her lips. "I didn't know you were capable of saying what you really mean. Being honest."

"I can be honest." My hands flex against her slender hips. "Maybe I'm withholding the truth because I know you can't handle it."

She throws her head back, laughing. Laughing at *me*.

"You're so cute," she says it with a slight, condescending

edge. "You think you're protecting me, am I right? Wrong, Jude," she says, not giving me a chance to respond. "It's yourself you're protecting, because you're too scared to admit the truth."

"And what do you think the truth is?"

"You," she pokes me in the chest, "are attracted to me."

I am. I so fucking am. "I'm not."

She stands on her tiptoes to reach my ear. "Liar. I can feel your cock. That's for *me*."

I never fucking imagined I'd hear the word cock on Millie's tongue and fuck if it doesn't make me want to wrap my hand around her neck to pull her lips to mine.

"It could be for someone else," I argue, trying to deflect.

She smiles breezily, her eyes hazy from the alcohol that's boldening her. "You're lying." She taps my nose. "And since your nose isn't growing, I wonder if something else is." She giggles, eyes dropping to my crotch.

I wrap my hand around her wrist, pulling her from the dancefloor. She follows easily enough until we stop in the darkened hallway near the restrooms and back exit. I cage her in against the wall, hands on either side of her head. She licks her lips, trying not to smile.

"Is the big bad Jude trying to scare me? I might be little and innocent, but you don't frighten me."

I bend down, pressing my nose to her neck. Fuck, she smells amazing. Like something both floral and sweet. If I didn't already think she was good enough to eat, I would now. One of her legs wraps around me, trying to pull me against her hips, and one of her hands fists the hair at the back of my skull.

"You should be fucking terrified of me, Little Madison."

Laughter lights her eyes. "You're not as scary as you think."

"I'd ruin you."

She smirks. "Maybe that's what I want." Biting her lip, she rises up, so her lips barely brush mine. It's not even a kiss. It's not *anything* and yet I feel it fucking anywhere. I'm sunk for this girl, and she hasn't even tried to reel me in like so many others have. All she has to do is *exist* and I want to drop to my knees and worship her.

I shake my head, trying to snap myself out of this trance she has me in. "Trust me, you don't. I'm not the happily-ever-after kind of guy. I'm not going to ride off into the sunset with you. I'm the guy that fucks you so good that no other man will ever be able to replace me and then you'll hate me for it."

She laughs, a soft sexy sigh of a laugh. "Someone thinks very highly of himself." She starts to pull away, so I let her. Over her shoulder she says, "Remember, Jude, I'm not the one that said anything about sunsets."

Fuck, she's right.

I run my fingers through my hair, watching her go.

DID I plan on getting saddled with taking care of Cree's drunk little sister?

No.

But here I am.

Millie heaves over the toilet in our shared bathroom, her hair down now and clasped in my hand so she doesn't throw up in it. With my other hand I rub circles against her back. Who the fuck have I become?

"How much did you drink?"

My only answer is her tears as she slumps against me.

"No more bars for you," I grumble.

I'm exhausted from my game and the late hour, but when it became obvious how wasted she was at the bar I hauled her ass home. I've tried to get water in her system, but since she keeps throwing up, I doubt any is staying down.

The only saving grace is Cree still isn't home. Something tells me he'd be pissed to find Millie in this state and somehow I'd get blamed for it, even though she'd clearly already had plenty to drink when I arrived at Harvey's.

"How's she doing?" Daire asks, appearing in the doorway to the bathroom through my room.

"How's it look?"

He cringes. "Not good."

"Exactly."

I groan, trying to adjust my legs since my right calf is wanting to go numb.

Daire takes in the scene in front of him, his eyes darting back and forth from Millie to me.

"You're into her."

It's a statement, not a question. "Mind your business."

"You can't go there," he warns, rubbing his jaw. His blond hair is a mess and I'm not sure if it's from a girl or him tugging at it. The guy has seemed extra stressed lately.

"I know," I reply.

"I mean it. Cree will never forgive you."

I swallow thickly. "I know."

Millie starts to cry, and I resume rubbing her back. Out of the corner of my eye I see Daire shake his head. "You go there and we're both fucked. Cree will figure I've known something."

"I'm not doing anything!" I yell loud enough that Millie whimpers. I'm sure she has a raging headache already and since she can't keep water down, I haven't even bothered trying to get ibuprofen in her system.

"Maybe not yet, but you will," Daire says cryptically, like I'm always destined to fuck things up.

"I won't."

He laughs humorlessly. "Yeah, we'll see."

He disappears from the doorway, leaving me with the drunk girl I'm supposed to feel nothing for but stupidly feel everything.

nineteen

Millie

"ARE YOU OKAY?" I LIFT MY HEAD FROM THE COOL surface of the wood table in the library's work room. The door softly latches behind Jonah. He sets his stuff down on the table and bless him he's brought me iced coffee and there's a whole box of donuts. Yesterday, when I drank an endless amount of margaritas and something called a Harvey's Hurricane I didn't take into consideration the fact that I've never had more than a few sips of beer in my life or that Jonah and I had agreed to meet this morning to work on our project. Apparently, I'm not the best decision maker.

I even had some weird dream that Jude was taking care of me while I was sick. Yeah, right. "Are you sick?"

"Hungover," I grumble. "Bad decisions were made last night." I rub a hand over my face. My brain isn't slamming against my skull as badly as before, but I know it won't take much to send me into a migraine. "Can I have one of those?" I point at the box of donuts.

"That's what they're for."

I open the box and grab one that has purple icing and rainbow sprinkles. "Sugar," I say with glee, taking a bite. "You, Jonah, are a saint. I think I might love you."

My psychology partner blushes at the compliment, which in turn makes me blush when I realize what I've said. Apparently, I completely lack any sort of filter when I've been drinking.

"Are you going to be able to work today?"

I sigh, pulling my laptop out of my bag. "I'm going to try my best."

He pushes the iced coffee closer to me. "This is for you too."

"If I didn't love you before, I do now."

His blush deepens.

Dammit, I've done it again.

Taking a fortifying sip of coffee, I open my laptop. "All right, let's do this thing."

THREE HOURS LATER, Jonah and I have finished for the day and are packing up our stuff. Trying not to think about some of the things I said to Jude last night—unfortunately I still remember most of them—I think about our conversation we had before, on things I could talk to Jonah about.

"So," I exaggerate the word, "you like swimming?"

He gives me an amused look. "Yeah."

"Maybe we could go to the pool together sometime?"

Oh my God why does that sound so cringe! I instantly want to smack my face with the palm of my hand.

Jonah pauses midway to sliding his laptop in his bag. He gives me a funny look, half-curious, half-confused. "Are you asking me on a date?"

"Maybe. Yeah." I'm not sure I could be more awkward if I tried, and screw Jude for his God-awful advice.

"I love swimming, but for a date..." He pauses, shrugging his backpack on. "Let's do something else."

"Like dinner?" I blurt.

His lips thin with thought. "I think I can come up with something better. How about Friday at six? I'll see you sometime this week so we can go from there."

"Make it seven," I say, since I teach a ballet class that evening and want enough time to come home and change.

"Seven," he agrees with a shy smile.

God, if we aren't two awkward human beings, but still surely Jonah is more experienced with dating than I am.

He walks me out to my car, and I say a prayer on the drive home that I don't make a fool of myself on this date.

I DON'T KNOW WHY, but it takes me a few days to get the courage to tell Jude about the date.

Knocking on his door that connects from the bathroom, I hear his muttered, "What?"

I open the door and find him at his desk, shirtless in nothing but a pair of athletic shorts. I don't know what takes over my brain, but I think about what it would be like if he were mine, and if I were more confident. I'd tiptoe across the floor and sink into his lap on the chair, maybe roll my hips into his—

"Millie?" He prompts, trying to hide his amusement.

"Oh, um." I toy with the hem of my old t-shirt. "So, I have a date Friday."

I'm not prepared for the various emotions that flicker across his face. Ranging from surprise, to worry, to ... jealousy? Before flattening into a smooth expression like nothing was there to begin with.

He clears his throat. "That's great. The swimming thing worked?"

"Not really," I hedge, sitting on the edge of his bed. I'm surprised to find it made and the rest of his room tidy. "But it got my foot in the door so to speak."

"And now you want my help with?"

I look around his room instead of at him. He hasn't added any personal touches that I can tell. "You know what I need help with," I grumble, not wanting to say it out loud.

He sighs, running his fingers through his hair and flips his laptop closed. "So, what, you want me to kiss you or something?"

My stomach flips and flops and does a complete somersault at that. "I don't know, maybe we could go out on a pretend date so I could get a feel for it?"

He pinches the bridge of his nose. "Now, you want me to fake date you?"

"Not like that." I frown, rubbing the side of my nose. It's itchy with nerves. "I just mean, that maybe we could go out together and it'd be like a practice run."

Jude rubs his face, his cheeks heavily stubbled with dark scruff. "Fine. Okay. But it's Wednesday, which means we have to do this tomorrow, is that good for you? And your brother can't know." He points a warning finger at me. "I like my dick attached to my body."

I smile, happy he's agreed. "You have a deal."

twenty

Jude

I'M THE BIGGEST IDIOT ON THE PLANET. SERIOUSLY, there's no one dumber than me. It's not possible. I never should've agreed to help Millie in the first place but agreeing to a practice date is even worse.

I keep reminding myself this isn't real, that it doesn't matter, it's all to help her, but it's harder to get through my head than I expected.

She's doing this because she's into a guy that isn't you.

That should be enough to kill my lust, sadly it does nothing.

I dress in a pair of jeans, my usual boots, and a navy t-shirt. She asked me to plan this pretend date since the guy she's going out with is doing the same and she figured she should be surprised by me as well.

I haven't gone on a proper date since Macy and I ended things. Even if this isn't technically a real date, it's close enough to freak me out.

Luckily, Daire and Cree aren't home. I'm so thankful that for whatever reason those two are MIA most of the time. Maybe Cree's making progress with that girl he likes.

Grabbing my cologne off my nightstand I spray a little on my shirt. I don't want to do too much and have it be overwhelming. Wiping my clammy hands on my jeans, I exhale in frustration. Why am I so fucking nervous? This isn't even a date.

Should I have gotten her flowers?

I've seriously lost my mind.

Leaving my room, I head down the hall to hers and knock on the door. "You ready?"

"Just a minute!"

I try not to groan, leaning my body against the opposite wall as I wait for her to finish up.

True to her word, a minute later the door opens. Millie steps out with a soft, sweet smile. Her hair is curled around her shoulders, and she wears a dress with some kind of flower pattern on it. Spinning in a circle, she stops in front of me, my eyes taking in the pair of heels on her feet and gliding back up her body.

"What do you think?"

Beautiful.

I clear my throat. "You look fine."

Her face falls and I feel like an asshole. I *am* an asshole.

"I guess we better get going," she says, and I can tell that she's retreating into herself all because I couldn't be honest.

I wrap my hand around her wrist. "You look good, Millie."

"Really?"

I look her up and down again. "Really."

That seems to satisfy her, but her smile still isn't quite as big as before.

"Are you going to tell me what we're doing on this non-date yet?"

"Nope." I follow her down the stairs. "Where's the fun in that?"

She shakes her head at me. "Fine, don't tell me."

Outside, I unlock my truck and open the passenger door for her, offering her a hand. She ignores it at first until she reluctantly accepts that she's not as steady as usual in her heels. I would think those things would be a piece of cake for someone who dances on her literal toes, but what do I know.

When Millie's settled in the seat, I close the door. "What are you in the mood to eat?" I ask when I get behind the wheel.

Her mouth opens in a surprised O and she lightly

smacks my arm. "You mean to tell me you haven't planned this non-date at all?"

I back out of the driveway, glancing over at her. "Oh, I have something planned, but you're picking the food."

Her eyes narrow like she doesn't quite believe me. Fair assessment, but I actually do have a plan.

"I'd actually love Thai."

"I know the perfect place." I call in an order with an assortment of things, Millie interjecting here and there with things she wants. "It should be ready by the time we get there." I put my phone in the cupholder.

"And then where are we going?"

I cluck my tongue. "Now, Little Madison, we've been over this. It's a surprise."

She sighs haughtily but when I look at her there's a playful glint in her eyes, so I know she's only kidding.

Ten minutes later I pull into the lot of the Thai restaurant and run inside to grab our food. When I get back to the truck, I pass Millie the bag of food. She's plugged her phone in, swaying along to the song playing

"It's not nice to take control of people's AUX cords."

She sticks her tongue out, rummaging through the bag. "Don't act like we don't have practically the same taste in music."

Where I want to go is another ten-minute drive from the restaurant. By some miracle Millie doesn't ask any more questions. Her playlist keeps her occupied, shuffling through songs and singing along softly. When I sing with her, she smiles over at me and for a second, just a second, I let myself imagine what it would be like if she were mine.

Riding around in my truck, her hair spinning around her shoulders. Holding her hand in mine. Free to kiss her when and where I wanted. She'd look at me like ... like I was everything.

I swallow past the lump in my throat, because I can't have that, not again, and definitely not with my friend's little sister.

I pull my truck over to the lookout spot, the views stunning. Millie's eyes widen in surprise at the view of the hills and valleys all around us. On campus and in the town surrounding it, it's easy to forget that places like this exist too.

"Is this where we're eating?"

"Almost."

She watches me curiously as I get out of the truck and lay down the tailgate. She slips from the truck, gasping in surprise at the blankets and pillows piled in the back. Her wide doe-like eyes dart from the back of the truck to me.

I rub the back of my head, suddenly nervous that this was a stupid date idea. I mean, it's not even a *real* date. It's just practice.

"You ... uh ... you said you preferred eating in the car than in a restaurant, so I thought I'd go along with that, but sort of..." I wave my hand at the shit in the back. "Elevate it, I guess."

Fuck, kill me now. I sound like a blabbering idiot.

I grunt in surprise when she crashes into my middle, wrapping her arms around me. The side of her face presses against my stomach.

"This is amazing," she murmurs, her voice muffled. "You listened to what I said and you came up with this."

I clear my throat. "Yeah."

She doesn't appear to be letting me go anytime soon, and I find my arms automatically wrapping around her. My body relaxes against hers as I hug her. My nose is pressed to the top of her head, and I smell her shampoo. It's the same smell that fills our bathroom. It smells clean and floral and perfectly Millie.

Her arms start to drop from my sides, and I reluctantly let go and step away.

This girl shouldn't mean anything to me, but she has me in a fucking chokehold and I haven't even tasted her lips yet.

"I'll grab the food." She gives a little dance, running back around the side of the truck. I adjust the blankets on top of the air mattress I put on the bottom to cushion us and climb inside, grabbing drinks from the cooler. When Millie comes back around I take the bag from her and then lift her up. She gives a little gasp, and I realize how close my thumbs are to her boobs.

Fuck.

I feel like a horny teenager again, the way my dick gets instantly hard around her over the smallest of things.

If Millie realized what a turn on everything she does is,

she would've never asked me for her help on this endeavor. She would've known that any sane male would find her attractive.

We get comfortable among the blankets and pillows, piling the food between us. The truck is parked so we'll have the perfect view of the sunset—which I definitely did not Google the exact time it would set, that would be ridiculous.

She digs into a box of noodles. "I'm sad summer is almost over. The warm days are already becoming fewer."

I lift a bottle of water to my mouth, chugging half since I suddenly feel parched. I'd love to have a beer, and one would hardly be enough to make me drunk, but I wanted to have all my wits about me since Millie's presence alone tends to make me crazy.

"I love fall," I admit, stretching my legs. Reaching for a container, I shovel food in my mouth, more from a desire to keep myself from saying anything stupid than from actual hunger.

"I do love the clothes," she admits with a small smile. "I guess that sounds so stereotypical to you."

I shrug, deciding for honesty. "I'm not the person to ever judge or poke fun at someone's interests." I motion to myself. "Some could say I'm the stereotypical jock, but that's just surface level and clearly coming from someone who doesn't actually know me. So what if you like clothes and dressing up? It's okay to like those things."

"What's something you like then that would surprise people?" She crosses her legs under her, sitting up straight

I laugh, realizing I have the perfect thing to tell her. "I collect Hot Wheels."

She gasps. "No, you don't! And you gave me the car from your Happy Meal and everything."

It wasn't a big deal to me. "You wanted it."

"I never would've pegged you for a toy car collector."

I snap my fingers. "And that's exactly what I'm saying. You can't ever really know someone if all you do is skim the surface."

"You have a point." She stares at her noodles like they hold all the answers in the universe.

"Your turn. What's something I should know about you?"

"Um…" She wets her lips, thinking. I can't help but look at her lips, so full and fucking kissable. "There was this one time when all I would eat were peanut butter sandwiches. I'm talking for every meal. I think it lasted for a few straight weeks. My parents took me to see a doctor thinking I might be deficient in something, but the doctor said I was just being a kid. All this after they ran a bunch of tests and blood work." She gives a soft laugh. "I can't look at a jar of peanut butter without thinking about it."

"I'm not sure I'll look at peanut butter the same either." Clearing my throat, I say, "You're doing well on this non-date. You doubt yourself too much."

She looks at me shyly. "That's because I'm with you."

I rear back, not understanding. “What does that mean?”

“I’ve gotten to know you, and we’re friends, I mean I think we’re friends.” Her nose scrunches like she’s suddenly insecure about this fact. “I’m comfortable with you.”

I clear my throat, reaching for another box of food. “We’re friends, Millie.”

She smiles softly, her hair falling forward to hide her face. “Good.”

twenty-one

Millie

We finish eating and Jude cleans up our mess, stuffing everything back in the paper bag and putting it in the truck. "The date's not over?" I ask when he climbs up into the back and lays down beside me. His shirt rides up, exposing a slip of smooth tanned stomach and the dark hair beneath his navel. My stupid brain conjures the image of the time I saw him naked.

Stop thinking about him like that on your fake-date! This isn't real! He doesn't want you like that.

"Nope, not over yet. We're waiting for sunset. It shouldn't be much longer now." He reaches over, opening the cooler again and pulls out a plastic container of mini cupcakes. "Dessert?"

"I'll never say no to chocolate and icing."

He opens them up and holds it out for me to take what I want. I grab two, one with hot pink icing and the other with blue.

Jude takes two as well and we're silent as we peel the wrappers off our cupcakes and eat them.

"You know," I say after a few minutes of quiet, "for someone who doesn't date, this is a pretty good one."

He laughs, humorless, bright pink frosting stuck to the corner of his lip. I don't know what makes me do it, but I swipe it from his lip with the back of my pinky finger, sucking the sugary goodness from my own finger. His eyes darken as he watches, a blush blooming across my cheeks.

"Millie?"

"Yeah?" I sound breathless to my own ears. It's pathetic how worked up he gets me without even trying.

Jonah, I remind myself. I like him. He's cute. He's a good guy. He could be a great boyfriend for me. Jude's not that type, and it would serve me well to remember it. But it's so hard sometimes when he makes me feel so many things I've never felt before.

He clears his throat. "You need to remember I'm not this guy." He gestures around us. The view. The blankets.

The pillows. "I'm not romantic. I don't date. This is..." He swallows like it's almost painful. "This is to help you, okay? That's it. Nothing more."

"I know."

And I do know, my brain at least does, but my heart? That's another matter altogether.

I look away from him, focusing on the view and where the sun is beginning to sink behind the hills.

While I watch the view, he watches me, and I don't know what that means.

I FEEL Jude's eyes on me as I come down the stairs for my date with Jonah. I wonder if he notices that I put more effort into myself for our non-date. It wasn't on purpose, but after the ballet class this evening I was tired and didn't have the energy to look as nice as I would've liked. In my defense I did get a text message from Jonah telling me to wear jeans and t-shirt for wherever we're going. He hasn't given me any clues beyond that, but I take that to mean it's a casual event.

Cree comes around the corner, stopping me before I reach the last step. "Text me when you meet up with this guy, and again when you get where you're going, then check in thirty minutes later, and—"

"Jesus Fucking Christ, Cree, let the girl go on her date."

This comes from Daire who steps out of the kitchen with a plate of food. “You’re not her keeper.”

“I’ll be fine.” I kiss Cree’s cheek. I know his worry, although annoying, comes from a place of love. “I promise to text when I can.”

“Fair enough.”

My eyes collide with Jude’s, and he gives me a thumb’s up, but there’s something in his eyes, a flare of jealousy I think, that he quickly tries to hide.

I say my goodbyes to the guys and drive over to the library on campus since Jonah asked me to meet him there and that he’d take us where we need to go.

When I park, I spot him leaning against an SUV. He sees me, a smile lighting up his face, and waves.

Taking a deep breath, I give myself a quick mental pep talk. I can do this. He’s just a guy and it’s just a date. No biggie.

“Hi,” I say, walking up to him.

“Hey,” he echoes, looking down at his shoes. “I hope this isn’t a bad idea.”

My heart drops. “What? The date?”

Oh my God, if he sends me packing before the date even starts that would be humiliating.

“No!” he blurts, waving his hands through the air. “I meant what I picked for our date.”

“What is it?” I hedge, nervous now.

“I was going to let it be a surprise, but that feels stupid

now. I thought we could do axe throwing, there's a place in town—"

"That sounds fun," I assure him. "Unless you're worried, I'll go all Lizzie Borden on you."

He snorts. "That thought didn't even cross my mind. We better get going then."

I hop in the car with Jonah and it's stupid, but I can't help but compare him to Jude. Jude drives his truck with one hand and the confidence of someone who's never doubted himself. Jonah keeps both hands on the wheel, constantly checking his mirrors, and making sure to use his blinker before he makes any lane change even if no other cars are around.

We arrive downtown at a brick building with large glass windows in the front. It's not far from the ballet studio.

"I think this will be fun."

Jonah glances at me, shutting off the ignition. "I hope so."

Jude is so confident in everything he does, whereas Jonah is more cautious and reserved.

Stop comparing them! They're nothing alike and Jude and you are never going to be a thing!

Jonah and I walk side by side to the front of the building, his hand hovering against my waist. Inside, he checks in and after we each sign a waiver we're led to the back where others are already playing. After some instructions and a quick demonstration, we're left on our own.

"Have you ever done this before?" I ask Jonah, testing the weight of the axe in my hand.

"Once with my friends and once with my family."

"That's cool. You wanna go first?"

"Sure." He stands in front of the target, holding the axe in both hands. He swings it back and then up, releasing it. It spins once, sinking into the center of the target.

Jumping up and down, I clap and cheer for him. "That was amazing. Don't laugh when I fail."

He grins. "I would never."

I take my turn, standing behind the taped line on the floor. I mimic the stance Jonah used, swing my arms up and — "Oh my God, why is this thing heavier than I thought." The axe clatters to the ground, halfway between where I stand and the target I was aiming for.

Jonah chuckles. "It can be deceiving, but you have the idea now. Try again." He retrieves the axe for me, passing it over. He stands out of firing range. "Come on, you can do it."

I try again, more prepared this time. It gets closer to the target but still hits the ground. Frowning, I get the axe.

"I can do this," I assure Jonah.

He grins, crossing his arms over his chest. He really is cute. Tanned skin, golden-brown floppy hair. He's sweet, thoughtful, perfect in so many ways.

"I'm cheering you on."

I swing the axe with more force this time. It flies

through the air and hits the target. It's not dead center like Jonah's, but it's in there!

I jump up and down in excitement. "Yes! I did it!"

Jonah picks me up, swinging me around. "I told you that you could do it."

I hug his warm, firm body. He smells like a mixture of cologne and chlorine. It's strangely alluring. When he sets me down, we both exchange smiles and Jude becomes the last thing on my mind.

I'M BRUSHING my teeth that evening, fighting a smile in the reflection of the mirror, when Jude's door opens, and he slips inside. He leans against the counter, arms crossed over his bare chest. A pair of sweat shorts clings to his hips.

"How'd your date go?"

I spit out my toothpaste, taking extra time to rinse. "It went great."

His tongue presses against the inside of his cheek. "Good." His tone makes it sound like good isn't ... well, a good thing.

"What's wrong?"

"Nothing." He runs his fingers through his hair.

"It doesn't sound like nothing."

He shakes his head. "It's a me problem."

I snort, brushing out my hair. "That's obvious."

His brows furrow together, his feet carrying him a step closer to me. “What’s that supposed to mean?”

“That I haven’t done anything to give you a problem.”

His mouth twists back and forth. “Do you still need my help with this whole thing?”

“Yes,” I blurt, without thinking. But sadly, I’m not ready to give up on his help yet. Blushing I add, “If this thing with—”

He holds up a hand, shutting me up. “I don’t want to know his name.”

I rear back. “What? Why not?”

A muscle in his jaw ticks. “It’s just better if I don’t know.”

“Fine, whatever. Anyway, I was saying if this thing keeps going with us, I need practice just being … you know.” I shrug like that gesture finishes what I was going to say.

He pinches the bridge of his nose. “No, I don’t know.”

“Like I said before, with the intimacy stuff,” I whisper the last part. “I don’t want things to progress and freak out on him.”

“Any guy that is into you isn’t going to care.”

“But I do!” I cry, setting my brush down. “I care. I don’t want to be bad at it.”

“I told you I wouldn’t have sex with you.”

“I’m not asking you to.”

“So what? You want me to kiss you? Touch your pussy?

Maybe lick it?" I blush fiercely at his words, but he's not done yet. "What am I? Your fluffer?"

"Fluffer?"

"They keep the guys hard in porn."

"I … I don't even want to know how you know that."

"You want me to get you primed and ready, so he reaps the benefits, and I don't like that at all."

I gape at him, my heart thundering so loud I can hear it in my own ears. "Are you jealous?"

He snorts like the idea of him being jealous is the most preposterous thing I could've said. "No. Why would I be jealous?"

"I'm not sure." I mimic his pose, crossing my arms over my chest, hip against the counter. "You tell me."

His nostrils flare. He looks like he's debating something. With a growl he says, "Fuck it," and in one stride the space between us disappears.

In one heartbeat his hands are on my cheeks.

In one breath his mouth is on mine.

I gasp at the feel of him, his tongue sweeping past my lips. I've never been kissed with tongue before and for a moment I freeze, panicking, but then he *moans* and my body relaxes, letting him guide me. My body sinks against him. He's so big compared to me. Tall, broad, muscular. I feel cocooned in his arms, like he could wrap his entire body around mine and protect me from any coming danger. I have to press up on my tiptoes to kiss him back, my body flooding with desire I've never felt before and I know that if

I slipped my fingers beneath my sleep shorts I'd find my pussy soaked, all from his kiss.

My back hits the door that leads to my room and I expect it to snap Jude out from whatever force has taken over his body, but it does no such thing. Instead, he picks me up, encouraging me to wrap my legs around his hips.

"Oh my God," I blurt. "You're huge."

I feel his hard cock pressed right up against my core. All that separates us are our clothes.

He grins against my lips. "It'd fit," he promises, rolling his hips into mine.

My fingers tug on his hair. He hisses at the slight bite of pain, but he doesn't tell me to stop. My hips grind against him and ironically that's one of the things I was worried about in this situation—that I wouldn't know what to do. Lo and behold my body just knows.

Tugging my bottom lip between his teeth, he lets it go and dives in again, deepening the kiss. I didn't know kisses like this existed outside of movies.

It feels like this goes on forever, but eventually he sets me back down. He braces one arm against the door, his chest rising heavily with each breath. His other hand is on my hip, keeping me anchored to the door.

Neither of us says anything for a moment. But then he's the first to speak.

"Was that good enough practice for you?"

Fire flares inside me. I shove at his chest, and he steps back on unsteady feet, his eyes half-glazed, half-angry.

"Fuck you."

He grins at that. "Tell me something I don't know you want to do."

I grind my teeth together, lift both my hands and wave the middle finger at him. He laughs, amused. Opening my door, I slam it shut behind me.

Fuck, Jude.

And not literally, like he thinks.

twenty-two

Jude

KEATON IS WATCHING ME FROM THE OPPOSITE SIDE of the gym—has been for at least a solid fifteen minutes now. I keep up with my set, my body drenched with sweat as I lift the barbell. Clinton is spotting me. I'm close to giving out, but I keep pushing because I'm hoping if I exhaust myself enough it'll get Millie off my mind, and I won't be able to think about what I ordered her last night. Granted, when it arrives it's not like I actually have to give it to her even if I think it could help her.

"All right, that's it." Clinton grabs onto the barbell, forcing me to put it down.

"Fuck you, I'm not done."

"I say you are."

"Whatever." I sit up, wiping my face off with my towel. My muscles are screaming, and I still feel like I have way too much energy.

I didn't mean to kiss Millie last night. I don't mean to do a lot of things I do, but here we are. And she was right, I was jealous hearing her talk about her date. What if she liked it more than the one I took her on?

That date wasn't real, I remind myself.

"Go shower," Clinton says when I bend over to grab my water jug.

"Don't tell me what to do," I mutter, even though my exact plan was to go take a cold, icy shower. Clinton shakes his head, wiping the bench off with a disinfectant wipe.

I have to walk by Keaton to get to the locker room and I'm not surprised when he turns, following me.

"What do you want?" I growl at him over my shoulder.

"There's something different about you."

"Like shit there is."

He chuckles. "Rumor is, you haven't been frequenting the bars or trying to bag every girl you can. Interesting. Makes me wonder if maybe you've found someone."

I whip around to face him. His eyes widen in surprise. "What are you getting at Keaton? Are you trying to rub it in my face that you got my girl? Good for you." I slow clap. "Enjoy my seconds. Eat 'em up."

I don't see his punch coming until I'm flat out on the ground. He stands over me, face red and angry. He points at me like a parent scolding a child. "Don't talk about Macy like that. You're better than this. And you know what, I've always let you get away with shit because of what you and Macy went through." My eyes widen and he gives a humorless laugh. "Yeah, I fucking know. She's my girl, and I'm going to marry her one day. We don't have secrets. I *want* to see you get your life together. You deserve that, Jude, but I won't stand by idly while you bad mouth Macy to my face. She deserves more than that."

I lower my head, chastised. He's fucking right. "I'm sorry."

I can tell my apology takes him by surprise which only makes me feel worse.

Keaton holds out a hand to me on the ground. I hesitate for about a second and a half before I take it. He helps me up, patting me on the back. Normally I would shirk the touch, but this time I don't.

"I'm not your enemy. I never was."

I nod. "I'm going to hit the showers."

FRESHLY SHOWERED, I walk across campus to grab a coffee instead of heading home right away.

My feet come to a halt when I spot Millie walking ahead of me out of the library. Her head is down and she's paying attention to her phone, not her surroundings.

I jog up to her side, slowing my steps to match hers. "Hey, Little Madison."

She jumps, dropping her phone. I bend down and scoop it up, placing it back in her palm.

"Where did you come from?" Her head whips back and forth, trying to deduce which direction I came from.

"The gym," I answer. "Thought I'd get a coffee before heading home. You?"

She tosses her head back, long brown hair flowing around her shoulders, and laughs. "Same, only I'm coming from the library. My psychology partner canceled on me, which is a first, so I worked on some other things for a while."

"This partner ... this the guy you're into?"

She gives me a funny look and nods. We reach the coffee shop; I hold open the door letting her slip inside first. The line isn't that long for a change.

I bend my lips to her ear. "What are you getting?"

She shivers, but it's not even cold in here. If anything, it's warm. "An iced coffee with almond milk."

"That it?"

"Maybe a cookie if I'm feeling spicy."

When we step up to the counter, I let her place her order and then cut in with mine, adding two cookies. I hand my card over to the cashier, ignoring the feel of Millie's probing gaze on me. Taking my card back and the receipt, we grab a table to wait for our order to be ready.

"You didn't have to get my coffee."

I lace my fingers together on the table, looking around the shop to see if I recognize anyone. This meeting is entirely innocent, but I know if someone recognizes me and Millie as Cree's sister then it's bound to get back to his ears. No one looks familiar so I relax.

"I know." I lean back, stretching my left arm over the back of the empty chair beside me.

Millie shakes her head, tucking her hair behind one ear. "You are the most confusing human being I've ever met."

My brows furrow. Leaning forward, I ask, "What do you mean?"

She wets her lips, glancing around before her eyes finally settle on mine. "I mean, you went from wanting to be my friend, to being kind of an ass to me, to my friend again and you've made it clear you don't like me in 'that way.'" She uses her fingers for air quotes. "And then you kissed me last night and not just a peck on the lips either, but here you sit like nothing happened." She takes a deep inhale of air after that long-winded speech.

"That's because..." I start, then struggle with how to explain myself. "Look, I'm not some knight in shining armor to sweep you off your feet and that's what you want, a fairytale."

She blinks at me like I've spoken another language. "I never said I wanted a fairytale. In fact, I've never said I wanted anything from you other than your help. Maybe it's *you* who wants something from me. Sounds to me like you've done a lot of suppressing of emotions over the past few years and it's time for you to take a look at yourself."

Our order is called then, and she hops up from the chair, grabs her coffee and cookie, and dashes out the door before I can call her name.

Getting up, I grab my stuff and follow her out, spinning to search for her, but somehow, she's vanished.

Millie's right though, just like my friends have been, even Keaton. I let my breakup with Macy change me so wholly that when I look in the mirror the guy that stares back at me feels like a complete stranger. Despite the years, I've spent trying to fit into this role of being fine, of being the guy who parties and drinks and fucks his way through campus, that feeling has never gone away.

And all it's taken is a petite brunette with the personality of a firecracker to finally make me question if this is the path I want to stay on.

twenty-three

Millie

IT'S MY TURN TO COOK DINNER FOR EVERYONE, which wouldn't be so bad if I didn't have to feed three male athletes who could eat an entire buffet if left to their own devices. The ground beef and potato skillet recipe I found online, luckily smells delicious and thankfully none of us are too picky.

"Smells good, Mills." My brother comes into the kitchen, snooping through the fridge for something to drink.

"Thanks." I use the wooden spoon to push the meat,

potatoes, and veggies around the skillet, so everything cooks evenly. "Hopefully it tastes just as good."

"Don't you worry about that," Daire says, joining us. "I'll eat anything." He brushes past my brother, giving him an annoyed look.

I swear, guys complain about girls and their drama when they're the more dramatic sex. I have no idea what's going on with those two, but there's been trouble in paradise practically since school started.

"I heard something about dinner?"

I want to whimper at the sight of Jude, still damp from a shower, his hair wet and curling against the nape of his neck, with a pair of sweatpants hanging loosely on his hips.

My libido goes into overdrive when he's around which is bad, since I can't have Jude like that. He's made it perfectly clear that he won't cross that line with me, which I might respect if he didn't make me feel so hot.

"I'm almost done," I say to Jude, but really, I'm telling all of them. "Get your plates ready."

They line up like over eager puppies and after they've shoveled food onto their plates there's just enough left for me. Sitting down at the table in the kitchen, I'm slightly amused by the fact that I'm having dinner with a bunch of jocks.

Cree sits beside me with Jude and Daire across from us.

"What's the verdict boys? Is this recipe a keeper?" I ask after I've had a couple bites and they've all shoveled at least half of their servings into their mouths.

"Hell yeah." Daire's voice is garbled by his full mouth. "Definitely top three, Millie."

My brother gives me a thumb's up and Jude meets my gaze, giving a nod.

After we eat the guys are on clean up duty since I cooked. I have some studying to do, so I head up to my room.

Opening the door, I'm surprised to find a few boxes on my bed. I hesitate, wondering what they are since I know I didn't order anything.

Hesitantly, like I'm approaching a wild animal, I tiptoe up to my bed.

My jaw drops when I realize what they are.

Vibrators.

Not one. Not two. But *three* different kinds.

"Who? What? Why?" I blurt out loud, picking up one of the boxes. It's kind of egg-shaped on one end with a separate piece that goes … *where?* I set it down on the bed, feeling my whole-body flush. I think I'm sweating.

I do a pit check.

Yep, definitely sweating.

I pick up another box. It's a purple flower-shaped device.

"Why do they all have shapes?" I hiss under my breath. "What am I supposed to do with a flower?"

I sound absolutely hysterical, and it's because I am. If I was nervous about intimacy before, I'm downright terrified now. Like how is this flower device vibrator thing supposed to make me feel better about all of this?

Oh, Jesus.

I'm hyperventilating now.

I run for the bathroom sink, splashing water on my face.

Maybe all this is a fever dream or something.

Yeah, that has to be it.

I look back at the bed. Nope, they're all still there.

The door adjoining the bathroom to Jude's room opens and I jump, hand flying to my chest.

"What are those?" I hiss at him in a hoarse voice, pointing toward my bed. He's the culprit of this, I know it.

He stands there all cool, calm, and collected.

"I thought even you'd know they're vibrators. Says so on the boxes."

"You bought me vibrators!"

"Shh." He slaps a hand over my mouth. "Do you want your brother to hear you say that?"

Right now, I want to curl up on the floor and die. "No," I say against his hand, and he lowers it. "What," I gesture wildly back to my room, "are you thinking?"

He crosses his muscular arms over his bare chest, and I want to curse him for his casualness. I need him to cover up that spectacular body around me because I don't trust myself when it comes to him.

"We've established you're a virgin and that intimacy makes you nervous. I thought maybe," he shrugs like this is no big deal, "if you ... um ... played with yourself a bit that it might make you more comfortable and understand what turns you on."

I blink at him. Once. Twice. Trying to sort my thoughts out. "This is both very sweet and kind of weird at the same time."

He winces. "I know but look at this as an assignment from me."

"My assignment is to pleasure myself?"

"Yep."

I shake my head, looking at the boxes on my bed. A light bulb goes off in my brain. "If I have to do this, then I'm giving you some homework too."

"O-Okay," he hesitates, watching me curiously.

Turning on my heel, I head into my room and scan my bookshelf, finding exactly what I want. I swipe it and spin back around to find Jude leaning against the doorway of the bathroom. His hair is dry now, curling against his forehead. There's a chunk of hair in the back that sticks out adorably like maybe he ran his fingers through it and forgot to smooth it down before it dried.

He's only helping you, I remind myself.

Clearing my throat, I hand him the book. "I'll try out those tonight." I eye the vibrators sitting oh-so-innocently on my bed. "If you read this tonight."

He eyes the colorful illustrated art on the cover. His forehead scrunches as he reads the title. "This looks weird."

I grin and I don't know what makes me do it, but I pat his chest, right over his hard pectoral muscle. He looks down at my hand, brows drawn in tight. I quickly swipe my hand away.

"Good luck, Jude-y."

He grunts at the nickname. "Same to you, Little Madison. Same to you."

I EYE the vibrators sitting on my dresser, all charged now, wondering how the hell I'm supposed to use them. *Sure,* it's self-explanatory and I *did* read the instructions, but considering I've never had anything other than a tampon near my vagina I'm a tad worried.

"What was he thinking?" I hiss to myself.

I grab the one that looks more like a wand and what I would expect from a vibrator and stuff it under my pillow. I stick the others in my dresser drawer and climb in bed.

"There's a vibrator under my pillow." I have no idea why I'm talking out loud to myself about this, but it does make me feel better.

My phone vibrates on the nightstand, and I lean over to look at it since it's charging.

Jude: What kind of alien smut porn do you have me reading?

I giggle to myself, more than a little amused.

Me: I have no idea what you're talking about.

His reply only takes a few seconds.

Jude: Liar.

Me: It's good! Give it a chance.

Jude: I'm trying.

Me: Try harder.

Jude: There's a lot of sex in this book.

Me: Just the way I like it.

Jude: I'll never understand girls.

Jude: You know what's even more horrifying?

Me: What?

Jude: I'm pretty sure I've seen my sister reading this book.

I laugh out loud, unable to control the sound as it bursts free from me.

Jude: I'm serious.

Me: I don't doubt you.

Jude: Don't forget your end of the deal.

I gulp, thinking about the device under the pillow.

Me: I won't.

I wait to see if I get any more texts from him, but when I don't I put my phone away with a sigh. My heart starts to race in my chest at what I have to do. I shouldn't be embarrassed about this. Pleasuring one's self is a perfectly normal thing. But I feel the same crippling fear I have when I think about dating and being intimate with a guy—the fear of doing something wrong.

I wet my lips with my tongue.

Distraction, I need a distraction before I do this.

I try to read. That doesn't work. I scroll Instagram. That doesn't work either.

With a small cry of frustration, I grab my phone.

Jude answers on the first ring.

"What's wrong?"

"I can't do this." *Can he hear the complete and utter panic in my voice?*

His sigh echoes through the connection. "You're in your head too much. You can do it. If you really don't want to, then don't, but if it's just because you're scared then try."

I bite my lip, covering my eyes with my hand. "I..."

"Do you want me to talk you through it?"

I inhale shaky breath. "God, no."

"Are you sure?"

I hesitate. "No."

"No, you're not sure, or no, you don't want me to?"

I bite my lip. "I'm not sure."

His sheets rustle and his voice is even deeper than normal when he says, "Pick up the vibrator."

"Which one?"

"Whichever one you want."

"It's the longer one," I whisper, pulling it out from beneath the pillow.

"This doesn't count as phone sex, Millie," he warns. "This is a friend helping a friend. That's all."

I try to ignore the sound of my blood roaring through my veins. "I know."

"Good," he says, clearing his throat. "Do you have the vibrator in your hand?"

"Y-Yes."

"Good girl."

I almost whimper at his words. "Now what?"

"Are your clothes on?"

I nod, then realize he can't see me. "Yes."

"Take your pants off." I do as he says, and he groans when he hears the sound of rustling fabric. "Now, I want you to slide your fingers under your panties."

"I-I'm not wearing any."

He curses on the other end of the line. "Jesus fucking Christ, Millie, you're going to kill me saying shit like that."

"Sorry?" It comes out as a question.

He sighs. "Don't be sorry. It's just … I shouldn't be getting hard from this."

"And you are?"

"Fuck, yes."

"That actually makes me feel better."

I hear him swallow and when he speaks his voice has gone husky. "You want me to get myself off while I help you get off?"

I don't even have to think about it. "Yes."

"Don't use the vibrator yet," he bosses. "I want you to take your hand and slide it down your stomach. Are you doing that?"

"Mhmm."

"Take your fingers lower, I want you to touch yourself, Millie. Right on that sweet pussy. Fuck, I know it would taste so good. Are you touching it?"

"Y-Yeah," I whimper, biting my lip.

"Are you wet?"

"I am now. So wet." I slide a finger in an out of my core, easily adding a second finger.

"Fuck, Millie, I wish I could touch you."

"You could."

"No, I can't. I-I'm not ... I'm not worthy of that."

"You are."

"No," he growls. "I'm not."

I don't want him to change his mind and stop this, not now that he's helped me get this far and I've never been so turned on in my life.

"Are you touching yourself?" I ask him, surprised by how strong my voice sounds despite my breathlessness.

He hesitates. "Yes," he admits. "You said you wanted me to."

"I do, I do."

"Where are your fingers, Millie?"

"I-In my pussy."

"Are you rubbing your pussy?"

"A little."

"What about your clit?"

"N-No."

"Rub it. Slow circles. I want you to picture me between those pretty legs of yours. My tongue's on your pussy."

I whimper at the visual. I want to know what his facial hair would feel like against my thighs and pussy.

"Are you ... how are you touching yourself?" I ask, wanting the reminder that I'm not alone.

"I am. Fuck, I'm gripping my dick so tight, and I shouldn't be thinking it, but I wish it was your pussy. I'd guide your hips and suck those pretty little tits. I could make you come so hard with my fingers, my mouth, my cock. I'd ruin you for any other man."

I whimper. I have no doubt that he could and that he would. "Why won't you?" I find myself asking.

He groans. "You're too good for me." And like he knows what I'll say, he adds, "And not because you're a virgin. It's who you are. So sweet. So vibrant. Where are your fingers at Millie?"

"Rubbing my clit," I whisper, putting my phone on speaker and setting it beside me. I should've done that sooner, but I felt closer to him that way.

"Good girl," he purrs the praise. "You listen so good."

"What do you want me to do now?"

"Where's the vibrator? Can you grab it and turn it on?"

"Hold on." With my free hand I pat the sheets, searching for the device. Wrapping my hand around it I find the button and turn it on. "Got it."

"Okay, baby, I want you to replace your fingers with the vibrator. You can hold it there. Rub it around. Whatever feels good to you."

"O-Okay." I press the vibrator against my clit and cry out immediately from the pleasurable sensation. It's not like anything I expected. "Oh my God!" I slap my other hand over my mouth, not wanting anyone but Jude to hear me. My chest rises and falls heavily with every panting breath.

"Does it feel good?"

"Y-Yes," I stutter the words out. "So good."

"Do you think you can come yet?"

"Almost," I admit, my skin flushing.

I feel hot all over. I want to take my shirt off, but I'm scared if I move this feeling in my core will go away.

Jude grunts on the other end of the line. "I'm almost there, baby. I'm going to come so fucking hard all over my hand. Make a mess of myself. You like that don't you? That you make me a mess?"

I cry out, biting down on my lip. My abdominals are contracting the closer I get to an orgasm.

"It's happening," I gasp. "Oh my God, I'm coming."

"Fuck," he shouts, such a guttural and animalistic sound. I wish I could see him right now, but I let my imagination do the work. I picture him sitting on the side of his bed, cock in his hand, both covered in cum. Some on his stomach too. The tendons in his neck would be visible. His eyes hot for me.

Soon, our collective breaths are the only sounds.

Eventually, he clears his throat. "Goodnight, Millie."

"Goodnight, Jude."

twenty-four

Jude

I CAN'T EVEN BE SURPRISED AT MYSELF AT THIS point, can I? I've proven time and time again that when it comes to Millie, I shove past all the barriers I put up. It's not her fault. It's entirely mine.

I stride down the sidewalk toward the burger joint I'm meeting Mascen at.

Despite graduating last year, he's still in the area, but we don't see him much since he's been traveling and trying to figure out what comes next in his life. God knows he wants to settle down with Rory but since she has more years left of school, he can't put all his plans in motion.

I'm honestly not sure what made me reach out and ask him if he'd meet me for lunch. The guy isn't exactly the best conversationalist, but I figured maybe he could give me some insight on this situation with Millie and since he doesn't have any skin in the game, I figure he'll be unbiased.

I hope, at least.

He's already sitting outside, perusing the menu with a disgruntled expression.

He looks up when I take the chair across from him. "Jude," he says in greeting.

"Mascen," I reply, picking up the other menu.

"What'd you want?"

That's Mascen for you—straight to the point. I don't think he knows any other way to be.

"I need your advice on something." I look at the menu instead of him even though I know I'll order the tried-and-true classic cheeseburger. There's one on the menu with peanut butter and jelly. Gross.

He grunts in response. "Do I look like I give advice? I'm not Dr. Phil."

"Dude," I look at him over the top of the menu, "can you not be a dick for five minutes?"

He smirks, rubbing his lips. "Five minutes? Start the timer." The waitress comes to our table, and we place our drink and food order. "Tell me what this is about. I'm curious now."

"There's this girl—"

He laughs, and it's a ridiculously shocking sound coming from him. The guy is always so serious. "Why is it always a girl?" He shakes his head, adjusting his baseball cap so it sits backwards.

"I like her," I admit quietly. It's the first time I've said it out loud. I've kept the thought to myself, I guess in the useless hope that it would disappear. "As a friend. As more."

Mascen shakes his head. "I'm not seeing the problem here? I know you've preferred hookups for a while now, but you've been in a relationship before."

"It's Cree's sister."

His lips part in shock and I realize I've rendered him speechless. Then he starts laughing *again*. This is the weirdest lunch ever.

"I'm sorry," he chortles, looking damn near tears from the hilarity of it all. "But how do you expect me to give you advice with that? He's going to kick your ass if you go there. You have to decide if she's worth being at odds with your friend."

"What would you do?"

He arches a brow. "If it was Rory ... friendship be damned. She's mine."

I let out a sigh. I had a feeling he'd say that. My jaw clenches when I think about what we did last night. I told her it wasn't phone sex, but that was a complete and utter lie. It wasn't even her I was trying to fool, it was myself.

"I'm not sure I'm cut out to be in a relationship again."

Mascen watches me through narrowed eyes. "Then don't fucking go there. Don't lead this girl on. Don't screw over your friend. Not if you don't think you're ready."

He has a point. "I'm so confused."

"What's there to be confused over? If you have feelings for her, do something about it. If you're on the fence, don't go there. Easy enough."

"She's this ... she's this *light*," I explain. "And when I'm with her, I feel like maybe some of that light shines on me and I'm not as bad as I think I am."

Mascen studies me, working his jaw back and forth. "I'm going to be upfront with you, until you work through the shit from your past, this can't go anywhere. That was the deal with Rory and me. I had to move on from things I was holding onto so I could actually see a future with her." Macy, he means. I have to confront that big hulking demon of my past. "Do that and you're golden. Cree's going to be pissed no matter what, but if you do go for her, my opinion is it's better to tell him sooner rather than later."

Liking Millie as more than a friend has made my life a hell of a lot more complicated.

I PARK outside the ballet studio. Millie's class should be finishing up any minute if it hasn't already. It's been a few days since my lunch with Mascen and I'm no closer to knowing what to do when it comes to her. I haven't been ignoring her, per se, but I have been making myself scarce around the house. I'm sure she's put two and two together. She's not dumb.

It would be so much easier if she was any other girl.

If I didn't like her as a person.

If I wasn't insanely attracted to her, inside and out.

If she wasn't my friend's little sister.

But who am I kidding, nothing is supposed to be easy.

Walking into the building, I nearly collide with the dude from the parking lot when Millie's car wouldn't start.

Aleksander. His name is a sneer in my thoughts. He's a good-looking guy, probably late twenties, and he's exactly the kind of guy I can see Millie going for even if he's too old for her.

"Sorry," I grumble.

He eyes me shrewdly and I know that means he recognizes me. "Attack any innocent men in parking lots today?" he asks, the words lilted with a slight accent.

"Nope, can't say I have."

He looks down at the papers in his hands, flicking his fingers lazily toward the stairs. "She's up there."

"Thanks."

I take the stairs two at a time and follow the sound of music down the hall.

Coming to a stop outside the room, I watch in awe as Millie dances. There are no kids, so her class must've finished up early.

She spins and twirls, her limbs graceful and elegant.

I've never seen anything quite like it. Her eyes are closed as she dances. She's *feeling* the music, letting herself get lost in it. I wonder if she feels the same way about dancing that I do when I'm on the field. Like nothing else exists.

I walk carefully into the room, taking soft steps so she won't hear my boots on the floor. I lean against the wall, crossing my arms over my chest and kicking one foot up against the wall.

When the song ends, she pauses catching her breath, but she never opens her eyes. The next song begins, and she starts dancing again.

I think I could watch her like this all night.

She dances through another full song before she comes to a stop and finally opens her eyes. She gasps, clutching at her chest when she sees me there.

"Jude," she breathes my name into existence.

"You're amazing," I tell her sincerely. "I've never seen anything like it."

Her cheeks flush deeper. They were already pink from exertion. "Thank you. I'm surprised to see you here."

I nod, rubbing the back of my head. "I've been ignoring you." No point beating around the bush since we both know it.

She smiles, sitting down on the floor to remove her dance shoes. "I know. Not sure *why*. I mean, what are a couple of orgasms between friends?" She winks at me, and I nearly groan. Everything this girl does is a turn on for me.

"I shouldn't have done that with you." Her smile falls and she looks away from me. "But I don't regret it."

Her head whips quickly back in my direction. "You don't?"

"No." I stride over to her. "I should, though."

She rolls her eyes at me. "You're always telling me what you should and shouldn't do. Why don't you tell me what you want for a change?"

"You," I answer baldly. I know I shouldn't have admitted it, but I'm tired of keeping it to myself.

She stares at me, lips parted, eyes blinking slowly like maybe she thinks I'm a mirage that's going to vanish at any moment.

"Don't say something you don't mean." She tucks her dance shoes into her bag and slips on a pair of sneakers. She lets her hair down. It falls like a curtain to shield her face.

"I do mean it." I pick up her bag as soon as it's zipped, tossing it over my shoulder. She looks up at me with those round doe eyes that make me stupidly weak in the knees. "Don't expect much from me," I warn her. "I don't even know what this means yet myself." I run my fingers through my hair. "I don't want to lead you on, and I know you like someone, that was the whole point of me helping you, but I'm so fucking attracted to you, Millie, that it has me torn apart on the inside. I didn't even want to tell you all this." She gets up from the ground as I speak, standing in front of me so there's only about a foot of space between us. "I'm *not* the guy for you. I'm jaded and broken. I'm—"

She covers my mouth with her hand, like I've done to her before. "How about you let me decide if you're the guy for me or not?" She lets her hand drop back to her side. "I'm not looking for any promises from you or you to propose to me. I don't know what I'm doing here." She waves a hand between us. "That was the whole point of me asking for your help."

"I can't be your boyfriend."

She laughs. "Didn't ask you to. It seems to me like you're overthinking this whole thing." She pats my chest. "It's kind of cute." She winks.

"Don't call me cute, Little Madison."

"Why not?" She bats her eyes innocently.

She reaches for her bag on my shoulder. I catch her wrist in the air, moving my hand up to hers to lace our fingers together.

"Because it makes me want to prove to you how not cute I am."

A smile curves her lips. "Let's not overcomplicate things, okay? We're friends, right?" I nod. "And there's a mutual attraction between us, so let's just see where things go. No labels."

"You can do that?"

"What? Because I'm a girl and inexperienced it means I automatically want to call you my boyfriend?" She rolls her eyes. "Welcome to the twenty-first-century, Jude, where women are free to do whatever and whoever they want. Labels or not."

"What about the guy?"

She sighs, tucking her hair behind her ear. She instantly knows what I'm talking about. "I like him, a lot. He's sweet and nice. He's a good guy and really cute. I … I could see myself with him if things were different."

"Different?"

She pokes my chest. "If I didn't like you the way I do."

"I don't want to hurt you," I admit, cupping her cheek. Her skin is warm, soft against my thumb when I rub it in circles. "And I will. I'll fuck this up. It's what I do. This guy, whoever he is," I squeeze my eyes shut, "he would be a safe bet."

When I open my eyes, she's grinning at me.

"Lucky for you, I like to gamble."

twenty-five

Millie

JUDE AND I AGREE THAT FOR THE DURATION OF US doing whatever it is we're doing we don't tell my brother unless it becomes serious. That's fine with me, because I know Cree would blow this ridiculously out of proportion.

My brother isn't aware of it, but he's a drama queen.

I walk into the bathroom stifling a yawn and find Jude at the sink brushing his teeth. His eyes scan me up and down, taking in the pair of tiny blue terry shorts I slept in and tank top. My nipples pebble against the fabric of my top, growing harder beneath his stare.

Grabbing my toothbrush, I stick it under the water, swipe on some toothpaste and brush my teeth. Jude smirks around his toothbrush, so I pull mine from my mouth and stick my tongue out at him. Laughter rumbles in his chest.

We spit out our toothpaste at the same time, but he rinses his mouth while I go back to brushing.

We haven't done anything like the phone-sex-he-doesn't-want-to-call-phone-sex thing again. He hasn't even *kissed* me again.

So rude of him, honestly. But it's only been a few days, so I'll cut him some slack.

"It's raining," he announces after he's wiped his mouth.

I spit out the last of my toothpaste and rinse my mouth with water and then mouthwash. "I know."

"We're going for a drive."

I smile to myself, liking a little too much the way he says it. *We're*. He's taking over my rainy-day tradition and I'm not even a little bit mad about it.

"What about classes?"

He rubs his jaw. "I think we both can afford to play hooky for a day, don't you?"

I grab my hairbrush, gliding it through my sleep-mess strands. "You're a bad influence."

His eyes flash with something. Worry, maybe? "I know. Are you in or not?"

"I'm always in. But what about my car? We can't leave one of our vehicles here or Cree will think it's weird."

He thinks for a moment. "We'll leave your car at the

CVS down the street. It should be safe there for a few hours."

"Good idea."

He glances at the watch on his wrist. "Can you be ready in thirty minutes?"

"That's hardly a challenge."

He grins. "Make it twenty then."

I PARK AT THE CVS, sitting in my car until Jude pulls in a few minutes later. Hopping out, I make a mad dash for the passenger side of his truck since it's raining cats and dogs. In the distance thunder booms.

I can't help the smile that comes over me at the sound. Jude shakes his head, amused.

"You know, for someone who's such a ball of sunshine it really surprises me that you like storms so much."

I strap the seatbelt across my body. "They make me feel alive."

I reach for the AUX cord, plugging my phone in. By now, there's no point in asking for permission. Kicking my shoes off, I rest my bare toes on the console.

He eyes my feet with narrowed eyes but doesn't ask me to put them down.

"Do you like the color?" I wiggle my toes, watching the color shift from pink to purple. "They're holographic."

"Holo-what?"

"Holographic. It's different than iridescent."

"You know what, never mind," he grumbles, turning out of the pharmacy parking lot.

I skip through my playlist, settling on 'Single' from The Neighborhood. They're one of my favorite bands.

"You just want me to drive around again? No destination?"

"Yep." I nod excitedly. "It makes it more fun that way."

"Don't you ever worry about getting lost, Little Madison?"

I shake my head, my hair swishing around my breasts. It's gotten pretty long and I'm due for a trim, but I haven't bothered to get one. "Nope, that's what GPS is for."

"And if you don't have service?"

"Then I'd drive around until I found it." He shakes his head, blowing out a breath from between his lips. "Keep 'em coming. I can do this all day."

"I'm sure you can."

Setting my feet down on the floor, I grab my purse and dig through it until I find my bag of snacks. "Want one?" I hold up a lollipop.

He takes his eyes off the road to glare at the stick of candy in my hand like it's personally offended him somehow. "Why do you have that?"

"Because I do." I hold up my snack bag. "I also have Twizzlers, some Milk Duds, sour gummy worms and—"

"Are we going to the movies?"

"No," I frown, setting the bag back on the floor, "this is standard road trip food. Don't you know anything, Jude?"

"Apparently not."

"I have to start the song over now. You disrupted the flow with your lollipop hate."

He grunts in response. "Give me one then." I gladly pass him a watermelon flavored one. "Ew, not that one."

"Jesus, so picky. What flavor do you want then?"

"Cherry."

"Excellent choice. I'll forgive you for your pickiness." I pass him a cherry-flavored one and grab one for myself.

He tries to hide his smirk, but I know no matter what he says or tries to portray, he *likes* me. I mean, he wouldn't have shown up at the ballet studio saying what he did if that weren't the case.

Sticking the lollipop in his mouth, he turns the volume up to help drown out the *swish-swish-swish* of the wipers.

A few songs play while I let my thoughts wander, but I find it impossible to stay quiet for too long.

"You've got me all alone now—what are you going to do about it?"

He glances at me, his eyes dark and intimidating. "Who said I was going to do anything about it?"

I feel a slight sting at his words but try not to let it show. I shrug off what he said like it doesn't hurt. "Your loss then."

He makes a noise in the back of his throat. "I just meant; I mean ... I don't want you to think that's why I asked you to play hooky. I *am* capable of having a relationship with a girl that isn't strictly sex."

Beneath his heavy stubble I catch the hint of red blooming on his cheeks.

"I know you are," I curl my legs under me, sitting criss-cross, "you're my friend. And you know what," I brighten, "since we're friends we should get to know each other better."

"Like what? Favorite colors and that shit? I already know yours is pink."

I gape at him. The broody man at my side has rendered me speechless. In the background 'Sweater Weather' by The Neighborhood plays.

"How do you know it's pink?" My voice goes higher than normal with the question, because frankly he's taken me by surprise.

He clears his throat, keeping his eyes on the road even though there's no one else around.

"Because I pay attention."

"I didn't think guys noticed that kind of thing."

"I normally wouldn't," he admits a bit reluctantly.

"Then why did you?"

He adjusts his position in the seat. "Because I find myself wanting to know things about you."

He's stunned me, which honestly, I didn't know was possible. I'm not easily shocked.

"What is it, exactly, that you've learned from your observations?" I challenge with a smile, certain there's not too much he could've noticed.

"You prefer iced coffee to hot, usually with some kind of nut milk and that's it, but you'll drink hot coffee if there are no other options. You like to read, although I still can't wrap my head around the alien porn you gave me." He takes a breath and goes on. "You have a thing for vampires, or at least I'm assuming so, because on top of watching 'Vampire Diaries' I've also noticed you watching 'Buffy' and 'Twilight'. You have a sweet tooth. You love kids. The way you light up talking about your students has enough power to fuel the entire east coast." He pauses, glancing at me. "Should I go on?"

Selfishly, I nod my head. "Please."

Hearing Jude say these things about me ... there aren't enough words in the English language to articulate how it makes me feel.

"Okay." He rubs his jaw in an effort to hide his smile. I want to beg him not to do that. He doesn't smile often enough, and I want them all. Each one he sends my way is like discovering a hidden treasure. "You're confused about what you want to do with your life, so you deflect whenever the conversation comes up with someone. You're young, you have time to figure it out, so don't feel bad that you don't know yet." I stare at the side of his face, in awe of all that he's noticed about me. Unfairly, I haven't given Jude enough credit. "You hate spicy food—when Daire made dinner the last time you looked like you wanted to vomit.

Apparently, you have tendency to hoard snacks, which I've only just learned today, and—"

I put my hand over his mouth. "You can stop now." My voice is soft, tears pooling in my eyes.

I don't think anything in my entire life has touched me the way hearing Jude say these things about me has. It's one thing for someone to remember something you've told them, and a complete other when they learn these things on their own.

"Fuck, don't cry. I didn't mean to make you cry."

"I'm not crying," I lie, wiping dampness from beneath my eyes.

"Liar," he grunts. Jude is always calling me on my shit, and I both love and hate it.

He pulls the truck off the side of the road. In the distance thunder rumbles over the sound of Halsey's 'Colors'.

"Come here." He undoes his seatbelt and clicks mine, tugging me over the console of his truck and into his lap. He scoots the seat back as far as it will go, which isn't much further with how tall he is.

But it doesn't matter to me. I'm in Jude's arms, in the middle of a storm. For me, no moment exists more perfect than this one. He smooths his thumbs beneath my eyes, removing any traces of moisture.

"I didn't mean to make you cry."

His lips are a breath from mine. All I would have to do is

lean forward the barest inch and kiss him. God, I want to kiss him again.

I never understood the term 'boy crazy' until Jude.

Now, I understand wholeheartedly, because lately all I can think about is him.

He fills my thoughts. Invades my senses.

"They're not sad tears." I trace the outline of his lips with my pointer finger. His lips are so soft it's unfair. "I don't think anyone's ever noticed so many things about me before."

He clears his throat, wrapping his big arms tighter around my frame like he's afraid if he doesn't keep me tethered to him, I'll float away.

"How can I not? You're magnetic. When I'm near you I can't help but be drawn to you. It's like my eyes don't want to look anywhere else and that fucking terrifies me."

"Why? Why does it scare you?"

He clears his throat, pressing his lips to the top of my head. "Because, I've never felt that way before."

"Not with—"

"Never."

I'm stunned.

My lips find his and the moment they collide it's like something explodes. We're kissing like our lives depend on it, not a care that we're currently parked on the side of the road. His fingers tangle in my hair, cupping the back of my head as he holds me to him. My elbow bumps the horn, but neither of us cares. I adjust myself in his lap so that I'm straddling him the best I can in the front seat. It helps that I'm shorter.

A whimper flees my lips at the feel of his erection rubbing against me. My hips start to grind against him of their own volition.

The music changes, 'RIP 2 My Youth' by The Neighborhood.

Jude reaches for my hoodie, pushing it up my body. I lift my arms, letting him pull it off me. As soon as it's gone, he buries his head against my chest, kissing the tops of my breasts above my tank top.

"C-Can I?" He tugs on my tank. I've barely started to nod when he says, "Thank fuck," and yanks it off too. I gasp when he tugs my bra down, exposing my breasts. His eyes are dark with desire when he zeroes in on them. He doesn't seem to care that they're small and that helps ease some of my nerves.

"Oh my God," I cry out when his mouth closes around one nipple. My fingers grip his hair as my head falls back. He moves to my other breast and my body pebbles with goosebumps. My breast is wet with his saliva and looking at it, at the proof that Jude put his mouth on me, nearly makes me shake. "Jude," I whimper his name.

He swirls his tongue against my nipple and lets that one go, diving back for my mouth. I swear he feels even harder against my core than he did before. That has to be painful right?

I move my right hand between us, rubbing him over his

jeans. His hips buck up at my touch. I start to take my hand away, worried I've hurt him.

"Don't fucking move your hand."

"I-It's okay?" I struggle to catch my breath. "Me touching you?"

"More than okay."

I reach for his belt, eyes on his to see if he wants me to stop. But he just watches me as I undo it. I struggle with the button on his jeans and he gently pushes my hands aside to help me. My breath is caught in my throat as I slide the zipper down. His cock springs free and I look at him with surprise.

"You're not wearing boxers?"

He shakes his head. "I rarely do."

I wet my lips with my tongue. "C-Can I touch it?"

"Fuck, Millie, are you trying to kill me with a question like that? I'd get down on my fucking knees and beg you to touch it if I had to."

I smile, my eyes flickering down to stare at his hard cock. It twitches and my eyes fly back to his. "It moved."

He groans, covering his eyes. "Yeah, it does that. God, you're too fucking innocent for someone like—"

I cut off his sentence by wrapping my hand around his cock. "Oh, wow," I murmur in surprise. "It's so soft and warm."

"Babe, my cock is as hard as it gets right now."

I giggle, biting my lip to keep the rest of the sound inside. "I meant your skin is so soft there." My face heats and I wonder if my chest turns blotchy with the embarrassment too, but I refuse to look down and check.

"I know what you meant." He grabs my hips, picking me up easily and adjusting my position on his lap. He puts his hand over mine around his cock, showing me how firmly he wants me to grip him and how fast to stroke. "This isn't why I brought you out here."

"We've established that," I say with a smile, rubbing my thumb over the tip of his dick. "It's not my fault your dick just fell in my hand."

He laughs, the smooth planes of his abdominals flexing. "Don't make me laugh when my dick is in your hand."

"I could put it in my mouth?"

"Fucking hell, Millie, don't say shit like that to me." He covers his eyes with the crook of his elbow. "You want to kill me. That's got to be it."

"If I kill you then I don't get to play with this." I twist my wrist and he curses. "And where would the fun be in that?"

I'm not quite ready to give him a blowjob, despite joking about it. With this all being new to me I want to savor every step, and there's something insanely hot about knowing Jude is losing his mind with my hand alone when this man has made his rounds around campus.

He lowers his arm, his eyes glazing over when he stares at my breasts. He dips forehead, taking a nipple in his mouth. I gasp, my eyes drifting closed. I don't know how it's possible with his mouth on my breast, but I feel my core pulsing with pleasure like there's a direct tie between his tongue, my nipple, and my pussy.

I stroke him faster, rolling my hips against his lap. I think I might even be able to come this way.

"Fuck, Millie, I'm gonna blow my load if you don't stop."

I know he's warning me, giving me a chance to stop before his cum gets all over me, but I keep going.

His hips jerk up into my hands and then he's cursing as his pleasure takes over. It spurts out, white and sticky and all over my hands.

I stare down in awe, shocked I was able to get him there with just my hand.

Huh, maybe this whole thing isn't as difficult as I thought.

Lifting my hand, I lick one of my fingers out of curiosity. Jude's lips part, the brown color entirely leached from his eyes, leaving behind nothing but lust-filled darkness.

He tears his shirt off and hands it to me. "Wipe your hands off and get in the back."

"What?" I stammer out, worried I've done something wrong. Is he sequestering me to the back like a pesky child? "What about your shirt? It'll get dirty."

"Back seat, Millie, now." He gives my ass a light swat as I crawl to the back seat. "And I have some spare clothes in my gym bag."

He hops out of the truck, looking like some kind of avenging angel as the rain pelts his skin. He's tucked his cock back into his jeans, zipping them but leaving them unbuttoned.

Opening the back door, he climbs in with me. The door slams shut behind him and then he's over me, crowding me against the narrow back seat. The leather is cool against my skin, but Jude's hot, like his skin is on fire.

"Do you want to take your pants off or do you want me to do it?"

I don't hesitate. "You."

He rids me of my black Lululemon leggings and panties, cursing when my pants get stuck at one point. I help him get them off the rest of the way and he tosses them on the floor. I sit up, taking my bra fully off.

Jude watches my movements with unabashed awe and pleasure as I lay down once more on the back seat. My right legs rests on the floor, my left bent on the seat, entirely exposing my pussy to him. I'm so very naked and surprisingly not even shy about it. The way he stares at me, like I'm the most gorgeous woman he's ever seen, keeps me from trying to cover myself.

He wets his lips, his top teeth digging slightly into his full bottom lip.

"Can I touch it?" he asks, staring at my pussy. I'm so wet it's probably getting on the leather seats, but that's something I refuse to worry about right now. I nod and he says, "Thank fuck."

He rubs his fingers over my pussy, groaning when he

feels how wet I am. He takes the wetness between his fingers, rubbing it over my clit.

"Tell me what feels good, Millie. You have to tell me what feels good and what doesn't, okay? That's the only way any of this can work with us."

"Are you going to fuck me in the backseat of your truck?" I'm surprised, not only by how bold the question is, but with how much the thought alone turns me on. I swear I feel myself get wetter.

"No," he says, "but I am going to taste your pussy. You have no fucking idea how badly I've wanted to know what you taste like."

Somehow, he manages to maneuver his big body down between my legs. He ducks his head, his soft brown hair brushing my thighs.

"On the phone," I gasp when his tongue licks over my clit, "I wanted to know what your stubble w-would feel like down there."

He looks up with a wicked smirk. "You imagined me licking this sweet pussy?"

"Y-Yes."

He grins. "Naughty girl."

And then I don't have to imagine it anymore, because he's licking my pussy, and his stubble scratches against my inner thighs.

But *oh* his mouth.

His mouth is heaven sent. It has to be.

Looping his arms around my legs to keep me in place

and open to him, he licks and sucks my pussy like it's a five-star meal and he hasn't eaten in a week.

I whimper, slapping a hand over my mouth to stifle my moans.

He stops what he's doing. "Take your hand off your mouth, Millicent. I want to hear every fucking sound you make, because they belong to me. Do you hear me?" I drop my hand, my mouth gaped open. I nod jerkily. He grins, his lips glossy with my wetness. "Good girl."

Oh, sweet Jesus.

I don't cover my mouth again, doing as he says. When he slides a finger inside me, my hips jerk and I feel him smile against me. "So fucking responsive."

I mewl in protest when his mouth leaves my pussy. He adds another finger and I bite my lip from the full feeling.

"You're so tight."

He curls his fingers up, pumping in and out of my core. He presses his thumb against my clit, and I go off, the orgasm rocking through my body. He keeps pumping his fingers, in and out, while pussy pulses with shocks of pleasure.

My eyes flutter closed. There's a sheen of sweat clinging to my skin. I feel utterly spent, and yet I want more.

When I finally manage to pry my eyes open it's to see Jude looking at me with wide-eyed wonder. I swallow thickly. The wipers are still beating rapidly against the windshield and now 'Stop and Stare' from One Republic is playing in the background.

"You're hard again."

He palms his cock over his jeans. "It's a permanent state of being around you."

I smile, putting my hand over his. "Are you going to fuck me in the back of your truck, Jude?"

He arches a brow. "Do you mean am I going to take your virginity in here? As tempting as that would be, and what a fucking amazing thing to think about every time I drive around here, the answer is no. You deserve better than this for your first time."

Frowning, I say, "But a truck would make for such an interesting tattoo."

"Huh?"

I laugh and his eyes glue to my boobs, watching them move. "I overheard these girls once, at my school, saying they were all going to get tattoos to represent where they lost their virginity."

He looks at me incredulously, his hand still absentmindedly rubbing his cock. "What the fuck kind of school did you go to?"

"Not a good girl Catholic school if that's what you're thinking."

He narrows his eyes on me. "Is that your backwards way of telling me to throw out my schoolgirl uniform fantasy of you?"

I bat my eyes. "I didn't say we didn't wear uniforms."

"Fuck," he growls, his body crashing over mine as he kisses me. He grinds himself against my core and I whimper from the rough feel of his jeans against my sensitive skin. "Sorry." He pulls back, looking down at my body with unabashed lust.

"Please," I beg. "I want to feel it."

He freezes and then it's like time slows all together when he lets the zipper down. He takes his cock out, stroking the base. "Just the tip. I can't—I won't…" He closes his eyes like he's pained. "I don't deserve more from you."

Gingerly I touch his jaw. "It's mine to give."

He shakes his head. "Take it or leave it. This is all I can give you."

I press my lips together. This beautiful man is way too hard on himself. Doesn't he understand that this is mine to give? But if he's not ready to go all the way today then I'll take what I can get.

"Take," I whisper.

"Thank fuck." He kisses my forehead.

Gripping the base of his cock, he guides it to my pussy, holding it there before pushing forward. He meets resistance and I try to contain the look of pain on my face. I didn't expect it to be that tight, to *hurt*, and I can't imagine what it would feel like if he pushed all the way in. He's so thick and veiny.

"You're so fucking tight, baby." He pulls out, pushing back in slightly. "Relax," he murmurs, brushing his lips lightly over mine. "Let me in. Just a little more and we'll be there."

I take several deep breaths, trying to calm my racing

heart. As my body relaxes, he's able to push in a little more. "I can't—" he grits his teeth "—I can't go any deeper."

I think he's telling himself, not me.

"You can," I practically beg, gripping his ass, "I'm telling you it's okay."

He closes his eyes, shaking his head. "N-No. This is all I can give you right now." He guides his tip in and out of my pussy, and we both watch the way my body grips his, desperate to be filled. He rubs his thumb against my clit and my hips move of their own volition, taking him deeper. "Just the tip," he mutters to himself.

He rubs me to another orgasm and curses as my pussy spasms. Grabbing his dick, he pumps his hand roughly over it until his cum spurts across my belly.

Both of us breathe heavily, like we've just run a marathon.

Jude grabs his shirt I used to clean my fingers earlier and wipes my stomach off. Tossing the shirt aside he wraps me in his arms, cradling me the best he can in the confined space. I never took Jude for a cuddler, but this man is constantly taking me by surprise.

Lips pressed to the crook of my neck, he murmurs, "I'll never look at rainy days the same."

I smile to myself. "Me either."

twenty-six

Jude

I SLIDE INTO A CHAIR ACROSS FROM MY BROTHER IN the dining hall. He pushes food around his plate, keeping his eyes down. He seems sad about something, and maybe a bit disgruntled.

"What's up?" I ask him, twisting the lid off a bottle of Sprite.

"Nothing." He continues to fork his food around.

Jonah isn't the type to pout or be sullen over something. My brother is usually annoyingly happy most of the time, so seeing him like this is strange.

"Nothing," I repeat with a sarcastic lilt. "I wasn't born yesterday little bro. I know when something is up with you."

He groans, shoving his food away. "It's the girl I like," he mumbles, barely audible above the other chatter in the room. "She … we went on a date, and I thought it went well, but when we got together to work on our project today, she said she really likes me, but she likes someone else too and doesn't want to lead me on." He tugs at his hair. "How did I inadvertently get involved in some love triangle bullshit?"

I'm shocked by the hurt and annoyance in my brother's voice. Bug doesn't normally let things get to him. I've always envied him for the way he lets things roll easily off his shoulders. Clearly, he really likes this girl.

"Aw, shit, Jonah. I'm sorry."

He rubs a hand over his jaw, his eyes sad. "I can't make her like me back, but I'm just bummed, you know?"

"Her loss." I twist the cap back on my Sprite. "You're a hell of a catch. The other guy can't compare."

"Doesn't matter if she has feelings for him," he mumbles, taking off the top of his burger and getting rid of the pickles.

"Well, I guess all you can do is show her what she's missing out on."

He arches a brow, finally taking a bite of his burger. "What do you mean?"

"Just be yourself."

He snorts. "That's the worst advice you could give me. I could've gotten that from a fortune cookie."

I sigh, scratching at my stubble. "All I'm saying is you're a great guy and she'll see that. How can she not? And maybe things won't work out with this guy."

Jonah glares at me, stifling a snort. "And I'm supposed to be okay being second best?"

"It's not second best if you're the best choice," I argue, pointing a fry at him.

He thinks it over and finally nods. "Maybe you have a point."

"Of course, I do." I tap the side of my forehead. "There's a wealth of knowledge up here."

"That you hardly use."

"Hey," I laugh, throwing a fry at him. "You don't know that. But if she's truly not interested, it's her loss, not yours."

With a sigh, he nods. "You're right," he says, but it sounds like he only half-believes it.

"HEY, MAN," Cree pokes his head in the doorway of my room, "can I talk to you for a second?"

For a moment, panic seizes me. My heart speeds up, every pump of the organ chanting *he knows, he knows, he knows*. It was only last week I had Millie spread out naked in my backseat, tasting her sweet pussy.

But then I quickly realize that if he did know, he certainly wouldn't be asking to have a conversation. Instead, he'd be trying to lay my ass out flat.

"Sure." I spin around in my desk chair. "What's up?"

He steps into my room, looking around. I haven't seen much of him or Daire lately. Cree's been chasing after that girl he likes and hardly ever around. Daire? I've heard rumors but don't want to believe they're true. If they are? The dude's fucked.

"I got a call from Teddy, and he needs to crash here Friday night with his mom." I frown, wondering why he'd need to do that. Cree notices my look and adds, "His mom is finally leaving his dad and he figured his dad wouldn't come here looking for her."

I rear back in surprise. "She's finally leaving the bastard?"

He nods, looking over the books on my shelves. There aren't many, mostly textbooks and other shit I put there. "Teddy finally convinced her to go through with a divorce so she's moving out while the bastard is out of town."

Last year, Teddy confided in our group of friends that his father was an abusive asshole. It came as a surprise, at least to me. Teddy was my roommate, my really good friend, and as upbeat as the guy always is, it didn't seem possible that he'd dealt with something so fucking awful his whole life. But Teddy is Teddy and he's pretty fucking resilient.

"Good for her." I grab my bottle of water, twisting off the cap.

"Anyway," Cree rocks back on his heels, "I just wanted to give you the heads up."

"Cool." I nod, twisting side to side in my desk chair. "It'll be nice to see Teddy."

"Yeah." Cree rubs his jaw, distracted.

"You okay, dude?" He seems irritated about something.

"Fine. I'm fine. I'm going to let Daire and Millie know what's going on."

"All right," I reply, watching him go.

No matter what he says, there's something on his mind. But the good news for me is, the more he has on his mind, the less likely he is to pay any attention to what's going on between his sister and me.

IT'S my turn to make dinner tonight, and I'm opting for simple with grilled chicken and salad. Millie chops up some peppers and other veggies to add to the salad. I didn't ask her to help, but when she saw me setting things out, she wanted to do something.

From the living room I can hear Cree and Daire talking.

Teddy is supposed to be here soon with his mom. Apparently, she's crashing in Cree's room and Teddy's taking one couch while Cree takes the other.

"Are you okay over there?" Millie asks, nodding her head at where I've paused in cutting up the chicken. I glance her way with a questioning look. "You seem lost in thought."

"I'm fine," I say, tossing the chicken into the bowl with

the salad. Turning, I swipe a beer from the fridge and remove the top. "I'll be right back."

"Okay," she says with a soft smile, flicking hair out of her eyes.

I graze my fingers over her arm as I pass, that small smile of hers growing and eyes lighting up.

Leaving Millie behind, I head into the living room where Daire and Cree are. "What's going on?"

Daire glances at me over the back of the couch with a gloating smirk. "Ophelia, the girl that has this one so moony," he points a finger in Cree's direction, "is going on a date tonight."

I wince, knowing that one has to sting Cree. "Shit, dude, I'm sorry."

He throws his hands up in relief. "At least someone feels sorry for me."

I take a swig of beer, wiping my mouth with the back of my hand. "Hope you fuckers are okay with grilled chicken and salad because that's what I'm making."

"Sounds healthy," Daire grumbles. "I mean, delicious," he adds when I give him a death stare. If he doesn't want that for dinner, he can cook his own shit. He subjected us to beef stroganoff earlier this week when it was his turn to cook, and he didn't hear me bitching.

"We can't eat so much junk." Daire is a junk food fanatic. Since he's a hockey player like Cree I'm surprised it's not making him sluggish on the ice.

I head back into the kitchen to finish everything up.

I've hardly started putting the salad in separate bowls, Millie sitting at the table now, when I hear Teddy's voice.

Instantly, a smile comes to me.

Teddy is the kind of person who instantly lightens the mood no matter what. Millie looks toward the sound of the voices but doesn't move from the table.

"I'll be right back," I tell her.

I poke my head out of the kitchen and grin when I see Teddy in the front hall. "Didn't think I'd be seeing you around these parts any time soon."

He smiles, lifting one shoulder in a shrug. "Eh, you know how it goes with family."

I laugh, lifting my hands to the top of the doorframe. I swear I hear Millie give a little gasp behind me. "Oh, I do. How's Vanessa?"

"She's good." Teddy sticks his hands in his jean pockets, looking around the house. He's been here a lot the past few years for parties. I wonder if it feels weird to him, being done with college. "She gives me hell but man," he shakes his head with a grin, "I love that girl. She's the best thing that ever happened to me."

I let Cree and Daire catch him up on the Ophelia situation and sit down with Millie to eat.

"That's Teddy, huh?" She stabs her fork into her salad repeatedly. "He's hot."

A growl rumbles in my chest. "He's taken, Little Madison."

She smirks, tucking a piece of hair behind her ear. "I didn't say I wanted to do him, just that he was hot."

"Who's hot?"

I groan, covering my face when Teddy waltzes into the kitchen with Daire. Cree is mysteriously absent.

"You are," Millie says unabashedly.

Teddy chuckles, grinning. "I know."

"Have you no shame?" I toss the question at him.

"Nope." He helps himself to food along with Daire.

"Where's Cree?" I ask.

Daire rolls his eyes at my question, so Teddy's the one to answer. "Going to get his girl." He grabs a piece of chicken from the salad with his fingers, shoving it in his mouth. "Said she was going on a date with some guy, and I told him he can't have that."

Daire and Teddy join us at the table.

Teddy takes the chair beside Millie, bumping her arm with his. "You're Cree's little sister, huh?"

With a straight face she says, "Nah, I just live here. They found me on the street and adopted me. I'm like the house mascot now."

Teddy's grin widens and he wags his finger. "I like you." I growl, kicking his shin underneath the table. "Ow, fuck, dude," he curses.

Daire's eyes dart between the three of us and I don't know what kind of dots he's trying to connect, but he needs to erase them right now. I glare at him, and he looks back, clearly confused. He better fucking stay that way too.

"I hope you're not letting this one bother you," Teddy goes on, speaking to Millie while pointing at me. "He was my roommate for two years. The stories I could—*ow*, motherfucker, do you have a twitch or some shit you need to get checked out?" From the smirk he sends my way I know he's enjoying this—pushing my buttons.

"Don't talk shit about me."

His smile gets impossibly bigger. "It's not talking shit if it's true."

"Teddy," I warn.

"Fine, fine." He puts his hands up in a placating manner. "I won't say a word."

He looks way too fucking amused, and I want to wipe the expression off his face. I wasn't worried about Teddy being here, but now I am. The guy has way too many stories he can tell on me. All of them, horribly, true. We finish up eating and there's definite tension in the air. I keep eyeing Teddy, ready to jump across the table and tackle his ass if I have to. But for the most part he remains on his best, for Teddy, behavior. Even if I'd rather him not talk to Millie. It's not even about what he might say, I just don't fucking like it, which is ridiculous. He's my friend, he's in a happily committed relationship, and ... and I have no fucking right to be jealous. I don't *own* her.

When dinner is finished, I normally wouldn't be the one washing up dishes since I cooked, but I stand and start stacking the plates. I feel Millie's eyes on me, watching me curiously, and I have no rational way to explain my behavior.

"I've got the dishes," I growl out, hoping they'll empty out of the kitchen.

"Sweet." Daire shoves back from the table so fast the chair nearly topples out from under him. He's gone lightning quick, like he's afraid if he's not out of there fast enough I'll change my mind. His feet thud up the stairs and the door to his room shuts.

Millie gets up, brushing her hair over her shoulder. "I can wash them, Jude. It's my turn."

Teddy watches from behind her, his eyes moving from her to me and back again like he's trying to solve some complicated math problem.

"Nah, it's okay." I can't help myself when I give her hand a gentle squeeze, instantly cursing myself when Teddy notices. Letting her hand go, I say, "You said you had homework, go take care of that. I've got this tonight."

"All right." She turns to Teddy. "Goodnight. It was nice meeting you."

He grins, rubbing his fingers over his lips. "Likewise. It's been enlightening."

Millie ducks out of the room and I face my former roommate with my arms crossed over my chest. It's a defensive pose, and I should know better, because his smile grows when he notices.

"Hot for Cree's little sister? Who would've guessed it? Not me."

"Don't talk about her like that." I turn the faucet on, watching it fill with water and adding some dish soap.

He throws his head back and laughs. "Oh, you've got it fucking bad for her, dude. Does this mean you're over Macy?"

"I'm not talking to you about this."

He gets up, standing beside me at the counter. "Why not? I know you better than most people."

"I'm not talking about it because there's nothing to talk about it."

He laughs again. "Either you think I'm stupid, or you're that stupid. You look at her like—"

"What?" I turn toward him, elbow deep in suds. "What do I look at her like?"

His eyes narrow and he sighs. "Like I look at Vanessa."

I choke down a bitter laugh. "No way."

Teddy and Vanessa are madly in love. What he's suggesting is impossible.

"Deny it all you want, but I saw it with my own two eyeballs." He points his index and middle finger at his eyes and then at me.

I focus back on the dishes. "You saw nothing."

"One of us here is a liar-liar-pants-on-fire and—" He makes a show of lifting his feet off the ground and patting his jeans. "It ain't me."

"Where's your mom?" I growl out, trying to change the subject.

"She went up to bed. She's exhausted." He gets a

haunted look, rubbing his jaw. "It's been a hard day but I'm proud of her." Smiling slowly, he wags a finger at me. "Don't think you can change the subject that easily." Lowering his voice, and his eyes taking on a warning. "That girl is young, and sweet. Not to mention she's your friend's sister, and it doesn't take a genius to figure out he's probably oblivious to whatever is going on. Don't hurt her."

"I haven't fucked her if that's what you're getting at."

He's quiet for a moment. "But you have done something with her? Am I right?" I don't give him any indication one way or the other. "Don't hurt her. She seems like a good girl and if you're not serious about her then she doesn't deserve to be strung along. And Cree's your friend, so is she worth it?"

Again, I don't answer him. I swallow past the sudden lump in my throat.

"Deny it all you want, but you have feelings for her, and if you're truly not over Macy still, or you don't plan on changing your ways to be with her—"

"I haven't fucked anyone in weeks," I whisper, glancing at him. "Over a month now, actually, I think. I haven't been keeping track."

"Huh." He looks me over. "I know you didn't ask my advice, but if you're going there with her, the sooner you tell Cree the better." I press my lips into a thin line, it's the same thing Mascen said. He raises his hands, backing out of the kitchen. "Just think about it."

I OPEN THE BATHROOM DOOR, Millie jumping when I step inside. She's in the middle of brushing her teeth and obviously freshly showered. She's only in a pair of tiny pink panties and a tank top, no bra, with her nipples pebbled against the fabric.

I can't help myself when I look her up and down. She's petite but extremely muscular from all her hours of ballet.

After my talk with Teddy the last thing I should be doing is standing here checking her out. But when it comes to Millie I'm fucking helpless.

She spits out her toothpaste in the sink, rinsing her mouth out. "What are you—"

I drop to my knees in front of her, shock rippling across her features. Wrapping my arms around her middle, I kiss the skin above her panties beneath her belly button, then each of her hips. Her fingers slide into my hair, pushing my head back slightly.

I've never been in this position with a woman before, practically submissive, but just seeing her standing there brushing her teeth is enough to bring me to my knees.

"What are you doing?"

"I don't know," I whisper, pressing another kiss to her stomach. "I don't know *anything* when it comes to you."

Her hand moves down to my cheek, cupping my jaw. "Why do you have to know? Why can't we just see where things go?"

I grip the backs of her legs, pulling her up as I stand. Her legs wind around my waist.

In the back of my mind, I hear that annoying voice telling me I shouldn't be doing this, but I can't stop. I'm not sure I've ever needed anyone more than I need Millicent Madison and that's the most shocking thought of all.

When Macy and I broke up, I was certain that that was it for me. I believed she was my one true love, and I was destined to never find someone who was my partner, my equal, ever again.

I never saw Millie coming.

My lips attack hers, our tongues tangling together. She wraps her arms around the back of my head, her fingers tugging roughly on my hair. I carry her into her room, laying her on the bed beneath me. My body crowds her, covering every inch of her much smaller body.

She moans, rolling her hips against my growing erection. My right-hand snakes beneath her tank top, rolling my thumb over her nipple.

"Jude," she moans my name, her fingers moving to yank on my shirt. I rise up enough to yank it off and toss it on the bed before I'm over her again. Her soft hands flutter against my bare chest, gently tracing every dip and curve of muscle I work so hard for.

"I have an away game next week." I brush my lips over her collarbone. She shivers from the touch, curling a leg around my waist. "I want you to come."

"Why?"

"I want you there." I tug her top down, exposing her breasts for my eager eyes. "I want to know you're in the stands, watching me play."

"I was there for your first home game," she confesses, her blush spreading from her cheeks to her neck and down her chest. "You were spectacular."

I pull back so I can I stare down at her. "Is that so?" Maybe I shouldn't be so surprised that she thinks that of me, but I am.

She nods, her pulse fluttering in her neck. "I couldn't take my eyes off of you."

"You know how to make a guy feel good."

She bites her lip, rubbing her pussy against my thigh where I've wedged it between her legs.

"Are you going to touch me?"

I wet my lips. "Do you want me to?"

"Y-Yes," she stutters as I duck my head down, sucking on her right breast.

"Oh God."

I flip her over, smacking her ass. She gasps, rocking back into me. I rub my hand soothingly over the sensitive skin. She looks at me over her shoulder, her hair falling forward. "What was that for?"

"Because I wanted to." I move her panties aside, pressing a kiss to her reddened ass. "Are you wet?" My fingers find the answer before she speaks. "Mmm," I hum. "You're fucking soaked."

I pull her panties down her legs, rolling her onto her

back again to get rid of them. She takes off her tank top, lying completely naked beneath me. She cups her breasts, not looking the least bit shy to be naked. Selfishly, that pleases me, because she came to me worried about this kind of thing, but she shows no embarrassment whatsoever. She's confident and it's sexy as fuck.

"What are you going to do about it?" She wiggles below me. Standing, I get rid of my jeans but leave my boxer-briefs on. She licks her lips, watching me. "You're so hot."

She tries to reach for me, but I duck down, wedging my shoulders between her thighs keeping her wide open. I inhale her sweet scent and she whimpers, her eyes hazy. I lick her sweet pussy, smiling against her when she slaps a hand over her mouth to stifle the sounds she makes.

Am I taking a big risk right now doing this in the house?

Yes, and I should care about that, but surprisingly I don't. I'm not sure what's overtaken me when it comes to this girl.

She's so fucking responsive that it doesn't take long for her to come. Kissing my way back up her body, I reach her mouth.

She cups my cheek, smiling almost shyly. "Hi."

I grin back at her. "Hi." I kiss her some more, luxuriating in just how fucking good kissing her is. Pulling back, I ask, "Where are the vibrators?" I follow her eyes to the drawer of her bedside table. "There?" She nods. "Do you trust me?" Another nod. I chuckle, kissing her. "I need to hear you say it, babe."

She takes a deep breath, letting it out slowly. "I trust you."

She has no fucking clue what those three words do to me. I close my eyes, taking a moment to relish in them. Reaching over, I open the drawer and grab the one I want.

Her eyes widen questioningly at the device. "What are you going to do with it?"

"You'll see."

I don't turn it on yet. Gliding it over her chest and around her nipples, I trail it down her stomach until I reach the apex of her thighs. She jumps when it starts up, even though it isn't even touching her yet.

"So jumpy," I murmur, kissing the skin beside her belly button. "Relax."

She blows out a breath. "Sorry."

"Don't apologize, baby." Pressing the vibrator to her clit, her hips buck up and she bites her lips. With my other hand, I slide first one finger and then another into her pussy. She's so fucking tight and wet. Warm too. Her pussy squeezes my fingers over and over like a pulse. "Does it feel good?"

She licks her lips, cupping her breasts. "Yes."

"Are you going to come?"

She nods. "Don't stop."

I grin. "You're not in control here."

She whimpers when my fingers leave her pussy and I take the vibrator away from her clit. Her whimper quickly descends into a moan when I slide the vibrator against her folds. I let it slide an inch, then another into her.

"Oh my God," she cries out when I roll my thumb against her clit. "Yes, yes, yes!" She cries out as she orgasms. I watch mesmerized at the way her pussy squeezes the toy. I desperately want to fuck her, but not yet. Just ... not fucking yet. She's not ready. She might think she is, but she isn't. We'll get there, though.

I never planned on taking her virginity, or even going as far as I have with her, but when it comes to Millie, I seem to be incapable of controlling myself.

As long as this thing keeps working for the both of us, I have no plans of stopping.

I turn the vibrator off, setting it on the table. I gather Millie in my arms, holding her naked body against me. She splays over my chest, struggling to get enough air.

She moves her hand over my chest, down to palm my cock over my underwear.

"Millie," I groan, crooking my arm over my face. "You're going to fucking kill me touching me like that."

She starts pulling my boxer-briefs down and my hips buck when she takes my cock in her hands.

"You have to tell me," she says, swiping her tongue over her lips, "if I do it wrong."

I lower my arm, peering down at her. "Do what wrong?"

I know what she means as soon as she lowers her head, licking the tip of my cock. My hips jerk and she giggles lightly, her breath ghosting across the sensitive skin of my dick.

My hips jerk at the sensation.

She licks me again, and growing bolder lowers her mouth over the top. I grip her sheets tightly in my fists, surprised they don't pull right off the mattress. She lets me go, jerking her hand up and down. Up and down. Her grip is firm, just like I showed her in my truck.

I brush her hair over her shoulder, my fingers lingering on her collarbone. "That's a good girl," I murmur when she takes me in her mouth again, going deeper. She gags slightly, but doesn't panic, relaxing her throat. "Fuck, Millie, your mouth is heaven."

She goes a little deeper and it's as far as she can take me right now.

I gather her hair in my fist, watching her bob up and down on my cock.

"Just like that, baby," I encourage, my body drawing up tight with pleasure. I won't deny I've had fantasies about Millie, but for some reason I never let myself imagine this. And I know for fucking sure that this is better than anything my brain could've conjured up.

"I'm getting close," I warn her. "Almost. Fuck, Millie, you have to stop." She releases my cock with a little smile, wiping the spit from her mouth. "I wanna come on your tits."

She nods, lying down. Her hair fans out around her like

a halo and she nods. "Okay." She plays with her breasts, pinching her nipples.

"Fuck." I grit my teeth, jerking my cock until I spill my cum all over her pretty little tits. "Look what a mess I've made of you."

I let myself get my fill of looking her over before I grab her up, eliciting a tiny scream from her. Tossing her over my shoulder, I spank her ass lightly and carry her into the bathroom. I set her down and turn on the shower, tugging her in with me.

I kiss her beneath the spray. Letting my hands roam up and down her slick body.

"No funny business," I promise.

But it's a lie when I end up dropping to my knees.

After she's come again, and we're thoroughly clean, I carry her to her bed. Our naked bodies twine together, and Millie drifts off to sleep with her head on my chest. I promise myself I'll leave and go back to my room in ten minutes, then fifteen, and then before I know it it's morning.

twenty-seven

Millie

"THANKS FOR THE COFFEE," I SAY SOFTLY, TAKING A seat in the same back room at the library Jonah and I have been using. My cheeks flush with shame that despite me telling him I was interested in someone else; he's still being kind to me.

I know it's stupid, but I almost think I'd rather him be angry.

It's what I deserve, even if I didn't intentionally lead him on, and if I'm being honest I still like Jonah in a way that could potentially lead to more, but I didn't expect this thing with Jude to turn into whatever it is.

Jonah nods his head at my thanks. "You're welcome. Should we get to work?"

"Oh, yeah, of course." I unpack my stuff and open my

laptop to my essay I've been working on. Setting out my notebook, filled with page after page of notes from the past I don't know how many weeks, I slip into a chair. "Do you want to start first today?"

"Sure." He smiles but it doesn't quite reach his eyes. I know he's hurt and it makes me feel sick knowing I'm the person who caused that pain. Jonah is a kind, sweet guy and I ... I suppose I should've never gone to Jude to help me feel comfortable being with a guy. I just ... I truly never expected it to turn into whatever this is.

We work for a few hours, taking turns interviewing each other as mock-patient and psychologist and working on our essay's. I'm not sure about Jonah, but I know mine will need a lot of editing. So far, I've mostly word vomited my thoughts into the Word Document, figuring I can go back and sort it out later.

Across from me, Jonah closes his laptop. "I have to head out."

"Oh." I look at the time, not realizing so much has passed. "I should get going too. I'm supposed to meet a friend for dinner." Jonah freezes, his shoulders bunched and I know immediately what he assumes since I told him there was another guy I liked. "Zara," I say, trying to play it off like I'm not obviously letting him know it's a girl I'm meeting up with. "I met her kinda-sorta by accident in the coffee shop and we became friends."

God, I'm fucking rambling like a lunatic.

But I don't like the fact that I've hurt Jonah's feelings.

"Cool." He clears his throat, stuffing his backpack full. "I'll see you later."

He doesn't look at me as he leaves, head down as he speed walks through the library. I watch girls at one of the tables near the room we use watch him go appreciatively.

My feelings for Jude are strong and complicated and not something I entirely understand. I'm not naïve enough to think he's my boyfriend and he hasn't promised me anything. Jonah would be the safer choice. A good one. He'd make me happy. But he doesn't evoke the same chemistry I feel with Jude—and it terrifies me that maybe no other guy ever will.

I SLIDE into the booth across from Zara at the restaurant.

"Sorry I'm late." I slip my purse off my shoulder, setting it on the booth beside me. After leaving the library, I decided to go home and change instead of coming straight to the restaurant to meet.

"No problem." Zara smiles, placing her menu on the table. Her dark hair is pulled back in a sleek ponytail, her makeup impeccable. I managed to dab some mascara on my lashes, add a bit of blush to my cheeks, and swipe on a pinky-nude colored lipstick before dashing out of the house. "How's it been lately? I'm sorry we haven't had much of a chance to get together." I blush instantly, thinking about all that's transpired with Jude since I last spoke with Zara. She notices my look immediately, gasping. "Oh my God, you hussy, did something happen with Jude? I mean, he is your roommate and he's definitely not shy about sex. Spill girl, I need details."

I find myself unloading everything upon her, only pausing to give our order. I tell her about the drive in his truck and what it led to, about the other night, and him asking me to go to the away game.

"Are you going to go? I mean, you have to." She sips her raspberry tea. "This is not something you can pass up."

"I mean ... yeah. How can I not?"

"Do you think you'll finally go all the way with him? I mean, they're going to be gone overnight so it makes sense you'd stay in the hotel with him."

"I don't know," I sigh, playing nervously with the ends of my hair. "I feel like if I tell my brother that I'm staying overnight for the away game he might get suspicious."

Zara rolls her eyes. "No offense, but your brother sounds like an overbearing dick. You're an adult. You can do what and whomever you want." She thanks the waitress when she drops off our appetizer of mini egg rolls. "I'm volunteering myself to go with you. We can drive down together, and it gives you the perfect excuse with your brother."

"I don't know," I hedge. There's no reason for Cree to suspect anything. It's only a football game and lots of people go. But after the way he acted when I went last time... "You know what, screw it, sounds like a plan."

"Yes, bitch." Zara grins, lifting her glass of tea for me to cheers. “We’re going to have a blast and maybe, just maybe you’ll actually get laid this time.”

I laugh. “We’ll see, but I’m not holding my breath.”

“Fine, I will.” She inhales a lungful of air, her cheeks puffing out.

We both end up dissolving into laughter, and I find myself so thankful that I’ve met this girl. It’s nice to finally have a friend.

JUDE LEFT EARLY this morning with the rest of his team, sneaking from my bed with a gentle press of his lips to my forehead. He’s been sneaking into my bed some nights and maybe it’s just my body playing tricks on me, but I swear I’m sleeping better when he does. We haven’t fooled around much this week besides one heavy makeout session. With my brother and Daire around we have to be careful. And even though neither is home much, you never know when they’ll be back.

I finish zipping up my overnight bag, checking the time on my phone. Zara should be here any minute, but she said she’d text when she was in the driveway and there’s nothing yet.

There are two soft knocks on my door, and I know who it has to be.

“Come in.” I grab my phone charger from beside my bed, stuffing it into the outside pocket of my bag. Cree opens the door, lingering there awkwardly. "Did you need something?"

He runs his fingers through his hair, sending his slightly wavy strands into disarray. "I just want you to be careful, Mills. It's a football game, which means lots of people and drunk guys, and guys can be stupid."

"I know," I assure him, grabbing up my bag. "I grew up with you." I stick my tongue out at him. "I'll be careful, and I'll be with Zara."

"Who's also a girl," he points out. "Just check in with me, okay?"

"Sure," I say, opening my arms to hug him. Even though my big brother can drive me up a fucking wall, I love him, and I'm thankful to have a brother who cares. "Try not to worry, though. Do something fun with Ophelia."

He's tutoring a girl named Ophelia that's super sweet with the prettiest red hair I've ever seen. I'm not sure if they're officially together yet, or not, but my brother is seriously moony over her. I swear he'd propose in a heartbeat.

"Just be careful. I love you."

"Love you, too. And don't forget mom and dad are coming into town next weekend for my first hockey game."

"I remember. I've gotta go. Zara's waiting." I felt my phone vibrate in my pocket two minutes ago.

Cree walks me out and as soon as I'm in Zara's car and we're a few miles away it feels like I can finally breathe.

We arrive at the hotel, a fairly nice one to my surprise. Athletes stroll through the lobby, some of the guys I recognize from our team, others I don't. Jude isn't anywhere to be seen. Zara checks us in since she reserved the room, and we head up in the elevator. I don't know why I feel like such a big ball of nerves. I don't *think* Jude asked me to come to his game with the intention of taking my virginity this weekend, but I can't help but think there's a chance it might happen. That means I have to be prepared.

Zara swipes the room key, pushing the door open and motioning for me to go in first.

"This bag is so heavy," she grunts, dragging her suitcase behind her. I have no idea why she packed so much for one night.

"Um…" I pause, finding just one bed. "I think they gave us the wrong room."

"Nope." She shakes her head, glossy dark curl flying. "This is *your* room."

"My room?"

"Mhmm." She lifts her suitcase onto the bed. "You know, just in case you *do* happen to want some alone time with Jude." She waggles her brows. "Aldridge might cater to the upper crust of society, but even our athletes have to bunk together." I frown, not having thought about that even though I should have. "This way, you have a room you can both stay without a roomie."

"You don't mind being on your own?"

She grins, her eyes lit with mischief. "Who said I was going to be alone?"

I gape at her. "Have you been holding out on me?"

She wiggles her shoulders in a little shimmy. "No, but there's nothing wrong with a little one-night stand and with all these hot football players milling around the lobby and hotel bar who can blame a girl?" She fans herself. "Anyway." She unzips her suitcase, pulling out a shopping bag. I don't recognize where it's from, nowhere I've ever shopped before, that's for sure. She holds it out to me on one finger, letting it sway back and forth. "For you, my friend."

"What is it?" I hesitantly take the bag, peeking inside to find a pile of tissue paper.

"You have to *look*."

Sitting on the end of the bed, I shove the tissue paper aside, gaping when I find the scraps of lace sitting at the bottom. "Zara." My eyes dart from the contents of the bag to her. "What did you do?"

She giggles, bouncing onto the bed beside me. "Come on, take it out."

I pull the garment out, staring at the lacy monstrosity. It's a pale pink color, completely see-through, and nothing at all like anything I would've picked out myself. I guess, that's the point.

"I ... how do I even put this on?" It has straps hanging off of it and it's so tiny I can't tell the front from the back.

"It's easy, really. Don't overthink it." She takes it from me and stands up, showing me how it works.

"Do I really need that?" I ask, a tad horrified.

"Well, no," she concedes. "But it's really pretty and I promise it'll make you feel bad ass. There's something about putting on nice lingerie that automatically makes you feel sexy and powerful."

"Thank you," I tell her, meaning it whole-heartedly.

She smiles, gently laying the lingerie out on the bed. "You're welcome and if nothing happens tonight, don't stress about it, and if it does, don't worry about that either."

I wrap my arms around her in a hug. "I'm so glad I met you."

She hugs me back. "Same girl. Now, let's get ready for this game."

I'M surprised by how many students from Aldridge pack the stands, but this game is only a few hours away from our campus so I guess I shouldn't be that surprised.

Following Zara through the stands to our seats, I adjust my sunglasses looking down at the field. The game doesn't start for a little while yet, but we wanted to get here, grab some food, and find our seats.

"This is going to be a blast," Zara says to me over her shoulder, shimmying down the aisle to our seats.

I check my phone, finding a smiley face reply from Jude when I told him we'd made it and were at the stadium. I quickly type out a good luck text and take the popcorn bag from Zara.

"I love football." She smiles giddily. "The guys are hot. The pants are tight. And the butts are impeccable."

"Wait until you learn about other sports," I joke. "Especially hockey."

"Ooh, your brother plays right?" She waggles her brows suggestively.

"First off, ew. Secondly, he's pretty serious about a girl right now. I think they're official or at least headed that way."

Her shoulders deflate. "Ugh, the hot ones are always taken. I still can't believe you bagged Jude Cartwright."

"Jude what?" I blurt, realizing I've never paid any attention to his last name. When I got his jersey it didn't have his name on it, just his number.

"Cartwright," she repeats, looking at me funny. "You didn't know his last name?"

"I'm sure I did." I wave a dismissive hand. "It sounds familiar, so I had to." I stuff my hand in the popcorn bag, taking out a handful to munch on.

Zara takes a bite of it and cringes. "This popcorn is stale. Give me that, I'm going to complain."

I laugh to myself as she makes her way back down the aisle with the popcorn to go chew out some poor employee. Rightfully so, stale popcorn is garbage.

While Zara's gone, I reply to my brother after he sent yet another text to make sure we found our seats okay. He's such a worrywart sometimes. While I'm scrolling Instagram a text comes in from Jude.

Jude: Sorry, I haven't been able to text much. Just wanted to say I'm happy my good luck charm is here.

Me: I'm your good luck charm? How?

Jude: Just by being you, Little Madison. I have to put my phone away but come down to the locker rooms after the game. I'll give them your name and Zara's too.

Me: Okay, thanks, and good luck again.

Zara is going to lose her shit that we get to wait by the locker rooms. She's going to be so excited.

She returns after about fifteen minutes with two fresh bags of popcorn. "They were nice enough to give me two for all the trouble. I tasted it just to make sure it wasn't stale so we should be good."

I take one of the bags from her and pop a piece of popcorn in my mouth. Definitely better, but I would've eaten the other anyway. I fill Zara in on what Jude told me and just like I knew she would, she bounces with excitement.

"Oh, this is going to be a blast." She sways back and forth in a little dance move. "You have checked in with your brother, haven't you? I don't need him sending out a search party and raining on our parade."

"Don't worry, I've updated him accordingly."

"Good."

When the game starts, I find myself sucked in just like I

was last time. Zara knows a decent amount about the sport and answers all of my questions even when I know she wants me to shut up. Growing up, my family was into hockey, and I danced. Therefore, I never really got into other sports and I'm not the kind of person who can only sit and watch. I want to understand what I'm seeing. It makes me more invested.

By the end of the game, my voice is hoarse despite the warm apple cider Zara went and got for us, and I've ditched my hoodie, leaving me in only a t-shirt despite the cooler temperatures. Apparently, my temperature rises during football games. But our school wins, *barely*, and knowing Jude that fact probably grates on him. He's probably the type who wants to win by a large margin.

Zara and I navigate our way through the stadium to get where we need to be to meet up with Jude. It takes us so long to get there that some of the guys are already leaving. We had to give my name to this big beefy security guy that completely intimidated me.

At my side, Zara checks out the guys as each one approaches.

"Hi," a small feminine voice says from nearby. "I'm guessing to be back here you must be a girlfriend, but I haven't seen you before. Who are you with?"

"Oh, hi." I smile at the girl. She's really pretty in a soft, natural way. She's not wearing much makeup, if any, and her brown hair is tied in a loose braid. "I'm Millie. I'm waiting for Jude. Jude Cartwright."

"Jude," she rears back in surprise, her mouth opening and closing like a fish. "He … wow. I'm Macy."

Surprise floods me. Macy. The girl everyone knows broke his heart and then went on to date his teammate. He's never talked to me about her. Never even uttered her name in my presence, but it's not like she's much of a secret. I've heard people talk about them on campus and bits and pieces have reached my ears just from living with Cree, Daire, and Jude. "I know you dated," I say when it becomes obvious, she's nervous to say more.

"We did," she confirms, trying to force a strand of hair back through her braid. "It's in the past, though. He's a great guy. He got lost for a little while, but he must be doing better." She looks me up and down, not in a mean way, but almost … approving. "He's never had a girl meet him after a game before. You must be special."

I feel a bit shaky, realizing I'm meeting *the* Macy. The girl he's been hung up on for literal *years*. "I don't know about that."

She gives me a soft smile. "Trust me, you are. I'm glad I got the chance to meet you. I'm sure I'll be seeing you around. That's my fiancé," she points to the newest guy to leave the locker rooms.

"It was nice to meet you."

"You, too."

She's almost to her fiancé when she turns around to face me again. "Be patient with him, okay? He needs someone who will tough it out and fight for him."

She doesn't give me a chance to reply before she's walking away hand-in-hand with her fiancé. He turns and looks back at me and she says something to him before they turn and disappear down the hall.

"Wow, that was..." Zara trails off with a whisper.

"Intense?" I supply, feeling a bit jittery after this encounter.

Sure, she was super nice and not what I expected, but she has to be special for Jude to have loved her for so long.

"Yeah," she agrees. "Are you okay?"

"I'm fine." And I am, even if I wish I knew more about their relationship and what led Jude to be ... well, kind of a man-whore. Not even kind of, a total man-whore.

We have to wait about ten minutes before Jude comes out of the locker room chatting with one of his teammates. The moment Jude sees me waiting for him, a smile transforms his face.

Eyes crinkling at the corners, he approaches me. I stand there awkwardly, not sure what he's going to do. He completely shocks me when he wraps a massive arm around my shoulders, using it to pull me in and up to him until I'm on my tiptoes and my fingertips are pressed to the hard planes of his toned stomach. I'm still unsure what he has planned so when his lips touch mine, it's like a shock to my system. I swear, my heart stops and restarts, beating faster than it ever has before. With his other hand he gently cups my cheek, urging me to open my lips with his tongue. I gasp, giving him the access he so desperately wants.

More guys must've left the locker room, because there's a chorus of cheers and I hear a male voice say, "Jude finally got himself a girlfriend."

My cheeks are warm when he releases me, gently brushing his nose tenderly against mine. "There's my girl," he murmurs, and my insides turn to goo. I like the sound of that way too much considering what we're doing is supposed to be a secret. As if sensing what I'm thinking he says, "The guys won't tell. Don't worry about your brother."

Stupidly, I allow myself to think about what if we *did* tell him. This thing between us seems promising, but maybe that's only to me and he doesn't want to risk ruining his friendship with my brother.

I refuse to let my thoughts go there and get hung up. I'm the one who proposed this whole ... *teaching* thing, so I have no right to expect more from him.

"Let's head back to the hotel and get changed."

"For what?"

"I'm taking you out to dinner, Little Madison."

My gaze darts to Zara where I know she's listening in. "Like on a date?" I want to clarify what he sees this as and not get my hopes up.

His smile grows and he presses a quick peck to my lips. "Exactly like a date."

ON THE WAY back to the hotel I properly introduced Jude and Zara since he'd really only heard of her up until tonight. Although, maybe he met her that night I got drunk at the bar. That night is a hazy blip in my memories.

Since Jude declared we're going on a date, Zara helps me get ready even though I told her she could meet up with someone if she had plans. I didn't exactly pack date clothes, but thankfully Zara did. The dress is sexier than anything I would've picked myself, but the fitted black dress makes me feel sexy and powerful. Or maybe that's the lingerie's doing since I decided to wear it.

Zara finishes putting my hair into a sleek bun at the base of my neck—declaring that Jude will have made a mess of it by the end of the night—and then starts on my makeup.

"This is fun," I tell her softly. "I've never had a friend to do something like this with before."

She pauses with her eyeshadow brush floating halfway in the air. "Don't make me cry, girl." She points a long fingernail at me in warning. "I spent a long time doing this." She turns her finger to her own face. "So that it would last all day and all night. I can't afford tears." She blends a color into the crease of my eye and says, "I'm really glad I met you, Millie."

When my makeup is finished, she air kisses my cheeks, wishes me good luck, and dashes from my room like some kind of fairy godmother.

I stare at myself in the mirror shocked by the transformation.

I still look like me, of course, just enhanced. My eyes are large and open, framed by a smokey eye with a shimmer of pink in the inner corners. My lips are a soft pink, but somehow look poutier than normal. My cheeks are bronzed and blushed, dusted with some kind of shimmer high on my cheekbones. She dusted that same shimmer stuff on my collarbones. Every time I shift the light in the bathroom catches it.

Luckily, Zara and I are only a half-size apart in the shoe department, so she left a pair of heels for me to wear.

I spray on a bit of perfume and that's when there's a knock on the door.

My heart takes off at a gallop.

Opening the door, I find Jude just like I knew I would. He's just as good looking, if not more so now that I know him better, as I thought he was the day he moved in.

He looks me up and down in the same way I'm doing him. He's dressed in a charcoal gray pair of slacks, and a white button down with the sleeves rolled up to show his corded forearms dusted with dark hair. His hair is pushed back from his forehead, like he put some effort into getting it to stay out of his eyes. He's cleaned up the scruff on his cheeks so it's more like stubble now. I itch to reach out and touch his cheek, but refrain.

"You're beautiful, Millie," he murmurs, sounding slightly in awe. "So gorgeous you take my breath away." I duck my head at the compliment, and he immediately tips my head back up with a gentle finger beneath my chin. "You don't believe me? Clearly, I haven't done a good enough job showing you how completely and utterly attracted to you that I am."

There's a sudden lump in my throat and I find myself having trouble swallowing. Yep, Jude has officially choked me up with his compliments. The way he is with me, the things he says, sometimes it's hard for me to wrap my head around the fact that this guy has been such a player. To me, he's just Jude. My Jude.

"You're not so bad yourself." I finally manage to get the words out of my clogged throat.

He grins. "Just admit it, Little Madison, you only want me for my body."

I shake my head. "No. It's *you* I like." And even though there are still lots of things I don't know about Jude, I love everything I do know, and I want to learn everything about him.

He cups the back of my head, pulling me in for a kiss that ends all too quickly. "Don't want to mess up your makeup," he explains. "Where's Zara?"

I didn't tell him I had the room to myself when he walked Zara and me back here after the game.

"I suppose she's at the bar, or maybe in her room."

He rubs his lips in thought. "In her room?"

"Mhmm," I hum, like it's no big deal. Bending down, I slip the heels on. "She booked us our own rooms."

His eyes heat with desire. “Remind me to tell Zara I really, really like her.”

“I might get jealous if I have to tell her that.”

“Not as much as I like you,” he assures me. “I don’t think I like anyone as much as I like you.” A shadow flickers over his face at the statement, like it only just occurred to him how he feels.

“We better go. I’m starving. That popcorn at the game didn’t do much for me.”

He takes my hand, tugging me toward the door. “Let’s go. You need your energy so that I can get my fill.”

“Fill of what?”

His brown eyes darken with lust. “You.”

THE RESTAURANT he takes me to is upscale, with live music being played by a group of musicians in the center of the room, with tables spread far enough apart to create the illusion of privacy.

The hostess leads us to a table, handing the menus to each of us.

“This place is nice,” I tell Jude in a hushed breath. “You didn’t need to bring me here.”

He shrugs, the corner of his lips ticking up slightly in amusement. “I can afford it.”

I haven’t talked to Jude much about his family life and where he grew up, but the majority of the students at

Aldridge are from *very* wealthy families. The best of the best.

Jude doesn't look at the menu for very long before he sets it aside.

When our waiter stops by to fill the water glasses on the table Jude orders a bottle of wine for the table.

"Are you trying to impress me?" I joke when the waiter leaves.

Jude shrugs, lacing his fingers together before he rests his hands on the table. "I'm always trying to impress you."

I smile, setting my menu down since I've decided what I want. "You already do."

He arches a brow, amused. "That's right, you would've preferred takeout in my truck."

I laugh, shaking my head. "See, you already know me so well. But this is nice too every now and then."

"Good to know."

Our waiter returns with the bottle of wine, pouring each of us a glass before leaving the bottle on the table. We give our order and then we're alone again.

"I met Macy," I tell him. Shutters come down over his eyes and I worry that maybe I shouldn't have said anything. "She seems really nice."

He nods, looking away from me. "She is." He clears his throat. "You … uh … you know about her?"

"I've heard some things, but I'd rather hear them from you. Can you … can you tell me about her?"

He arches a brow, curious. "You want me to tell you about another woman?"

I take a sip of my wine, hoping it'll help strengthen me. "If it helps me get to know you, then yes. I mean, she was a big part of your life."

"Who told you about her?" I know he's evading my question, and I guess I can't really blame him since I sort of ambushed him with it.

"No one. Everyone." I shrug easily. "People talk about it on campus, so I've overheard things there and at home." Jude looks away, a muscle in his jaw pulsing. "You don't have to tell me anything about her, about your relationship. It's okay."

He lowers his head, letting out a weary sigh. "No." He straightens, plucking at his sleeves for a distraction. "You should know. Maybe it'll help you."

"Help me, what?"

He frowns, scratching his jaw. "Help you to learn not everything is a fairytale."

"I know that," I start to argue, but he shuts me up with a look.

"I haven't told anyone about what happened to us. Not my parents, or my siblings, or even my friends. For a long time, they thought she cheated on me with Keaton, fuck some of the guys probably still think that, and I just let them, because it was easier, and I thought that was true myself. It took me a while to accept that neither of them was lying when they said they got together after we broke up."

"You really don't—"

He cuts me off. "I want to Millie. I want you to know and understand me."

"O-Okay," I stutter.

"I'm going to start at the beginning, okay?" I nod, keeping my mouth shut so I don't interrupt him. "Macy and I started dating in high school. She was a cheerleader; I was a football player. It was all so stereotypical." He chuckles humorlessly. "It was first love. Pure, young, so innocent now that I look back. We applied to the same schools, agreeing to go to the same one, so that's how we ended up here." He pauses, catching his breath. There's a shadow in his eyes, like he's haunted by something from this time in his life. "We had it all planned out—or at least I thought we did. We knew we wanted to get married after we graduated so I figured I'd propose our junior year. We'd get jobs, buy a place together..." He gauges how I'm handling this and must decide I'm doing okay, because he goes on. "It was the start of our sophomore year when Macy got pregnant." My heart stops for a moment, panicking that Jude has a child, but then I quickly realize there's no way that's the case. "Macy was terrified, and I was scared too, but I figured it was fine. I'd just move the plan up, you know? We'd get married then and it'd be fine and a baby? I was happy about it. Sure, it was sooner than we wanted, but we'd talked about having kids." I can tell this is hard for him.

I reach across the table, taking his hand in mine I squeeze it, reminding him I'm right here with him. "And I wanted that. I wanted to be a dad and I wanted that baby so fucking much. A girl or boy it didn't matter."

He grows quiet, so I ask, "What happened?"

His hand is slightly shaky in mine when I reply. "She got an abortion and I know, I fucking know, it was her body and her choice but it fucking stung that she didn't even talk about it with me beforehand. We'd been together years at that point, and I thought I was owed at least a conversation about it, but that's not what happened, and it hurt. She said she wasn't ready to be a mom and it made her think about us and..." The pain in his face is so raw it's like this only just happened to him. I *ache* for him. Jude is so much better of a person than people give him credit for. He's so incredibly caring. "She broke up with me, said that getting pregnant made her realize that I was all she ever knew, and she wasn't sure I was the one. Here I was, thinking she was a sure thing, planning a whole future, and she thought of me as temporary." His eyes meet mine and he grimaces. "I'm sure you don't want to hear this shit. It's in the past, I swear. I'm over her, but..."

"But it's the baby, isn't it? That's what bothers you so much."

He nods slowly, and neither of us says anything while the waiter places our dishes on the table. I'm not very hungry now, and I doubt he is either.

"I think about that kid all the time. How old he or she

would be. What they would've looked like, grown up to be. I was so angry at her to start with."

"And now?" I squeeze his hand softly, reminding him I'm still here and I'm not going anywhere. This isn't going to send me running. If anything, it pieces together so many things.

"Now, I understand why she did it. We were young, we still are, and being a parent changes everything. Neither of us was ready, it was just a thing that happened. Nothing much would've changed for me. It would've been a lot harder on her becoming a mother than me a father."

"You'll make a great father one day, Jude." And I mean it wholeheartedly. "Can I ask something else?" He nods for me to go on. "How did this lead to you sleeping around so much?"

"I didn't at first," he admits, tapping the fingers of his free hand on the table. "But then she started dating Keaton, and he's on my team and that just…I guess, I couldn't handle that, and I decided to move on the only way I knew how. I didn't want attachment, so that meant sex, and hookups, one-night stands and—"

"And what?"

"Just some questionable sexual conduct."

"Questionable?" I repeat, my brows knitting together. "You're going to have to elaborate on that."

He looks embarrassed, shameful and maybe since I have zero experience besides what I've done with him he expects me to judge him, but that's not my place.

"More than one woman at a time."

"Oh." My eyes widen. "That's..."

"Awful, I know."

"I was actually going to say impressive. You must have incredible stamina."

He laughs, looking like a weight has been lifted off his shoulders. "I'll show you that impressive stamina some time."

I smile slowly, glad that he's not running away from this—from me. "Good."

"Do you mind if we get this to-go?" He waves a hand at our food.

"That sounds like the best idea ever."

twenty-eight

Jude

I WAKE UP WITH THE SMELL OF MILLIE'S SHAMPOO invading my nostrils, not that that's so unusual these days since I find myself slipping into her bed most nights lately.

Her body is splayed across mine like a starfish. She sleeps peacefully and I hope she's dreaming something good.

Last night, I knew she expected me to take things all the way, and I'd thought about it before I spilled all the details about Macy. After that, I was emotionally spent and not entirely with Millie mentally. If I'm going to have sex with her for her first time, then I need to be present, and I wouldn't have been last night. That's not what she deserves. I want to give her all of me, not half.

I brush her hair off her shoulder, drawing circles on her back. She's so small compared to me that she almost seems breakable, but I know Millie is made of the toughest shit.

I told her everything I've kept bottled inside for years and it didn't send her running.

I wasn't supposed to, and I'm still trying to deny it to myself, but I'm falling for this girl. And if I'm completely honest with myself, what I feel for her is stronger—or has the potential to be stronger—than anything I felt for Macy. Which is terrifying for many reasons, but especially because then I have to reconcile with the fact that Macy was right, what we had was young love and not meant to last.

Gliding my fingers through Millie's hair, I brush my lips against the top of her head. I need to get going soon, back to the room I'm sharing with my teammate Carter since that's where all my shit is and I'll have to catch the bus while Millie heads back home with Zara.

Millie stirs, and I know she's close to waking up.

A few minutes later, she blinks her eyes open, stifling a yawn.

"What time is it?" Her voice is raspy with sleep. It sounds of sex and if I wasn't already hard, I would be now.

"A little after six. I have to go back to my room soon."

She nods, closing her eyes. "Five more minutes."

I chuckle, Millie's head bobbing up and down with my

laughter. Millie is slow to wake up, whereas years of early morning workouts have programmed me to get up and be ready to go for the day.

"Whatever you want." I go back to playing with her hair.

She moves her head, resting her chin on my bare chest so she can look at me. We're both naked despite the fact that nothing at all happened last night.

She traces her finger around the shape of my lips. "I'm glad you told me."

"I am too." I try to bite her finger and she yanks it away with a little giggle.

"Do you feel better? Having told someone?"

I let out a sigh, thinking it over for a moment. "I didn't think I would, but yeah, I do."

Keeping something like that bottled inside me for literal years hasn't been healthy. I know I should've told someone before now, but I'm glad it was Millie.

"I'll grab us some breakfast from the buffet before we have to go."

She lets me go from her koala hold and wraps the sheet around her. Stifling another yawn, she says, "I'm going to hop in the shower."

I yank my clothes on from the night before, not caring what anyone thinks or cares, and head down to the lobby. Grabbing a tray and some plates, I pile a smorgasbord of options onto each since I'm starving and I'm not sure what Millie wants.

Turning to head back to the elevators I see Keaton and Macy seated at one of the tables.

I spot the diamond ring on her finger as she moves her hand around, telling him some sort of story, and I feel … nothing. I don't feel angry, or sad, or anything at all.

For too long I let myself think that the one got away and I didn't let myself think about how I really felt. I loved Macy. She'll always have a special place in my heart as my first love, but now, I don't miss her. I don't ache for her.

Not the way I do with Millie even when she's only a room away.

And holy shit is that thought terrifying.

Macy notices me staring and waves. I dip my head in acknowledgment.

Keaton looks over his shoulder to see who she's waving at. His eyes narrow slightly, and she says something to him. He sighs, waving at me too.

I take the elevator up and Millie's still in the shower when I get there. Setting the food on the table, I check the bathroom door and find it unlocked. Stripping off my clothes, I step into the shower behind her.

"I'm almost done and then it's all yours."

I wrap my hand around the back of her neck, pulling her slightly until she looks up at me. Spinning her around into my arms, I kiss her deeply. She lets out a soft moan, relaxing against me. Her wet slick body presses against mine. It's the biggest turn on ever, but I didn't join her in the shower for this. I just wanted to be with her.

When her lips fall from mine, she stares up at me with a heavy-lidded gaze.

"What was that for?"

Because I can. Because you're mine. Because I—

I brush my nose against hers, and whisper, "Because I love you."

Millie gives a startled, surprised gasp. "What?"

I grin, pressing a quick kiss to her stunned lips. "You heard me, Little Madison. I love you."

"Me? You love me?"

She sounds in utter disbelief that I could feel such a thing for her. "Yes, you."

"I ... Jude..." She bites her lip, her eyes swimming with unshed tears. "I love you, too."

Telling her about Macy gave me the freedom to take a look at myself, at my thoughts and feelings, and realize that what I feel for her is strong, stronger than anything I've ever felt before, and she deserves to hear it. I want her to know that even though I didn't plan for this, it happened anyway.

I kiss her for a long time in the shower, until we both start to prune and then hurry to finish washing up. Our breakfast is cold by the time we get to it, but I don't think either one of us cares.

"I don't mean to put you on the spot, but does this mean we're dating now?" She grabs a grape, looking at it from all angles before chewing it. "Remember, I'm not very adept at this whole relationship thing."

I scrub a hand over my face. Stalling for more time, I

slather some cream cheese on a bagel. "I've only dated one person, so I'm not exactly an expert myself, but if you mean do I want things to be serious between us? Then the answer is yes, but—"

"But my brother?" She finishes as a question. I nod. "He's going to be pissed. Let's just ... wait a little while if that's okay with you?" Her eyes are filled with concern, and I know she feels bad for asking me that. I won't lie, it takes me by surprise. I wasn't going to suggest waiting, but if that's what she wants...

"We can keep it a secret."

It fucking sucks that she wants to keep quiet about us now that it's real, but I can't say I blame her either. It's what I deserve after the reputation I've made for myself. I'm the last guy Cree would ever want to see his sister with.

Millie smiles at my agreement. "Thank you. We'll tell him soon, I promise."

Soon is relative. It could be days or weeks from now, maybe even months. My stomach sours with the thought of it taking that long.

Millie wraps her arms around my neck, murmuring against my ear that she loves me.

Closing my eyes, I tell myself, *this is enough.*

And for now, it is.

twenty-nine

Millie

MY MOM AND DAD ARE COMING INTO TOWN FOR Cree's first hockey game and that means they're going to be meeting Ophelia. I've met her a few times, but I can't really say I know my brother's girlfriend all that well. She seems super sweet, but shy.

I'm riding in the back of Cree's restored Bronco when we pull up outside her dorm.

There's a part of me that's a tad jealous that Cree is introducing our parents to his girlfriend while I can't say anything about Jude. It's my own fault, I'm the one who asked Jude if we could keep this a secret longer, but it's still annoying. I know Cree is going to lose his shit when we tell him, and I don't want to deal with it. I only want my brother to be happy for me and it annoys me that, that seems to be too much to ask for. I'm an adult, not a child, but my brother doesn't see me that way. He's always going to see himself as so much older and wiser than me.

Ophelia walks out of her dorm, her head ducked low. She dressed nicely, but I can sense her nerves from here. "Your girlfriend is so freaking cute. I don't know what she sees in you."

He puts his hand on my face, shoving me into the back. Brothers. "Shut up, Mills." Ophelia opens the passenger door. "I was going to get the door for you, babe."

"Babe? You call her babe? Aww." I can't help but taunt him. It's way too much fun. He swivels around, glaring at me in warning to keep my mouth shut. Not likely.

Ophelia laughs at our joking banter, smoothing her red hair down. She smiles at me in the backseat. "Hey, Millie."

"Hi, Ophelia. I was just telling my idiot brother here that I don't know how he landed you."

Ophelia frowns, looking worried. "What do you mean?"

I didn't think what I said would upset her, but I feel like it has. "Just that you're way better than him, clearly," I joke. She better get used to me ribbing my brother. As his little sister it's my full-time job. I mean, if he's going to treat me like a little kid I might as well get to act like it.

"Ignore her," he tells his girlfriend, reversing out of the parking space. "She's in rare form today."

He heads downtown to the hotel our parents booked for their stay. There's a restaurant in the lobby, so they asked us to meet for dinner there.

"Do you think your parents will like me?" Ophelia's question comes out quiet as a mouse, but since the car is small, I hear her easily.

"Are you kidding me? They'll love you. You're kind, sweet, smart, and beautiful. Like I said, way too good for this one." I tap my brother on the shoulder.

"She was asking me." He makes eye contact with me in the backseat.

I roll my eyes, hoping he sees. "Are you telling me my answer is wrong?"

"No, but—"

I cut him off. "That's what I thought."

Ophelia's laughter fills the vehicle. "You two bicker like I do with my brother."

"I can't help it," I lean up between the seats again, knowing Cree's likely to bitch about it, "I've been stuck with him for my entire life."

"Right back at ya, Millicent."

"Bleh." I mock gag at my full name. "Cut the Millicent crap. Only Mom and Dad call me that sometimes, and our grandparents always. It makes me sound like an old lady who owns a million cats."

Not that there's anything wrong with cats. I'd love to

have a cat one day—just not enough to become Millicent the Cat Lady.

Cree ignores me. Shocker. "What are you reading lately?" he asks Ophelia.

Her face scrunches up like she's tasted something nasty. "I need to start a new book. I didn't finish the last one I read after the hero said he hoped her birth control failed and he could knock her up." She sounds completely appalled, frankly I am too. "Forced pregnancy is not sexy to me. It ruins the fantasy of it all. Nope. No way." She shakes her head rapidly back and forth like she wishes she could dislodge the memories of that book. "That is not my kink."

I laugh, slapping a hand over my nose and mouth when a snort tries to slip out. "What is your kink then?" I gag as soon as the question has left my mouth. Why-oh-why did I have to ask that of all things? "Oh, God, forget I asked. You're dating my brother. I don't wanna know. Why did I ask that? I hate myself. Ew." Now I'm the one shaking my head and trying to get rid of a nasty thought. "Cree, take me home. I feel dirty. I need a shower. One hot enough to melt my skin off."

He pinches the bridge of his nose. "Can you stop being dramatic for five seconds?"

As if *he's* never dramatic. My brother is the biggest drama queen I know.

"Me? Dramatic?" I gasp, feigning hurt. "Do you hear this slander, Ophelia? I'm never dramatic. I'm hurt that you'd think so, brother."

Cree groans, turning the volume up on the radio to end the conversation. Fine by me.

It's a little less than ten minutes later when we make it to the hotel. He parks in the garage, grumbling when it costs a hefty amount. Not that the money is a problem for us, but Cree tends to get hung up on the principle of things. He parks the car and I hurriedly scramble out of the backseat, stretching my legs before we go inside.

I let Cree and Ophelia have a moment, making my way to the elevator to wait.

They clasp hands and start for the elevator, looking adorable as fuck and making me ache once more that Jude isn't with me. "Come on you two love birds, time is a-ticking." I tap the pretend watch on my wrist.

They join me and we hop on. Cree hits the button for the lobby.

He suddenly seems outrageously nervous, which is silly if it's about Ophelia. Our parents are going to love her. I have no doubt our mom will already be planning the wedding after this weekend.

The elevator chimes when we reach the lobby, the doors sliding open to reveal our parents in the distance.

A smile overtakes me, and I hop out of the elevator, running in their direction to hug them. I just saw them earlier today with my brother, but it doesn't matter. I have to soak this up while I can because I won't see them again until the holidays, which isn't too far off, but I love my parents.

I smack a kiss on each of their cheeks just before I hear my brother say to Ophelia in a hushed voice, "You have nothing to worry about."

Our mom smiles from ear to ear the moment she lays eyes on Ophelia.

Cree looks nervous, but happy, his hand resting softly on Ophelia's waist. "Mom. Dad. I'd like you guys to meet my girlfriend, Ophelia. Ophelia, this is my mom, Hillary, and my dad, Grant."

I stand off to the side as the introductions are made.

Ophelia's hands tremble slightly at her sides. "Hi," her voice shakes slightly with nerves, "it's nice to meet you both."

She holds out a hand to my mom, but she waves it off. Ophelia looks stricken for all of one second when my mom says, "None of that nonsense. Give me a hug."

"Are you kids hungry?" My dad asks after he's greeted and hugged Ophelia as well.

"Starved," my brother replies. I'm pretty hungry myself too.

Our group heads toward the hotel's restaurant on the other side of the lobby. After my dad gives his name, we're ushered to a private table. There's a massive aquarium filled with exotic fish in the center of the restaurant.

"Isn't it gorgeous?" Mom makes sure her dress is wrinkle free before sitting down. My brother and Ophelia take the seats across from our parents, which puts me on the end by myself. I try not to let it show that it bothers me.

It's not the being stuck on the end that's the issue, it's just another reminder that Jude's not here when I really wish he was. "It reminds me of you," she says to Ophelia, and I focus back in on the conversation.

"Me? Why me?" Ophelia asks, genuinely confused.

Looking around at the ocean décor, I know immediately what my mom means.

"Oh, I just..." My mom looks around, embarrassed. "You remind me of The Little Mermaid. Ariel. With the red hair." She tugs on her own strands of hair as if to demonstrate what she means, even though it's completely unnecessary. "I'm embarrassing myself. I'll stop."

Ophelia gives a soft, shy smile. Her eyes briefly go to Cree and he gives her a reassuring nod before she speaks. "It's okay. I get that a lot. I'm not going to lie; thanks to the movie I was certain I would sprout a fin as soon as my legs touched the water. I spent months afraid of a bath or shower. It was a nightmare for my parents. It doesn't help that my brother would leave sand around my bed and try to convince me I was in the ocean every night in my sleep."

My parents laugh at her response, and I can tell they're already head over heels for her. She really is a great match for Cree. I know I shouldn't allow myself to sulk, but I wonder if they'd approve of Jude. They don't know his past like Cree does, so their first impression would be genuine.

I think they'd like him, maybe even love him, and I know he'd go out of his way to try because he'd know it would make me happy.

We won't be a secret forever, though, and I'll get my chance to introduce him to my parents just like Cree.

I FELL asleep in Cree's car on the drive home from the restaurant. I drag myself up the stairs, not at all surprised that Ophelia is staying the night.

In my room, I quickly change out of my clothes, take the quickest shower of my life, and pull on my comfiest pjs. There's nothing at all sexy about what I have on, but I don't care, and I know Jude doesn't either. When I ease open the door to his room, I find him lying on his bed, one arm crooked behind his head while he watches a game on TV. As soon as he hears the door, his eyes slip from the door to me and he smiles. It's a smile that says, "There she is. That's my girl," and that makes me feel like the luckiest woman alive.

"Whatcha' doing, Little Madison?" I shrug, still standing in the doorway. "Are you going to come over here or not?" He crooks a finger and I'm helpless as my feet carry me across the room to him. He opens his arms to me. "Come on, baby."

I dive onto the bed and into his arms. He smells fresh and clean, like the woodsy smelling soap he keeps in our shower. "I missed you," I murmur into the warm skin of his neck.

His lips press a gentle kiss to the top of my head. "I missed you, too. How'd dinner go?"

"It was great." I wiggle in his arms, trying to get comfortable. I end up in my favorite position with my head on his chest, my arm across his torso, and my leg wedged between his. "My parents loved Ophelia."

"That's good." He plays with my hair, rubbing my neck.

"I wish you were there," I admit, waiting to see how he handles that confession.

He peers down at me, his tongue wetting his lips. "You do?"

"Mhmm." I nod against his chest. "I wanted to introduce you to them." I wait for him to stiffen, or pull away, or even to say that it's too soon.

But all he does, is gently tip my head up to him and kiss me. "One day, Little Madison," he promises. "One day." I nod against his chest, still drowsy from dozing off in the car, but not ready to go back to sleep yet. "Want me to put 'Vampire Diaries' on?"

"You don't mind turning the game off?"

He groans, stretching to reach for the remote. "It's just a highlight reel anyway."

He switches the TV over to Netflix and starts the show up where we left off. I hope when we finish all the seasons, he wants to watch something else with me. I've loved rewatching the show and experiencing it with him.

We've watched one whole episode when I say, "Can I ask you something?"

He pauses the next episode before it can start. "Sure." He stretches his arms above his head.

"It's about Macy." I want to give him a chance to back out from answering if he doesn't want to, but he nods, urging me to go on. "My brother, your friends, all think she cheated on you but that's not what happened, so why do they think that?"

He looks away, shame clouding his face. "Because it's what they assumed when she started going out with Keaton, and I didn't correct them. In my mind, she did cheat on me. She walked away from the life we were creating and started building that with someone else. It felt like..." He pauses, rubbing his jaw. "It felt like everything I felt for her had been a lie and I didn't want to talk about the baby. And in the beginning, I thought she *had* cheated on me, because Keaton went public with her only a few weeks after we ended our years long relationship. I know now that's not true, but that doesn't change how I felt, and I know I should correct my friends, but I don't like opening those wounds. That's why you're the only person who knows the whole truth besides Macy, Keaton, and whoever else she told."

"I'm really sorry you had to go through all that." I hug his torso tighter, his heart thumping steadily against his ear.

"It's okay." He brushes his lips against the top of my head. He does that a lot and I wonder if it's more to comfort himself than for me. He chuckles softly. "For the first time, that's not even a lie. All that shit, it fucking sucked, but without it I'm not sure I'd be lying here with you right now. I don't even care if that makes me sound whipped."

Sitting up, I swing my leg over his body so I'm straddling his lap. He's only wearing a pair of sweatpants and I feel the press of his quickly hardening cock against my core.

"You like being with me?" He nods at my question. "Just right here, watching this show and lying in bed?" He nods again. "You never think about other girls? Or parties? Or—"

He shakes his head rapidly. "Never. Wherever you are, that's where I want to be."

I smile, poking his stomach. "You totally *are* whipped."

He sits up quickly, taking me by surprise. A small squeal flies out of my throat and he presses a hand to my mouth to stifle the sound. His other arm is wrapped entirely around my torso. "Careful," he murmurs huskily, "we can't have your brother figuring out you're in here."

I shrug and his hand falls, that arm wrapping around me too. "It's okay. He has Ophelia over so I'm pretty sure he's getting laid and completely unaware of anything else." I wrinkle my nose in distaste. This is the gross part of living with my brother.

Jude grins, gliding his fingertip over my cheekbone. "That so?"

I nod and another squeal of surprise flees from my lips when he rolls me over onto his bed beneath him. He kisses me, stealing what little of my breath is left. My tank top has ridden up, exposing my stomach. His hand is hot on my skin when he grabs onto my waist, urging me to wrap my leg around his hip. I gasp at the feel of his erection pushing against my core.

"Jude?"

He pulls away slightly, gazing down at me. He sees what I'm going to say in my eyes before I even voice the words. "Are you sure?"

I nod eagerly. "Please."

His mouth is on mine in an instant, his tongue tangling with mine. My hands are on his cheeks, urging him closer. His body is a heated cocoon surrounding me. I'm enveloped in his warmth, his scent, everything.

He takes his time kissing me, cherishing me, making sure I know that this, us, is different.

We're not hurried this time as we take what little clothes we have on off.

Jude tilts my head back, kissing my neck and making his way down to my breasts where he pays careful attention to each of them. His hair tickles my stomach as he keeps going, kissing above my bellybutton and further down until he reaches my pussy.

"You're so fucking wet," he remarks, kissing my clitoris before sucking on it. My back bows off the bed, my fingers grappling for purchase in the sheets. "And so fucking responsive." His voice rumbles against my core.

I whimper when he swipes his tongue over my pussy. Sucking on my clit, he slides his middle finger inside. It's tight and full feeling with only his finger, I can't imagine his cock filling me.

He brings me to an orgasm, quieting me by pressing his mouth to mine in a fierce kiss. I can taste myself on him, and instead of being grossed out by it, I'm only more turned on.

Reaching over to his nightstand, he digs through the drawer and produces a foil packet. He holds the condom up between us. "Are you sure about this, baby?" I nod, encouraging him to go on. "I need you to say it."

"Yes, fuck me, please," I beg, not even caring that I sound pathetically wanton with desire.

He shakes his head, his hair brushing my forehead as he does. "No, baby. I'm not fucking you." I open my mouth to protest but he presses his thumb against my lips, urging me to stay quiet. "You're more than a quick fuck to me," he explains, his voice husky. "Make no mistakes, Little Madison, I'm gonna be making love to you. Doesn't matter if it's slow, fast, hard, gentle, or rough—it's all making love with you." He rips the condom open, rolling it down his length. My hands are shaky, and he notices. "Shh," he croons, "I've got you." He grips the base of his cock, lining it up with my entrance. His eyes flick up to mine. "Don't hold your breath."

I inhale, not even realizing that I'd been holding it. "You're so big. I-I know it'll fit, but I'm scared it'll hurt."

"If I could make it not hurt for you I would in a heartbeat." He pushes in about an inch, stopping to gauge my reaction. "How are you feeling?"

"Not bad, but we've done this much before."

He grins, eyes twinkling. “I remember.”

He pushes in a little more and I wince, wiggling at the pinched feeling. “Too much. Too big.”

He shakes his head. “Relax.” My eyes meet his and he must sense my panic, because he hesitates. “Do you want me to stop?” He starts to pull out.

“No!” My fingernails dig into his ass cheeks, urging him to stay where he is.

“You want me to go slow or get this part over fast?”

I think it over for a moment. “Fast.”

He pushes all the way in before I can process what he’s doing. His mouth slams against mine, stifling my cries. “Such a good girl.” He rises up, looking at where our bodies are joined. My eyes follow his. “Look how fucking tight your pussy is gripping me. Fuck, Millie, I swear to God nothing has ever felt this good before. This pussy was made for me.”

He gives me a moment to adjust, his eyes never leaving mine as he pulls out and pushes back in. I wince slightly, the pinch still there, but after only a couple of strokes it eases and pleasure replaces the pain.

“I’m okay,” I tell him, urging him on. “It feels good now.”

“Are you sure?” He hesitates, sweat beading on his forehead from the strain of holding back.

“Yes.”

That one word is all it takes for him to let go. He grabs my hands, interlacing our fingers and holds them above my head as he rocks his hips against mine. I'm surprised, and I can tell he is too, when an orgasm shatters through me.

"Fucking hell, Millie, your pussy is gripping my dick so hard."

"I'm sorry."

"Don't be sorry. It feels good. Too good. I'm not going to be able to last much longer." He kisses me, silencing whatever I might say next. He shudders in my arms and moans his pleasure when he comes. I've heard girls complain about guys being too quiet in bed when expressing their pleasure. Not Jude, though. His moans become the biggest turn-on I've ever heard in my life.

He gathers me in his arms, pressing kisses all over my face and chest while he's still inside me. It's a few minutes before our breaths slow and he pulls from my body to dispose of the condom, and I roll out of bed to pee. I'm surprised to see only a little bit of pink when I wipe. We settle back down in his bed, and he tucks the covers around us.

I'm exhausted, my eyes heavy-lidded with the need to sleep. My body is sore in all the right places, a reminder of the fact that I'm not a virgin anymore. I yawn, cuddling into Jude's side.

"Go to sleep," he encourages softly, sounding tired himself.

I nod against his chest.

I'm almost asleep when his doorknob rattles. Jude

curses, eyeing me. There's a knock and he gets out of bed, yanking on his sweatpants to check the door.

When he opens it, it's shoved open wider, and I have zero chance to hide. Luckily my entire body is covered by the sheets.

My heart soars into my throat when Daire looks from me to Jude and back again before settling on his friend. "I fucking knew this shit was bound to happen."

"What do you want?" Jude growls at him, looking like he wants to murder the guy.

"I heard you guys, and you're lucky that Cree and Ms. Muffet have been going at it too or you'd be fucking dead."

My face drains of color.

"What are you going to do? Tell?" Jude asks mockingly and I want to beg him not to taunt Daire. He's too much of a loose cannon lately—hardly ever home and then a humongous jerk when he is.

Daire snorts. "Nope. Not my place, but if you two think you can fuck in this house and Cree not find out then you're both stupider than you look."

Jude grinds his teeth together. "Is that all you had to say?"

"Yup."

Jude shuts and locks the door, running his fingers through his hair.

He looks worried as he climbs back into bed. "We have to tell him. Soon."

"Soon," I echo.

thirty

Jude

THE HOUSE IS QUIET AND EMPTY.

I think it's the first time I've been here that no one else has. Normally, I'd appreciate the alone time, but Millie and Cree are spending the day with their parents and Cree's first hockey game of the season is tonight.

I rub my hand absentmindedly over the pink glitter smiley face sticker that Millie playfully stuck to my shirt this morning after we finished brushing our teeth.

"For an A-plus job taking my virginity," she had joked before I kissed her breathless.

Just when I think I can't love this girl more; I do.

I don't quite recognize myself anymore when I look in the mirror. I'm happy, really fucking happy, and I can't say I've felt that way in a long time. Millie brings out something inside me that I thought ceased to exist when Macy broke up with me. Now, I'm starting to realize that Macy had a point. We were all each other knew. We were comfortable, complacent, and in the long run that probably wouldn't have worked out in our favor.

It's a little after ten when I put a pod in the Keurig to make some coffee. I have no idea where Daire has waddled off to. He probably knew I was pissed about him busting Millie and me last night and wanted to avoid me bitching at him about it.

Rifling through the fridge while my coffee brews, I pull out the makings for a sandwich.

There's a knock on the front door, but as far as I know no one is supposed to show up for repairs or anything like that.

Leaving my sandwich makings on the counter, I go to check the door, grinning when I find my brother on the other side.

"Dude," I wave him inside, "what are you doing here?"

He shrugs, stepping into the front foyer and looking around the home. To my right, his left, is the living room. Straight back is the kitchen and a half bath and then there's a door that leads to the basement. "I got breakfast out with my friends and thought I'd stop by."

"I'm making a sandwich. I slept in this morning."

I lock up and have him follow me to the kitchen. He pulls out a stool at the island, looking around. "Where are your roommates?"

"Out," I answer, sticking my bread in the toaster. My coffee is ready, so I add a little bit of sugar before taking a hearty sip. I already feel a thousand times better from one little sip. "You wanna do something today?" I ask, grabbing my toast so I can start assembling my sandwich.

"Nah, that's okay. Like I said, I was close by, and I haven't been here all year, so I wanted to see the place." I place shredded chicken breast, some lettuce, a tomato, and a bit of mayo on my sandwich, taking a hearty bite. "What's with the sticker on your shirt?"

I grin around my food. "I got it for excellent participation skills."

My little brother shudders, cringing. "Is that some kind of weird kinky sex shit?"

"Maybe." I take another bite. "Don't knock it til you try it."

"That would require actually getting laid."

I arch a brow, picking up on something in his tone that surprises me. "Bug," I hesitate, not wanting to embarrass him, "are you a virgin?"

My little brother's ears turn bright red. "It's not a big deal," he grumbles, staring at the countertop.

"It's not," I agree, finishing up my food. "I'm just surprised is all."

He rubs at his hair, making it stick up in the back. "I didn't date in high school, you know this, and hookups … I don't know, it doesn't feel like my thing."

"Jonah," I swipe two water bottles from the fridge and pass him one, "there's nothing you have to justify."

"I know, but you're … you."

I snort. "What's that supposed to mean?"

He rolls his eyes. "I might be a freshman, but I've heard stories about you. You're like a legend to a lot of these guys."

"A legend," I scoffed. "That's ridiculous."

"Is it true you did like six girls at one time last year?"

I cringe, hating that this is the kind of shit people talk about when my name comes up. What a fucking embarrassment I must be to Millie.

"It was three, not six," I mutter reluctantly. That stunt got Teddy in a shit-load of trouble. I've changed so much since the start of this year that it's hard for me to reconcile the fact that I was such a dumbass.

"How is that even possible?"

I finish my coffee, rinsing it out in the sink. "I've got a dick, two hands, and a mouth. You do the math."

Jonah's face scrunches up like he's grossed out. "I think I'm more of a one-woman kind of guy."

"Cheers to that." I tip my water bottle at him. "It's the better place to be."

He arches a brow. "Are you seeing someone?"

I hesitate, not because I don't want to tell my brother

about Millie—I want to fucking brag about her more than anything—but because I'm not sure she'd want me to tell anyone yet. "No," I lie and my tongue tastes sour after I say it, "just thinking it's time to settle down."

"Mom will be happy."

I grunt. "Any updates with that girl you like?"

Jonah's shoulders deflate. "Nah, like I said she's into someone else. I'm not going to try to fight off another guy when she clearly likes him. She's a good person, but I guess not my person."

"You'll meet the one, Jonah, and she'll blow your fucking mind."

He laughs, unscrewing the water bottle cap. "I hope so."

"You will," I promise.

If anyone deserves to meet the girl of their dreams and be happy, it's my little brother. This girl must be an idiot if she can't see what a catch he is.

thirty-one

Millie

A PARTY OF DAIRE'S MAKING RAGES DOWNSTAIRS. I sit on Jude's floor, painting my toenails a soft pink color aptly named Ballet Slippers. Jude sits at his desk, writing a paper, but peeking back at me every other minute.

I point the nail polish wand at him in warning. "You better finish that and stop looking at me."

He pouts, his handsome face looking way too adorable with a puffed out bottom lip.

Sticking my tongue out slightly—it helps me concentrate—I focus on painting my toes. A curse slips free of my lips when I struggle with the pinky toe.

"Done," Jude declares, sliding his chair away from his desk and spinning around. He laughs when he sees me struggling on the floor. "Need some help there, Little Madison?"

"I'm fine."

He unfolds his body from the chair and sits down on the floor in front of me. "Give it here." He flicks his fingers for the nail polish bottle, grabbing my legs with his other hand and placing them in his lap.

"Jude," I say his name with a hint of a smile, "are you going to paint my toes for me?"

He flicks his hair out of his eyes, getting the amount of polish on the brush that he wants. "Don't tell anyone. I'll lose my street cred."

Carefully, and methodically, Jude applies polish to my pinky toe. Satisfied with that, he moves to my other foot that I haven't even started yet.

"This might sound weird," I whisper, not wanting to disturb his concentration, "but this is really turning me on right now."

He looks up, brown eyes glimmering with mischief. "Do you have a feet kink, Millie?"

"No." I roll my eyes. "I have a *you* kink." He smiles, his eyes crinkling at the corners, and I would even swear there's a hint of a blush on his cheekbones. He leans over, careful to avoid my freshly painted toes, and pecks a quick kiss on my lips. "I'm adding this to my spank back."

He throws his head back with laughter. "What else you got in the that bank, Little Madison?"

"The whole list?" He nods for me to go on. "You shirtless in sweatpants, you cooking, you washing dishes, you in your football uniform." I lick my lips, ticking each thing off on my fingers. "When you drive your truck with one hand. You doing basically anything, really. Thanks for those vibrators by the way, they really freaked me out to start with, but with all this material they're really coming in handy."

Lust warms his eyes. He looks like he wants to pounce on me which sends a shiver down my spine. He taps the side of my foot. "No moving."

"I can't help it. You make me all squirmy."

He arches a brow. "Do you want to mess up your toes?"

"No."

"Then be good."

"What do I get for being good?"

He inclines his head toward the ceiling like he's saying a prayer. "I've unlocked a sexual deviant with you."

He finishes with the color, putting the cap back on and holds his hand out for me to give him the topcoat.

"How did you learn to paint nails?"

"My little sister. I'd paint hers."

"That's right. You have a brother too. I think you said he goes here? Do I ever get to meet him?"

"Sure, after we tell your brother."

"Soon," I promise.

I want to tell my brother. I hate hiding this, because that makes it seem like we're doing something wrong when we're not, but I know Cree will freak and things are so good that I want to bask in it just being us for a little while longer. Is that so horrible of me?

Something crashes downstairs. "Fuck," Jude curses, his eyes meeting mine. Luckily, he's finished my toes. He sets the polish aside and stands, holding a hand out to me. Once I'm standing, I follow him down the stairs to investigate. I don't think my brother knows Daire was throwing a party and is probably going to shit a brick when he gets here, despite the fact that apparently until this year he was quite the partier himself.

I don't realize Jude's still holding onto my hand until I hear my brother's voice and quickly yank my hand from his. The wounded look he sends me makes me feel about an inch tall.

People are gathered in the living room where the show-down must be taking place. Everyone watches with rapt attention as Cree and Daire bicker like an old married couple.

"Shackled? Do you hear yourself?" My brother scoffs at his friend. Ophelia stands by Cree, looking like she's about to flee any second. "You've had an issue almost this entire semester, and I've been your friend long enough to know something else is up, and you're being an ass because that's what you do. You take your anger out on everyone around you instead of dealing with it like a man."

Daire rears back like my brother punched him in the jaw, even though, as far as I can tell, no punches have been thrown yet. I feel like a creeper watching their friendship meltdown from the sidelines, but then again I guess that makes *all* of us creepers. I'm not sure how many people are stuffed into the downstairs of the house, but every one of them is zeroed in on the drama playing out and someone has even turned down the music.

"Like a man?" Daire bellows, getting up from the couch. There was a girl on his lap and she falls to the floor. I think he completely forgot she was there. She shoots an annoyed look around, crawling away on her hands and knees since there isn't room for her to get up. Daire shoves my brother roughly, who stumbles back a few steps. Jude glances back at me, wondering when or even if he should intervene. "What about you, huh?"

"Me?" My brother laughs manically.

God, the two of them are seriously having trouble in the paradise of their friendship. Daire's been a jerk the past few months, but I guess I was too lost in my Jude-haze to notice how much it was weighing on my brother.

"Oh, come on," Daire throws his arms out, his upper lip curled, "I highly doubt you've told her the truth." Daire's eyes slide to Ophelia and now I'm curious as to what he's talking about. "I guess it doesn't really matter, does it? At the end of the day, we're *all* liars. Me, you, Jude, Millie, and

I bet even your girl there has lied about something." He spins in a circle, swaying drunkenly. He cups his mouth to yell, "I bet everyone in this fucking room is a goddamn liar!"

I start moving through the crowd, trying to get to the group. Jude's plowed forward and reached them.

"Dude," Jude says, pulling on Daire's arm. "You're drunk. Shut up, you'll regret this in the morning." I know he's trying to keep him from being a complete asshole and telling my brother about us. God knows Cree won't like this, but if he finds out from Daire...

Jude's eyes meet mine briefly as I come to a stop beside Ophelia, and I see the worry there.

Daire has to keep his mouth shut. It makes me sick thinking about him saying something before we can. My arm brushes Ophelia's and she looks up, startled. I wonder if she can see how scared I am.

Keep your mouth shut. Don't say anything. Please. I silently beg Daire, as if that will do any good.

"Are you okay?" she asks me in a hushed tone. "Are you sick?"

I shake my head. Not sick. Not yet at least. Tears start to burn my eyes and I will them away.

"Don't tell me what to do, fucker!" Daire jerks his body away from Jude. He nearly falls flat on his ass, which frankly he'd deserve. He's acting like a petulant child and for *what*? This can't really be about my brother, or Jude, or even me. Something bigger is going on here, but what? "Are you all listening?" He spins around again, gesturing with his arms to make sure all eyes are on him, even though they already have been. He swipes a cup from a guy nearby. He grins, gulping down the liquid before he throws the empty cup on the floor. "I think it's time for some lies to come to light." He smirks, basking in the attention of all the partygoers. "You wanna know why I've been such an asshole?" He pokes my brother so hard in the chest I'm certain there will be a bruise. "Because all you care about is your little girlfriend." He sneers at Ophelia, hatred rolling off of him. "And I needed you." I actually feel bad for Daire when he says that to my brother, because he genuinely looks so hurt. "Turns out, your boy is a dad." He laughs uproariously. Pain is evident in his expression and he looks like he might actually cry. "Had no fucking clue until I saw the kid, and then I just knew he was mine." The room is stunned at this proclamation. Holy shit, Daire has a kid. "Oh, and guess what? I'm fucking hitched now." The shocking twists keep coming. Have we been kidnapped and placed in a soap opera and someone forgot to tell me? He grapples awkwardly for his pockets, feeling around until he produces a ring. He slips it on the ring finger of his right hand, oblivious to the fact that he's put it on the wrong hand. "And no, not to the baby mama. She's a professor and a real bitch because she didn't tell me she was pregnant. She really thought she could keep him from me, but I won't let her. No, sir. So, now I'm married to Rosie—yeah, you know that girl I can't fucking stand—because ... well, that's not important." His hands fall to his sides and I actually feel bad for him, his eyes are filled with tears that threaten to spill over at any moment. "Oh, but guess what, there's more."

His eyes skim over Jude and then me. He hooks an arm around my brother's neck, tugging him close as he pivots him toward Jude.

My secret-boyfriend shakes his head. "Don't do this, man," Jude pleads with Daire, with his words and puppy dog eyes.

Daire's obnoxious laughter fills the room. I don't think I've ever wanted to punch anyone more than I want to sock him in the face right now. This is way worse than when I was six and Cree ruined my Barbie Corvette and I *did* punch my brother then. "But why not? It's so fun!" He squeezes Cree even tighter. My brother is focused on Ophelia with worry, and for the moment at least, seems to not have put together what Daire is trying to tell him. "Are you listening, buddy?" Daire jostles Cree, making sure he has his attention. "This is a big one. Are you ready?"

I half-expect Daire to break out into a drumroll. Other than leaving my razors in his shower what did I do to this guy for him to pull this stunt?

My brother pushes him away roughly, but Daire only laughs, not at all bothered by the less than playful shove. He's beyond drunk. The guy is completely obliterated, but everyone in the house is hanging onto everything he says with baited breath, knowing if they're patient enough they're going to get rewarded with juicy gossip.

"What? Well, what is it?" My brother's voice has lost all volume, he looks worried as his eyes slide to Jude.

Jude presses his lips into a thin line, hands on his hips. His gaze is zeroed in on me.

I'm sorry, he says with one look. I know he feels terrible, because he feels like his reputation defines him and we both know that in my brother's eyes it will when he finds out his friend is with me.

Don't be, I say back with my eyes, because I'd walk through fire for this man. This will be a battle, sure, especially with Cree finding out like this, but we'll fight it together and come out stronger for it in the end.

Daire clears his throat, lowering his head almost shamefully. He briefly looks at Jude and I can tell he's apologetic.

"It's not important." Even though no one makes a sound, I swear I can hear the whole room groaning as they realize they're not going to get the gossip they were hoping for even though they've already gotten plenty.

Cree stares at his best friend incredulously, anger rolling off him. "I think it must be, for you to be putting on this whole fucking debacle." He lifts his arms, gesturing to the messy room, the people, and Daire himself who looks ready to pass out from how much alcohol he's consumed.

Jude's eyes drop from mine. He stares at his shoes, or maybe it's the floor, like it's the most fascinating thing he's ever seen, and I feel it—the wall he's erecting between us.

Don't do this.

He swallows thickly, his Adam's apple bobbing. He shoves his hands in the pockets of his jeans.

Look at me!

He doesn't.

But Daire isn't done yet. He has enough anger rumbling inside to keep him going even if he should be passed out by now.

He wags a finger tauntingly at my brother. "Oh, don't be so quick to jump to conclusions, my dude. It's not like you're some holy saint," he practically spits the last part. "Nah, you like to think you're a good guy, but you're a liar just like the rest of us—and here's another little secret—*good guys don't lie*. Your sins might not be as shitty as the rest of us, but a lie is a lie *is a lie*." He taps his own nose, whistling as he pulls his finger straight out in a mocking gesture of Pinocchio.

Beside me, Ophelia starts to shake. I'm not sure she even realizes that she is.

Daire smiles at Ophelia, but it's a feral kind of smile, like the cat that ate the canary. He's having way too much fun with this and I kind of wish Jude would punch him and knock him out cold, but he seems to be frozen, still staring at the floor.

To Ophelia, Daire says, "Good ole boy Cree here wasn't supposed to be your tutor. Bet you didn't know that? Nah, he's spent a year looking for you, and apparently, you mistook him for your tutor, and this fucker used that situation to his advantage."

He tries to grab Cree around the neck again, but my brother isn't having it and shoves his friend back forcefully.

"Shut up! Just shut your fucking mouth, dude!"

Ophelia pales, holding her breath. She looks like a cornered rabbit, and I think we all know with the way my brother's not denying it that Daire is speaking the truth. It doesn't seem like that bad of a lie to me, but I think if I was in Ophelia's place I'd be pretty horrified too, because if he can lie about something like this, what other truths might he omit?

Now, it's not just Daire I want to punch, it's my brother too for hurting this girl. I've seen him with her, and I know he cares about her a lot, but that doesn't justify him being a complete and utter idiot.

Jude shakes his head, seeming to snap out of whatever dimension he let himself vanish into.

"You need to sober up." He closes the distance between them, trying to seize Daire, who somehow manages to dodge him. Then, Daire starts to giggle. Not laugh, no these are literal hiccupping giggles.

I'll have whatever he's having, I think to myself; because after this I desperately need a drink.

"Seriously?" His face is red as he pushes Jude away from him. He's still surprisingly strong despite being absolutely shit-faced drunk. Then again, he's a hockey player like my brother so it should come as no surprise that he's holding up so well. Those guys are fucking *built*, like solid steel walls of pure muscle. "You're going to act like *I'm* the bad guy right now? That's all you." He wags a finger tauntingly in Jude's face. It's a warning, we both know it. If Jude tries to corral him again, he *will* spill the beans.

My brother's eyes bounce around from Jude and Daire to Ophelia and back again. He seems lost, like he doesn't know what to do or say. I think he was at the library with Ophelia, and he certainly didn't expect to walk into all of this. A part of me feels sorry for him, but if he did lie to Ophelia then that's on him and he can deal with the fall out, just like Jude and I will have to handle his inevitable meltdown when we tell him about us.

Beside me, Ophelia wraps her arms around herself. She looks stricken as she melts into the crowd. As soon as my brother notices she's gone he's shoving people aside to go after her. The pain in his voice when he calls her name is palpable.

Jude looks around at the mess, shaking his head. "All right, everybody! Nothing to see here! Back to the party." Someone turns the music on again, turning up the volume. "You're coming with me." He grabs Daire around the back of the neck, all but dragging him out of the room and upstairs.

I follow behind, chewing my lip worriedly and looking back to see if Cree has come back inside. Out the second-story window that faces the front, I see him pleading with Ophelia. It's raining now, but neither of them seems to notice they're soaking wet.

Jude pushes Daire into his room, where the guy stumbles over his own feet but somehow manages to make it to his bed. “What the fuck, man?” He curses, spittle flying from his lips. “Do you want me to go out there and find Cree because I fucking will. I’ll tell him all about you two.”

Jude raises a finger in warning. “Don’t you fucking threaten me. Your life is imploding. We all see that, but stop trying to drag the rest of us down with you. Take a shower and sober the fuck up.” Daire’s lip curls with anger and he rises from the bed. Jude immediately shoves him back down. “I’m not playing, man.”

“And I’m not either.”

I step forward, arms wrapped loosely around my body. “What did we ever do to you?”

For some reason, that question seems to penetrate his pea-sized brain and he actually has the decency to look ashamed. “Fuck, guys, I’m sorry.” He runs his fingers through his blond hair. He looks away, jaw-ticking. “I’m being an ass. I guess, I just … I’m miserable and seeing everyone else so fucking happy all the time was eating at me.”

“Miserable,” Jude huffs a laugh, “and apparently married?”

“Yep,” Daire looks at the ring that is still on his wrong hand, “and a dad. Me, a fucking father.”

“You could’ve told me you needed condoms,” Jude jokes, trying to bring some levity to this whole thing.

“The kid’s practically a toddler now,” Daire goes on, his eyes glassy. I’m not sure he’s even aware we’re still here. “I hate this. I hate myself." He rolls over, burying his face in his pillows. Somehow, seconds later, he's snoring.

Jude turns around, facing me, and something inside me cracks.

His eyes are shuttered, his face wiped clean of emotion.

He's shutting me out.

"No." I lift a firm finger, stepping in front him. "Don't you dare do this, Jude. Whatever you're thinking—no. Don't go there." He shakes his head, chest rattling with a sigh. He won't meet my eyes and that physically pains me. "I love you."

He sighs, his shoulders falling as he finally looks at me. Cupping my cheek, he leans down, pressing a tender, lingering kiss to my lips. "I love you, too. More than anything."

Rising on my tiptoes, I kiss him deeper and he lets me, but he quickly ends it when Daire sputters awake.

"Did I fall asleep?" he asks no one in particular. "Fuck, I gotta get back to my party."

He lumbers out of his room and down the stairs, the two of us watching him go.

Jude takes my hand, lacing our fingers together.

Neither of us says a thing as he tugs me into his room and onto his bed. He wraps his big body around mine, tucking his face into the crook of my neck. His hands don't wander or anything of the sort. He only holds me, like if he holds on long enough and tight enough he'll never have to let me go.

thirty-two

Jude

I'M AVOIDING MILLIE.

It's pretty obvious at this point and I feel like such an asshole. Every time I ignore her, or disappear, something in her eyes fades like I'm not the man she thought I was and she's disappointed. She should be, because I'm a fuck up. I'm not the guy you bring home to mommy and daddy, or the one you introduce to your brother as your boyfriend even when you live under the same roof together.

I'm not good for her. Not good enough, either.

It's been almost a week since the party incident, and I

know I can't avoid my girl forever. She deserves to know where my head is at and an explanation as to why this is over. I can't—I *won't*—put her through the inevitable shit-storm that would take place if we were honest with Cree.

I keep replaying over and over again the way he looked at me the night of the party when Daire was about to reveal our relationship. Cree looked ... fucking horrified, not just angry, but like the thought of me and his sister made him ill, and I guess that's a normal reaction, but I keep thinking about how that look might never go away and that I can't subject Millie to that. I know if Cree didn't support us, it would eat at her. She loves and admires her older brother. I don't want to get in the way of that.

Little kids are leaving the dance studio with their parents, so I figure that means I'm just in time to catch Millie on her own for a chance to talk.

I park my truck in the lot, waiting until everyone else has left. There aren't any vehicles left in the lot besides Millie's. Even though I can't stand that prick Aleksander—Millie might be oblivious to how he looks at her, but I'm not—I can't stand the idea of her left alone in the studio even more. It's not safe.

I head to the building, not at all surprised to find the door still unlocked. I lock it behind me, and follow the sound of music upstairs to the studio. I wonder if she takes time to dance after all her classes. This is only the second time I've popped in like this, but both times I've found her dancing.

I always think she's beautiful, but when she dances Millie becomes transcendent. She's strong and graceful, the way she moves across the room commands the attention of everyone, but I'm the only one blessed enough to see this show. She notices me, a small smile gracing her lips before her eyes close and she allows herself to just feel the music.

Stepping all the way into the room, I sit down on the floor and watch her.

Millie Madison makes me feel alive in a way I never have before. It's like before she graced my life with her kaleidoscope of colors I was living in black and white. There was nothing wrong before, but now my life is so much better because she's in it.

That makes what I have to do all the worse.

Millie dances to another song and another, until she finally comes to a stop in the center of the mirrored room and faces me. Her body glistens with sweat, her chest rising and falling rapidly as she tries to regain her breath.

Getting up from the floor, I close the distance between us in a few strides. Cupping her face in my hands, I kiss her because if I don't I'm not sure I'll survive. Fucking pathetic of me, I know, but this girl brings me to my knees.

She pushes at me lightly, so I'll break the kiss. I leave my hands on her cheeks. It's like holding the sun between my hands. She's just so fucking brilliant.

She grabs my wrists but doesn't make to pull my hands off of her. Instead, it's like she wants to touch me too, to remind herself that we're real.

"You've been ignoring me."

It's not a question and I don't treat it as such. "I have."

Her eyes fill with hurt even though that's exactly what I'm trying to avoid. The last thing I want to do is cause her any pain. But it's better to end this before we get even deeper and it's worse.

"Don't do this," she pleads, her lower lip trembling. She already knows what I came here to do without me saying a word.

I kiss her again and she lets me, her arms going around my neck. Her body curls into mine. She's soft and warm and feels like mine.

She grabs my shirt, lifting it up. I help her, looping my thumbs into the back and yanking it over my head. This is the last thing I should be doing right now, but I can't seem to help myself when it comes to this girl. Her fingers splay across my abdominals, moving lower to my belt. She fumbles with the buckle, and I place my hand over hers, halting her movements.

"This isn't why I came here."

"I know." She dives back in, biting my bottom lip. She releases it with a pop, her eyes burning.

She steps away from me, pulling down the top of her leotard and exposing her gorgeous tits. I wonder what she's thinking, why she's doing this. I hope to fuck she doesn't think she can use sex to get me to change my mind, but I'm too fucking weak to resist her.

This has to be goodbye.

"Fuck, Millie," I growl at her little strip tease. She pulls her shorts off and the leo the rest of the way. She's completely fucking naked except for the ballet slippers on her feet.

Jesus, fuck. I didn't know I had the fantasy of fucking her in only those before, but I do now. She's reflected back at me from a million different angles, looking like a fucking angel on earth.

I drop to my knees.

Millie's the kind of girl who deserves to be worshipped.

Wrapping arms around the back of her legs, I encourage to spread them.

The second she does my mouth is on her. She gasps, grabbing the hair on top of my head. "Jude," she moans my name, and it makes me smile against her sweet pussy.

I flick my tongue against her clit and she moans again. She's already wet and I'd like to think she has been since the moment I walk in. I haven't touched her like this since the day of the party after everything went to hell. I didn't lie when I said this isn't why I came here. I wanted a clean break, but my girl wants me and that's impossible to resist even if I should. Selfishly, I want to ruin her so that no man ever fucks her as good as I can.

Sliding two fingers into her pussy, I bring her to an orgasm. I relish in the way she falls apart above me, legs shaking. Her eyes are glassy when I stand and pick her up. Kissing her long and deep I press her back into the mirrors, her ass resting on the barre.

"Did I ever tell you I took ballet?"

She licks her lips, still out of it from the orgasm. "You did?"

"Mhmm." I suck the sweet skin of her neck. It might leave a mark behind, and I should care about that, but I don't. Her brother will have no fucking way of proving I'm the one who left it there.

"Were you any good?"

I grin. "Yes."

I don't give her a chance to ask any more questions, capturing her lips and tongue in a long, slow kiss. She finally yanks my belt out of my jeans and undoes the button. I grab my wallet from my back pocket, pulling out a condom and handing it to her. Dropping my wallet on the floor, I kick off my boots and jeans.

She opens the condom wrapper, holding it out for me to take. Shaking my head, I say, "No, babe. You put it on." She looks nervous, but doesn't protest. She's still sitting on the barre, using my body to keep her balance. Rolling the condom down my length, she looks up at me from beneath her lashes. "You've got it, baby," I encourage.

When the condom is on, I grip her hips and slide into her pussy. She's so fucking wet and ready for me. She holds onto my shoulders as I pound into her. I'm not gentle this time. This is rough, and fast.

"Fuck," she curses, her eyes glazed with lust, "that's hot." I turn to see what she's looking at and realize she's watching me fuck her in the mirrors. “Don’t stop,” she begs when my thrusts slow. “Keep going.”

Looping my arms around her thighs, I open her wider.

“Fuck, baby,” I growl, mesmerized, “look at us. Look at how I fuck you. Your little pussy loves my cock, doesn’t it?” She whimpers in response. “You’re such a good girl, Millie. You take my cock so good.”

Her back arches as she comes, her fingers clawing at my chest, and it takes every ounce of self-control I have not to blow my load.

The second she recovers, I set her down and she whimpers when my cock leaves her slick warmth. Not for long though. I flip her around so she’s facing the mirror, arms braced on the barre. Lifting one of her legs, I position it on the barre too and then grip the back of her hips, fucking her from behind.

“Watch us,” I command, meeting her eyes in the reflection. “No one’s ever going to do this as good as I can.”

She whimpers, the sound turning into a gasp of surprise when I slap her ass. I smooth my hand over the reddened skin.

“God, Millie.” I wrap my arms around her from behind. “You were fucking made for me.”

And that makes this hurt so much more. I thought I wouldn’t recover from Macy, but now that I know what I feel for Millie is a thousand times deeper, there won’t be any coming back from this.

I’ll always, in some way, belong to my Little Madison.

"Don't do this," she begs, looking back at me in the mirror. "Don't break us."

I close my eyes, unable to meet her gaze. I don't want to, but I have to.

Millie's hand presses to the mirror as she shatters apart a third time. This time I go with her over the edge, burying face in the back of her neck as I come.

I wrap my arms around her torso, holding onto her for as long as I can. I finally pull myself away from her and get rid of the condom, trying to locate my clothes. Millie is already tugging her leotard back on. Her chin wobbles, eyes filled with tears. As soon as the straps are on her arms and her breasts are covered, she storms over to me, poking my bare chest. I've only managed to get my jeans on and half-zipped.

"You're a coward."

I shake my head. "If I was a coward, I would do nothing. You think ending this is easy for me? When this is the first time in years, I've felt something real? When I love you more than I've ever loved anyone?" Her doe-like eyes widen. "This is the hardest thing I've ever had to do, Millie."

"We'll tell Cree and—"

"And what?" I bend down and swipe my shirt from the floor, holding it in front of me like a shield. "Your brother is never going to accept us being together and that matters to you, don't deny it."

"He'll get over it."

"Not likely." I shake my head, yanking my shirt on. "I'm the last guy on the planet he'd want to see you with."

"You've changed, he'll see that," she pleads, tears falling down her cheeks now. It fucking pains me that I'm the one making her cry. I don't want to break her heart, it means too much to me, but I don't know what else to do.

I'm not sure there's another girl for me, not after her, but I think she has the chance to move on and find someone else. Someone with a much better reputation than mine.

"No, he won't. All he's ever going to see is the player who got his heart broken and fucked around. To him, I'm nothing but a broken boy who can't love. Definitely not someone worthy of you."

"Forget about him!" she yells. "This is between me and you." She flicks her finger between us. "We're the only two people that matter in this relationship."

I throw my arms out wide. "What relationship, Millie? The one where we sneak around, and you don't want to tell anyone? *That* relationship?"

She swallows thickly. "That's not fair."

"You're the one who hasn't wanted to tell him all this time. Do you think I'm so dumb that I don't know why?"

She wraps her arms around herself. "Why don't you tell me?"

"You're ashamed of me, because if you weren't then you would've wanted to stop this secretive bullshit."

She grinds her teeth back and forth, sniffling. "Forgive me, for wanting to enjoy it just being us for as long as possible. Yeah, I didn't want to tell my brother, but not because I was ashamed. I knew he'd try to insert his opinion when it's none of his business. I'm not a child. I can make my own decisions and I chose you."

I lower my head, looking at the floor. "It's over, Millie. Nothing you say can convince me otherwise."

She lifts her chin haughtily in the air. "Then I stand by what I said."

"And what's that?"

Her nose twitches as she holds back more tears. "That you're a coward."

I swipe my wallet from the floor. "Bye, Millie."

I walk by her, my arm brushing hers and close my eyes, pretending I feel nothing.

My boots thud against the stairs and when I reach the door to leave, I hear her break.

Her sobs are like a knife being jammed into my chest over and over.

I make myself stay there and listen, I deserve to hear how I've broken her, to live with those sounds for the rest of my life.

Finally, I open the door and leave.

thirty-three

Millie

ZARA WAVES ME OVER TO A TABLE IN THE BACK OF the coffee shop. She already has an iced coffee waiting for me and a cake pop too. Bless her.

"Hi," I say, leaning over to hug her before taking a seat across from her.

I filled her in over the phone last night about what happened with Jude, and she demanded that we get together for lunch today. Honestly, it's been the last thing I wanted to do after hours spent crying and a fitful night of sleep, but I know sequestering myself to my room isn't the answer.

"You look awful," she says, not beating around the bush. "Sorry." She cringes. "That didn't sound nice, I just mean you look sad."

I shrug, stabbing my straw into my drink with more force than necessary. Zara notices, arching a brow, but she doesn't call me out on it. Taking a bite of the cake pop, I chew, stalling for time. It's silly since she already knows all the sordid details, but talking about it in person instead of over the phone feels different.

Zara lets me finish the cake pop before she pounces on me with questions. "Did you see him this morning?"

I shake my head, stirring my iced coffee so that it's fully mixed with the cream and sugar. "No, he was already gone. Probably to the gym or something."

"I hope he looks as bad as you do."

A short bark of a laugh flies out of my lips. "You sure know how to make a girl feel pretty."

Zara smiles. "You know what I mean. You're clearly exhausted and … sad." She tacks on the last part somewhat reluctantly.

I sigh. "I should've known it wouldn't last. It was naïve of me to think otherwise. I think Jude still has a lot of unresolved things to work through with his ex." Even though it's obvious Macy has moved on, and honestly that Jude has too, they were together a long time and there was a hell of a lot of trauma in the end of their relationship. "I think because of how much of a player he's been, he doesn't feel good enough, and doesn't want to come between my brother and me. Which is stupid, Cree would get over it."

"I don't even know your brother, but I want to nut punch him after some of the things you've told me."

I lower my eyes to the table. Cree is the typical older brother, and I know he's only trying to look out for me, but he's said enough crap to Jude that the poor guy thinks there's nothing he can do to make my brother see him as a good fit for me. But we're the only two people in the relationship. All that matters should be how we feel.

"He's just trying to look out for me," I finally say. "He just doesn't go about it the best way."

She hums, sipping at her latte. "What are you going to do?"

I take a sip of my coffee, stalling. "I can't make him change his mind, so I guess things return to how they were before."

A life pre-Jude seems so boring and lackluster in comparison. Being with him makes me happy. We don't even have to be doing anything exciting. Just watching tv with him, or when he painted my toenails. Those little moments are—*were*—everything.

Zara pops the lid off her coffee, dropping in a pack of sugar to the already almost milk-colored drink. Not that I can judge. "And how were things before?" She stirs the sugar around, letting it dissolve, all while staring me down with an elegantly arched brow.

"Lackluster," I answer honestly. That's not exactly true.

Nothing was *wrong* with my life pre-Jude. He just made it better. "It's going to be weird at our house for God knows how long."

"Because of how you and Jude feel for each other?"

"Partly," I hesitate. I'm not sure how much I want to tell Zara—not because I don't trust her, but because not everything is my story. "There's just been a lot going on for all of us. Cree's girlfriend broke up with him ... I think at least. He won't talk about it. And Daire—"

She jumps into the conversation with an excited gleam in her eyes. "I heard *all* about his drama."

"Well," I wave my fingers dismissively through the air, "then you know how it's going at home."

"I'm sure Daire will move out soon. Right? I mean, he has to, he's legit married now. There goes my chances with him," she jokes with a wink.

"Eh, he's kind of a dick so you dodged a bullet there."

She cackles. "Don't you know that's how I like them?"

"Nah." I wipe crumbs off the table and into my hand, holding on tight. I'll toss them in the trash can on my way out. "You need a good boy."

She snorts. "Like who?"

As if I've conjured him, Jonah approaches our table. "Hey, Millie," he says with a soft, shy smile. His long fingers are wrapped around a coffee cup, his hands so large they nearly swallow the cup whole.

"Jonah, hi." I force a smile, not because I'm not happy to see him, but because smiling is the last thing, I feel like doing right now. “This is Zara. Zara, meet Jonah. We’re in psych together and working on a project.”

“It’s nice to meet you.” He extends a hand politely to Zara.

She takes it, darting wide eyes to me. “Nice to meet you, too, Jonah.”

They shake hands for an awkward amount of time, neither one seeming to want to let go. Okay, then.

Jonah finally shakes his head, clearing his throat, and lets her hand drop. He takes a step back, shoving his empty hand into his pocket. His cheeks are redder than I’ve ever seen them and even Zara looks flustered and not her normally calm, cool, and collected self.

“Text me whenever you want to get together this week for the project.” Jonah takes a step back, then another. “I’ll see you around.”

He turns, hurrying out of the coffee shop. Zara watches him go, and I swear her eyes are glued to his ass.

“He is *cute*,” she enunciates the word. “Is he single?”

“Yes. He’s nice and sweet, go easy on the guy.”

She bats her eyes innocently. “Who? Me?”

THE HOUSE IS dark and quiet when I get back. My brother’s Bronco is the only vehicle in the driveway, which should be a relief but isn’t. I’m unreasonably mad at him, considering he has no way of knowing what he did, but he's the reason Jude is running from me.

I set my bag down by the stairs, planning to head to the kitchen when my brother's head pops up from the couch.

"Jesus Christ!" My hand flies to my heart. "Why are you laying in the dark like a creep? At least put the TV on or something," I sputter, trying to regain control of myself.

"I fell asleep." His voice is a deep, raspy rumble like he has in fact been sleeping on the couch, and for a long time at that.

"Well, you still didn't have to scare the living daylights out of me."

He groans, rubbing his mussed hair. "Where have you been?"

My hackles rise. "You're not my keeper, Cree. You don't need to know where I am or who I'm with every second of every day. Can you imagine if roles were reversed, and I did that to you?"

"Jeez," he lies back down, disappearing from view, "it was just a question, Mills."

"I was getting coffee with Zara."

His disembodied voice says, "I'm not sure I like her."

Something in me snaps. Storming forward, I grab a throw pillow and smack my brother repeatedly with it.

"Okay, okay." He rolls to the floor away from me. "I get it. You're in a mood. Are you on your period or something?"

I gasp, stunned. "You did not just say that to me."

"What?" The idiot looks up at me from the floor. His brows are furrowed, completely confused.

"No wonder your girlfriend dumped your ass, you ignorant potato head." There are a thousand better insults I could've come up with, and yet, potato head fits him perfectly.

"So, you're not on your period?"

"No!" I storm away.

Ugh.

I swipe a La Croix from the fridge, nearly colliding with my brother when I whip around.

"What's wrong with you?" He looks truly concerned, which makes me feel a tad bad. Some of the fight leaves me.

"Nothing." I brush past him.

Nothing I'm going to talk to him about anyway. I can see how he'd react now—which dammit if that doesn't make me understand where Jude's coming from, even if I know given enough time Cree would move past it. But the fact is, I'm not wasting my breath telling my brother about us when there is no us, not anymore.

Cree groans, following me out of the kitchen. "I don't know why I waste my time trying."

"Maybe," I whip back around, "instead of moping around here, you should go find Ophelia and make things right."

He looks away from me, staring a hole in the wall. "She wants space, so that's what I'm giving her."

My heart pangs for him, because if he's feeling anything near what I am right now...

"I hope she forgives you."

He swallows thickly, gliding his fingers through his dark brown hair. "Yeah, I hope so too."

thirty-four

Jude

If I thought my breakup with Macy was rough—and it was—breaking up with Millie is a hundred times harder.

It's been two weeks already and I feel like complete shit. I barely eat, my weight is dropping which has my coach concerned, and I'm moving through life like a fucking shadow. I do what I have to—class, homework, and football—and no more than that. I haven't even been to Harvey's.

My feet pound against the treadmill, the pace I'm running is vicious and punishing, exactly what I need.

Keaton steps in front of the treadmill, motioning with his finger for me to remove my ear buds. I shake my head. Fat chance.

He points to his ears again.

I can tell he's annoyed, but thankfully he walks away—or at least I thought so until a hand shoots out and swipes the safety key from the treadmill, bringing it to an immediate standstill. It's a good thing I have good reflexes or else I would've hit my face hard enough to cause a broken nose.

I rip my earphones out, and level him with a glare. "What the fuck, dude? You could've hurt me."

"You're hurting you," he argues, jabbing a pointed finger into my chest. "Hit the showers, and we're going out."

Has he lost his fucking mind?

"Out?"

"Yeah, you know that thing you do where you go somewhere different, a lot of times it involves things like food which you clearly need." He looks at me like I'm a sack of bones, which isn't true, but I know the weight loss shows.

"Why?"

"Because you clearly need someone to talk to and for whatever reason, it looks like that's going to be me."

I grind my teeth together, pissed off by this whole thing, but I know Keaton well enough to know he isn't going to let this go.

IF SOMEONE HAD TOLD me a few months ago that I'd be sitting in Keaton's car while he drives us to get something to eat, I would've thought they were full of shit.

But here I am.

I can't blame the guy for assuming I'd drive off if given the chance to go in my truck. He covered all the bases.

He picks a place off the beaten path that other students aren't likely to frequent, and I appreciate that fact.

The car engine shuts off and he turns to me. "I didn't make you talk while we're in the car, but once we go in there, your ass better start speaking. You clearly need to get some things off your chest."

"Why should I talk to you?" I grumble, reaching for the door.

"Because you're clearly not talking to your friends about whatever this is, so you've got me."

We head inside the restaurant, not having to wait long to be seated.

I peruse the menu, nothing at all sounding remotely appealing.

Keaton peers at me over the top of his own menu. "I can tell you're already thinking about not ordering anything, and to that I say, nice try."

I narrow my eyes on him. "You do realize nothing is keeping me from decking you in the face, right?"

"Sure." He shrugs, unbothered. "But I can take your ass." He's probably not wrong. Even when I haven't lost weight the dude is more jacked than me. He gives me a reprieve from talking until after the waitress has taken our food and drink order. "All right, dude, start talking. I haven't got all night. My girl is waiting for me." He arches a brow in surprise. "Wow, you didn't even narrow your eyes at that comment. Does this mean you're finally over Macy?"

I drag the container of sugar packets closer to me, rearranging them in a neat and tidy order. "Yes," I grind out.

He leans back in the booth, completely surprised. "I take it that means you moved on?" I look away from his probing gaze. "Definitely, moved on, but you're more of a sullen asshole than usual so I take it she dumped you?" I shake my head and his surprise grows. "You dumped her?" I nod. "Not because you wanted to? And use your words this time, Cartwright. I know you can."

"No, I didn't want to." The words are like acid on my tongue.

I've barely seen Millie at all these past few weeks. I'm sure she's avoiding me as much as I am her. I thought the less I saw of her, the easier it would be, but it's so much fucking worse.

"Then why did you?"

I curse, rubbing at my face. "You're like a dog with a bone, aren't you? You just won't let it go."

"Not when you clearly need to get shit off your chest."

I swipe my tongue over my parched lips, muttering a thanks when the waitress sets down our drinks. "She's my friends' little sister." It feels good to say that out loud, to finally talk about her with someone. "I wasn't supposed to fall for her, but I did. She's sweet, and funny, so smart, and fucking gorgeous." I tug at my hair. "She's perfect, all right? But her brother…" I pause, gathering my thoughts. "She didn't want to tell him about us and I respected that, even if it bothered me. I love her, and I didn't want to be some dirty secret, but he almost found out about us and I could see it, how fucking appalled he was by the idea alone and I don't want to put her through that. He doesn't trust me, and she loves and respects him, so eventually she'll see what he sees."

"And leave you?" He fills in the blanks.

"Yeah," I mutter. "I guess. It makes the most sense."

"What I'm gathering from this is, you don't think you're good enough for her?"

"There's no thinking about it. I'm definitely not."

"Good."

My mouth opens in shock. "Good?" Do I sound as horrified to his ears as I do mine?

"Yeah, you heard me *good*; because as long as you think you're not good enough for that girl, you're constantly going to be trying your fucking hardest to get to that point. I sure as fuck don't think I'm good enough for Macy, but I'm going to spend the rest of my life proving to her, and myself, that I'm the only guy for her."

It's weird, hearing him talk about Macy and not feeling any sort of jealousy or anger. She was a part of my life once, and I'll always care about her in that sense, but she's no longer this giant emotional hang-up in my life.

Lowering my head, I shake it back and forth, realizing the reason I don't feel anything anymore is because over the past few months Millie has stitched the hole back together and made it new again.

"You're thinking about her, aren't you?"

"Macy?" I blurt, shocked he's come to this conclusion. "No."

Keaton rubs his lips, trying to hide his smile. "No, not her. The girl you fell for. What's her name?"

For a moment, I think about not telling him. That's stupid though. "Millie."

"My question for you is, how are you going to feel when Millie moves on? Not *if* but when, because if it hasn't occurred to you yet, she will. Do you really think some other guy out there is going to treat her better than you can?"

My fingers curl into twin fists on the table. The idea of Millie with another guy makes me want to commit murder. As cheesy as it fucking sounds, I'm not sure my heart could handle seeing her with someone else. It would be so much worse than Macy with Keaton and that was hard enough.

"I understand your reasoning," Keaton goes on, and we both sit back when the waitress comes by to drop off our food, "but you're a fucking idiot." He adds the last part after the waitress has walked away.

"I know I am," I grumble, picking up a fry. I look it over before I pop it in my mouth. Tastes like shit—just like everything I've tried to eat lately.

"Then maybe try not to be?"

I glare at my teammate. "Thanks for the advice. I'll take it into consideration."

He chuffs a laugh. "No, you won't. If there's anything I know about you, Cartwright, it's that you're stubborn to a fault. But listen here, all I want you to think about is this; is she worth her brother being pissed at you, and eventually getting over it? Because if she is, man the fuck up and apologize to her. Stop overcomplicating things, you dumbass."

"Can we go now?"

He grins evilly. "Nope, I'm going to eat a burger. Suck it up and order an Uber or wait for me to be done. Your choice."

I should get up and leave, call that Uber like he says, but something keeps me sitting there.

Even though what he said isn't exactly what I want to hear, I'm reluctantly starting to think that maybe Keaton isn't the bad guy I've made him out to be.

thirty-five

Millie

Weeks go by, and I barely see Jude. When I do see him, he doesn't make eye contact and shuffles by me in the house like I'm a ghost. He can't see me, can't hear me. I'm vapor. I'm nothing.

And I *hate* it.

More than once I've been tempted to kick him in the shin.

Then I would be more than a ghost to him.

He wants to ruin us? That's fine—I mean not really—but at least acknowledge my existence. Our short break for

Thanksgiving is fast approaching, and I dread what it's going to be like when we come back. If I'm non-existent now… God knows what I'll be to him by then.

I put the finishing touches on my makeup, turning the bathroom light off.

It's amazing how we never have any run-ins in our shared bathroom now. Jude is the king of avoidance.

In my room, I dig through my closet for something to wear.

Zara invited me to a party at one of the frat houses. I didn't want to go, but I knew otherwise I'd just mope in my bedroom, so I figured dressing up and going out was the better option.

I find a glittery pink dress in the back of my closet. I don't even remember packing it, but I'm thankful I have something a little sexier to wear tonight. Since it's cold out, I'll put on a long black belted coat with it. I'm sure a lot of girls will opt not to wear a coat, but I'm not out here looking to freeze to death just for the sake of fashion.

Slipping the dress up my body, I shimmy it into place, awkwardly jumping around to zip it up.

Once the dress is in place, I dig around for some shoes. I grin when I find my favorite pair of silver studded booted heels.

"Perfect."

Sitting on the end of my bed, I put them on and then check myself out in the floor length mirror in the corner of my room to make sure everything looks good. My hair is long and loose, in soft waves, and my makeup is a shimmery pop of silver that matches the boots. The dress fits like a glove, and if Jude weren't actively avoiding me, I'd love to see his reaction to it. Before he ended things, I know he more than likely would've taken one look at me and marched me into my room just so he could carefully remove it from my body, and we'd end up spending our night making love.

I swallow past the lump lodged in my throat.

I still love him, and I miss him so much.

But I'm still angry at him too, for giving up on us instead of fighting for us.

Taking a deep breath, I smooth an errant hair back into place just as my phone vibrates with a text from Zara letting me know she's here.

Dashing back into the bathroom for my tube of gloss, I run smack into Jude—well, not physically, but there he is, looking all kinds of tall, dark, and handsome. My treacherous pussy clenches with need.

Down girl, now's not the time.

His hand is warm on my elbow, my skin tingling from his touch. At least he saved me from going splat on the floor. I open my mouth to say thank you when his face screws up with—horror? Repulsion?

"What the fuck are you wearing?"

I gape at him, stunned to silence. "W-What? A dress." I yank my arm from his hold since he still hasn't let me go.

He shakes his head roughly back and forth. "Where are you going?"

I swipe my gloss from the counter. "Not that it's any of your business, but a party with Zara."

"No."

I laugh, incredulous. "*No?* Like you have any sort of control over me." I tap his chest, his eyes narrowing on my finger as I pull it away. "Kiss my ass, Jude."

He grumbles something, but I ignore it, walking out of the bathroom and into my room. Grabbing my clutch, I slip the gloss in and hurry downstairs.

"Whoa, whoa, whoa—where do you think you're going dressed like that?"

I whip around to face my brother as he gets up from the couch. "Sit your ass down, Cree Whitford Madison."

"Not the middle name," he groans, absolutely hating the old-fashioned family name.

"There is absolutely *nothing* wrong with the way I'm dressed. If it bothers you? That's on you. If you think this dress gives guys the wrong idea—again, that's on you and *any* dude that thinks how a woman is dressed determines if they're asking for it or not." I gather my breath. I could go on a rant about this all day, but I have a party to attend. "Think about that the next time you want to remark on what I'm wearing or question a girl's morals based on how she's dressed."

I know my brother is over-protective, and he's coming from a place of love, but fuck that. I'm sick and tired of the double standard that guys can sleep around and party it up in college, but I'm not supposed to because I'm a girl.

Whipping back around to head out through the garage, I spot Jude at the top of the stairs. I can't help myself when I stick my tongue out and give him the finger.

Zara's car is parked on the street out front, and I practically run down the driveway in my heeled platforms to get to her, just in case one or both of the guys tries to detain me again.

When I open the door, she's blasting 'Don't Blame Me' from Taylor Swift.

"I love this song," I tell her, closing the door and reaching for the seatbelt.

"Same, girl!" She yells, then lowers the volume. "Sorry, I blast my music at obnoxious levels when it's just me in the car."

"Where's this party at?"

I'm trying not to think about that moment in the bathroom with Jude, but *ugh* my brain wants to play it on loop. I need to forget about him tonight and let go.

"It's really close by, actually. Only a few blocks." The car eases to a stop at the stop sign. "What's up? You seem to have something on your mind."

I sigh, pinching the bridge of my nose as she eases the car forward. "I ran into Jude before I left."

She sends a sympathetic look my way. "I'm sorry, girl."

"Like I literally ran into him," I go on, wanting to get this off my chest. "Then he went all caveman on me, talking about my dress, then telling me I couldn't go to a party. The alpha male bullshit thing just rubs me the wrong way. Don't tell me what I can and can't do. I'm not a fucking object. It makes me feel like I'm a toy he played with for a while and got bored of and that pisses me off."

"Whoa, girl. I can feel the anger radiating off of you from here." She turns onto a street lined with vehicles. "Try to put that idiot out of your mind and enjoy tonight. It's your first college party, let loose and have fun."

That sounds easier said than done.

"I'll try." I flash her a half-hearted smile. I don't want to let Jude rule my thoughts, not when I'm trying so hard to move on—not even with someone else, but just to put us in the past. I don't want to be that person who lets a breakup define them. I'm still my own person and I'm allowed to miss him, but I've got to get back out there and stop sitting in my room sulking.

Zara parallel parks between a Mercedes and a Range Rover—she's much braver than I am—and cuts the engine. She makes no move to get out yet, turning in her seat to face me instead.

"You are gorgeous, brilliant, and a kick ass friend. You deserve a guy who treats you as such. So fuck that football player—not literally since you already did that—and go have some fun. And don't accept a drink from anyone. Get it yourself."

"You got it, Mom," I joke, feeling a little lighter after her speech.

She smiles. "Let's go."

We hop out of the car, walking down the street to the house where the party is held. Despite the chilly temperatures people hang on the front lawn, red Solo cups clasped in their hands. I don't know how those cups became the unofficial mascot of college parties, but hats off to the superb marketing.

Zara grabs my hand, leading me to the door. "Let's get some drinks and dance." She shimmies her shoulder as she drags me after her.

Inside, the house is thudding with the heavy bass of the song playing.

The lights are dim inside, with some kind of strobe going instead.

I'm definitely going to leave here with a headache.

I follow Zara into the kitchen which is covered in various bottles of liquor on almost every surface, a keg in the corner, and some 'chick beer' in a cooler. There's literally a sign on it that labels it as such, and someone even came along and doodled a chick coming out of an egg.

"Chick beer," Zara snickers, swiping one for me and then her. "I feel like I should be offended but I'm not. The last thing I'm doing is trusting any of those bottles in a frat house," she motions to the mess of alcoholic beverages, "or drinking warm ass bland keg beer." She pops her cap off and I do the same, looking around the room to see if I spot any familiar faces. A couple I do recognize from classes. "Cheers, my girl," Zara says, bringing me back to her.

We clink our bottles together, both taking hefty gulps. "That's really sweet. It doesn't even taste like beer."

"Eh." She looks at the bottle. "It'll do."

Grabbing my hand, she tugs me through the house and down a set of stairs to the basement. The music is even louder down here. Lots of people dance, some guys play darts—not very well, I might add—and another group of people sits on two oversized couches smoking what I assume is weed.

This isn't my scene, I'm not a party kind of girl, but after the past weeks I need to get out and pretend to be someone different for a night.

Zara lets out a hoot of excitement, her black hair falling in a curtain behind her as she shimmies her shoulders. "Come on, Millie, let's dance and get that asshole off your mind."

'Caught Up' by Gryffin plays over the speakers, making me think of Jude which doesn't help at all with the whole getting him off my mind thing.

Zara closes her eyes, grabbing onto my waist with her freehand. She lets herself go, dancing with me and feeling the music, so I do the same. I put one hand around her shoulders, determined not to think about Jude.

My body moves freely to the music. Even though ballet is my love and passion, I have studied other forms of dance over the years.

When I open my eyes, I notice that Zara and I have gathered quite the crowd watching us dance. There's nothing inherently sexual about the way we're dancing, but it's certainly sensual.

Sweat beads along my skin and I take a swig of the sweet tasting beer.

"Millie, you're so hot. Jude is an idiot," Zara shouts. "You're wifey material." I laugh, feeling looser the more we dance. "His loss is my gain." She waggles her brows.

"Thanks for getting me out of the house."

"Any time, girl."

Across the room, I spot a familiar face and smile at Jonah. He's watching us with heated eyes, but I think he might be paying more attention to Zara than me, which is sort of a relief. I like Jonah, a lot, but he's not Jude.

I sway back in Zara's direction, her eyes closed again as she drags her hands in a slow glide up her torso to cup her breasts beneath the corset top she wears. When her eyes open, they're heated with excitement and lust.

"Have you ever kissed a girl?"

Her question takes me by surprise. "No."

"Do you want to?" My lips part, unsure. "Mr. Tall Dark and Infuriatingly Handsome just walked in and a little girl-on-girl action might just break him." I start to turn my head, but she grabs my chin, her long fingernails almost scratching me. "Don't look. He can't know you know he's here." She licks her lips. "I should preface this by saying you're my friend, and I know you're straight so I'm not trying to take advantage—"

"Advantage?" I ask stupidly.

She grins, her top teeth lightly grazing her bottom lip. "I'm bi-sexual, Millie. But if you want me to kiss you to make him jealous, then I will."

"I—no..." I blush, because now that she's planted the thought in my brain I *do* want to kiss her. Not to make Jude jealous, but to know what it's like to kiss a girl. I've never thought about kissing a girl before, but she has me curious. It has to be different than kissing a guy, right? "Kiss me," I say and her smile grows, "but not to make him jealous."

"Oh?" She arches a brow as I blush. "Why then?"

"Because now you have me wanting to know what it would be like to kiss you."

"You don't have to tell me twice."

We're both on the short side, and since we're both wearing heels, we're evenly matched in height. Her eyes are on mine, giving me a chance to back out, but I won't. She cups the back of my head, pulling me in.

And then her lips are on mine.

They're soft and sweet, tasting of the beer and something vanilla, maybe her gloss. She makes a tiny sound that I feel, more than hear, and parts my lips with her tongue. The kiss is both somehow gentle and possessive. It's nice and I make no move to stop her. Instead, I skim my hands over her hips and up her waist. She shivers beneath my touch.

Oh.

I like this.

The room around us cheers, and I don't realize until Zara pulls away that they're cheering at us.

"Fuck off." She gives the finger to all the guys cheering at us. "Are you okay?" she asks me, and I can tell she's worried that maybe I wasn't into it.

"More than fine," I reply and she smiles.

"Good."

Across the room, my eyes accidentally collide with searing brown eyes where he stands in the corner sipping a beer with friends around him.

I turn away hastily. "I'm going to find a bathroom," I tell Zara. "I'm fine, promise." I don't want her to think I'm suddenly freaking out about the kiss when that's not the case at all.

"Do you want me to come with you?"

"No, no. I'm fine. I'll be right back."

I head upstairs from the basement in search of a bathroom. I find a long line coming out of one, so I head for the second-level instead.

Thankfully, I manage to locate the bathroom and only have to wait for one person.

Once it's my turn, I shut and lock the door. I pee and wash my hands, fixing the mascara streaked beneath my eyes. It's nothing too noticeable but I can't stand when black specks transfer to my skin.

Someone knocks on the door. "Almost done," I tell whoever it is. I smooth down my hair and fix my dress back into place when there's another knock. "I said I was almost finished."

My tone is a tad bit snappy, but I can't bring myself to care. It's honestly a miracle I haven't been snappier lately.

Inhaling a breath, I swing the door open and stifle a scream when the guy busts inside. My scream cuts off the second I realize it's Jude. He slams the door closed, pushing the lock.

He glowers down at me, crowding me against the wall. "Little Madison," he growls, "I don't know what the fuck kind of stunt you're trying to pull but—"

"I don't know what you're talking about." I stick my chin haughtily into the air.

"Bullshit."

"Quit with the fucking caveman attitude. I don't owe you anything, least of all an explanation, so back the fuck off—"

His mouth slams down onto mine, cutting off my tirade as I moan into his kiss.

He grabs my hips, his hands sliding down so his fingers dig into the back of my thighs. His tongue works some kind of devil magic along with his fingers, as he somehow manages to get me to spread my legs.

Gliding his left hand between my legs, he pushes aside my thong, so his fingers find my throbbing core.

"Fuck," he draws out the word, "I knew you'd be soaked." I whimper at his touch, feeling boneless. He holds my weight effortlessly though. "Is this okay?" I nod. "Thank fuck."

He sinks two fingers inside me, pumping them slowly at first but then increasing the speed and pressing his thumb against my clit.

"Jude," I moan his name, but it's also filled with the sound of my emotional pain.

"You're killing me, Little Madison," he murmurs into the skin of my neck. "I've never wanted anyone as much as I want you."

Whatever I might say next turns into a cry of pleasure as my orgasm hits me. Holy shit that was fast. He keeps pumping his fingers as my pussy pulses and squeezes his digits. Somehow, that one orgasm falls into another. I feel like I might collapse onto the floor, but Jude keeps one arm around me when he finally pulls his fingers from my soaking wet pussy.

I'm pretty sure my eyes are deceiving me when he takes his fingers into his mouth and sucks them clean. He stares me down, his brown eyes dilated and filled with a wide-range of emotions from lust to confusion to heartbreak.

I struggle to regain my breath.

He finally breaks eye contact with me, and I can feel the change come over him, the instant regret over what he's done.

When he looks back at me, it's like my heart is breaking all over again. "Don't you dare. Don't you dare say you regret this." I push past him, trying to get to the door. "Fuck you, Jude."

I swing the door open, promptly slamming it behind me, shock flooding my system when I see Jonah leaning against the wall on the other side.

"Hey," he says, looking me over with concern. "I saw you take off and I was worried about you. I just wanted to check on you."

I rub my hand over my face, flustered. "I'm fine. Thanks for thinking of me."

I make it two steps away from the bathroom when the door opens again, and I can see the confusion on Jonah's face.

The three of us stand awkwardly in the hallway, my face turning red as a tomato. I didn't *ask* Jude to follow me into the bathroom, but it's pretty easy for Jonah to put the pieces together as to why we'd be alone in there.

I clear my throat, trying to fill the silence. "Um, Jonah. This is Jude." I toss my thumb at the big guy. "Jude, meet Jonah."

Jonah lets out a petrified sound. "We've met."

"I … oh … um … okay, then." For some reason my feet won't move me forward.

"Did you know?" Jonah asks Jude, my gaze bouncing between the two of them.

"Know what?" Jude sounds completely clueless, and I'm baffled at what's happening.

"That she was the girl I liked. Did you fucking know,

and make a move on her, to what? Play some kind of fucked up mind games with me?"

"Huh? What is going on? Someone explain, please," I beg, my body shaking with nerves. "How do you guys know each other?" This seems to be the vital piece of information I'm missing.

Jonah lets out an incredulous laugh. "Millie," he says slowly, carefully, so I won't miss a word, "meet my brother."

Ice fills my veins.

I had to have misheard him.

"What?" I direct my question to Jude, hoping I heard him wrong.

Jude's not looking at me, though. His eyes are fixed to his ... to his *brother*. The guy I had a crush on, the guy I was originally asking for Jude's help with.

"I didn't know," he says to Jonah, his hands raising in a pleading gesture. "I swear to you, I didn't know."

He takes a step toward Jonah, who shoves him when he gets too close. "Bullshit. I don't believe you."

"Millie's my roommate, and I—"

Jonah, clearly not wanting to hear what his brother has to say sends me a sad look before he heads for the stairs.

To me, Jude says, "It was my brother, wasn't it? The guy you liked. I just inadvertently stole the girl my brother was into?"

Now it's my turn to say, "I didn't know." I lift a horrified hand to my mouth. "Oh my God." I start to cry, the tears coursing down my cheeks.

"Fuck," Jude curses, slamming his fist into the wall. His eyes plead with me for understanding. "I have to check on him. He's my brother and I—"

"Go," I say softly. "I'm..." I clear my throat. "I'll be okay."

Jude gives me one last pleading look, and then he's gone.

I go in search of Zara and she takes one look at my face, and knows I'm ready to leave.

She doesn't ask what happened, and I appreciate that since I'm still trying to process it myself. When she drops me off at my house, I promise to call her tomorrow.

Somehow, I manage to make it to my room before I break down sobbing.

SOMETIME LATER, my bed dips down with the weight of someone else's body. I jolt awake, sitting up so quickly that my head swims. Putting a hand to my forehead, I groan, letting the fuzzy shapes of my room take form.

"Hey, I didn't mean to startle you." Jude's voice is a husky whisper in my darkened room. I managed to change out of my dress into some sleep pants and a t-shirt—definitely not my cutest pajama attire but it's not like I should be wanting to look presentable for this dickwad.

"What are you doing in here?" I hiss at him, shoving at

his shoulder in an attempt to dislodge him from my bed. "Go away. I don't like you."

His eyes narrow on me. "You don't like me anymore, Little Madison? Explain why my fingers were in your pussy some hours ago." My nose crinkles, and he smiles annoyingly since he knows I have no rebuttal. "That's what I thought."

I want to wipe that arrogant smirk off his face, but I remain where I am, trying not to pout and look ridiculous. Crossing my arms over my chest, I ask, "What is it you want that you're willing to sneak in here?"

He runs his fingers through his hair, letting out a gruff sigh. "I wanted to say I was sorry I left you there. I knew you'd understand, but fuck, I didn't mean to just run off on you. I also um," he clears his throat, "that bathroom thing—I wanted to talk to you, I didn't plan for that to happen. I don't know what the hell that it says about me either that watching you make-out with Zara was the hottest fucking thing I've ever seen."

I blush. "So you were watching?"

"Mm," he hums. "I think everyone was. What was that about anyway?"

I sit up more fully, grabbing a pillow and holding it in front of me like a shield. "Well, I didn't know before tonight that Zara's bisexual and she asked if I'd be okay if she kissed me and I wasn't sure about it at first, but it made me curious." I shrug like it's no big deal.

He hesitates for a moment. "Did you like it?"

I blush. "Yes."

"More than kissing me?"

"It was different than kissing you. I can't really compare it."

With a shake of his head, he clears his throat. "I'm sorry. I shouldn't have asked that."

"Was Jonah mad? I swear I had *no* idea you were brothers. I mean, now I sorta see the resemblance. You're more rugged and gritty where he's cute and sweet. His hair is a couple of shades lighter than yours, but you have the same eyes."

"He's mad at me, not you." I can see the pain in his eyes at the hurt we inadvertently caused his little brother. "He doesn't want to believe that I didn't know you were the girl. But I swear when he came to me for advice, he never told me your name and I didn't ask. It wasn't my business. Jonah doesn't really come to me for things like advice, even though we're close, so I just wanted to help."

I laugh softly, tucking my sleep mussed hair behind my ears. "Don't you find it funny that we both came to you for relationship advice?"

Jude shakes his head, a self-deprecating smile on his lips. "Shows how dumb you both are that you trusted me with that of all things." He stands from my bed. "Anyway, I should let you sleep."

This is the most we've spoken in nearly a month, and I hate how much I crave his presence and thrive on being near him.

"Okay," I say, instead of begging him to stay like I so desperately want.

He heads back to the open door of the bathroom, but pauses, turning back. "I never meant to hurt you, Millie. And I ... I fucking miss you, okay? But I..." His jaw clenches. "I need to sort some things out."

I nod woodenly, not opening my mouth to say anything because I'm worried I'll either beg him to forget about sorting himself out and just be with me, or more than likely I'll say something scathing.

It doesn't take a genius to know that Jude's had a massive chip on his shoulder for a long time and if he's finally going to deal with his problems then I need to keep my thoughts to myself and let him do that.

He deserves to move on from his past and understand that despite what happened, he deserves love as much as anyone.

thirty-six

Jude

THE ENTIRE DRIVE BACK HOME FOR THANKSGIVING, my brother doesn't speak to me.

Not one single word.

Not even when I ask him a flat-out question, like, "Are you hungry?" or "Do you need to use the bathroom?"

He just stares straight ahead, steadfastly ignoring me. I can't say I don't deserve it, but I hate my little brother being pissed at me. We've always been pretty close, sure we fought like typical boys growing up, but we haven't really had any serious spats as adults.

Until now.

Stopping my truck in front of the gates that lead up to our house, I don't put in the security code yet.

"Jonah—"

He huffs, looking out the passenger window and showing me the back of his head.

"Look, for the hundredth time, I didn't know she was the girl. You know, I'm a lot of things, but I'm not a liar and I wouldn't screw over my brother. Believe what you want, but can we please go in here and be civil for Mom? She's missed us and doesn't need to know you're pissed at me."

Jonah doesn't move a muscle. "Fine." The word is nothing but a low grunt.

I know that's as good as it's going to get so I roll down my window and put in the code. The gate swings open and then it's another mile before we reach the house.

The sprawling mansion doesn't exactly scream homey, but it wasn't a bad place to grow up. My dad stayed home with us kids while we were growing up, I mean he still does since Jade is a junior in high school, so we were never really lacking parental care and attention. Even though our mom is a CEO of a major retail company she always made time for us, whether it was limiting phone hours, or showing up to games.

I feel lucky that we grew up with love and support, unlike so many other kids. Especially in our tax bracket most parents shuck their kids off to nannies and boarding schools, but our parents wanted our life to be as normal as possible.

I hate to tell them that the indoor swimming pool and full-size outdoor tennis court don't exactly scream normal.

Parking my truck in the garage beside an antique Rolls Royce, I shut off the engine.

Jonah silently grabs his bag, heading inside. I watch his retreating figure, wondering how the fuck I'm going to fix this. If he wants me to tell him I regret Millie, then I can't do that. I *won't*. Regret is the last thing I feel for her.

I really fucked things up with her, letting my insecurities get to me and I don't know how to make it right, not yet, but I'm working on it.

Swinging my duffel bag over my shoulder, I head into the house myself, Jonah already having disappeared. Fucker.

In the kitchen, I find our cook, Ellie, putting the finishing touches on tonight's dinner.

"Smells delicious, El."

She jumps, swatting at my chest with a towel. "Mr. Jude, don't sneak up on an old lady like that."

"You're not old." I set down my bags, opening my arms to hug her.

Having household staff is all I've ever known, so it never seemed weird to me. Ellie feels like family. So does Barry who takes care of the grounds, and Octavia our ... butler of sorts, but she's really just there to keep things running and scheduled.

"Do you see these gray hairs?" She points to the top of her head. "They're from you lot and they say I'm old."

"Sixty isn't old."

"Well," she smiles, "I'll just take the compliment then."

"That's my girl." I wink.

"Oh, you cheeky thing."

"Where is everyone else?"

"I think everyone is in the game room."

I kiss her cheek, grinning when she blushes. "Thanks, El."

The game room is in the basement, outfitted with several pinball machines, a pool table, a putt-putt course, and other games like skee-ball. I set my bag down by the main set of stairs before venturing to the basement.

I find them all—Jonah included—hanging around the air hockey table.

My little sister's face lights up when she sees me. When I'm away, it's easy to ignore the sting of missing my family, but the moment I see them again it's like all those months of being away comes rushing back.

"Jude!" She shrieks my name at a decibel that I'm pretty sure breaks the sound barrier.

Jade launches herself at me. She squeezes me in a death grip as I swing her around.

"I missed you, Jadie." I finally set her down, looking her over. It's only been a few months, but I swear she looks older. Even though we've Facetimed it hasn't been the same as seeing her in person.

"I missed you, too. How was the drive? Jonah's being tight-lipped." She eyes our brother with a shrewd gaze.

"It was quiet," I reply.

"Huh," she mutters, looking between us. "Interesting."

My mom gently coaxes Jade to step aside. "My turn to hug my first-born."

"Hey, Mom." I can't help but grin at my mom. She's a kind, fierce, badass that has handled running a company as well as raising kids, flawlessly. Not many could do the same.

She hugs me an extra-long time, like if she doesn't let go it means I won't leave.

Our break for the holiday is short, only a few days before we'll head back to campus this weekend.

"I swear you grow another inch every time I see you."

"Mom," I groan, trying not to laugh, "no I don't. I'm pretty sure I stopped growing a few years ago."

"Whatever you say." She lets me go and my dad takes her place.

"Missed you, son."

"I missed you too, Dad. It's good to be home."

And it really is. Don't get me wrong, I like being away at school and having my own life, but my family will always be important to me.

Dad looks at his watch. "Ellie should have dinner ready now, so let's head up."

Nobody protests, so I think it's safe to say we're all starving.

Dinner is its normal affair, except for the tension

between Jonah and me. Even our parents comment on it, to which we both give grudging grumbles of an explanation.

I fucking hate this—Jonah being mad at me.

I know I need to talk to him, force him to listen in a way he hasn't yet, because I don't want to return to school with my brother still hating me.

Even if I deserve it.

JONAH'S ROOM is right across the hall from mine. I wait, until I know everyone else has gone to bed, and that he's still up playing video games before I knock on his door. I don't bother waiting for a response.

Swinging the door open, he's reclined in a beanbag chair with a headset on and all his focus on the game.

I stand in front of the TV, and he curses.

"What the fuck? Move, dude." He sways back and forth, trying to see the screen behind me.

"We need to talk."

"I'm busy."

I shake my head, crossing my arms over my chest. "I've spent too much of my life ignoring shit—I'm not doing that anymore. Turn the game off."

He glares at me, but after a moment sighs and removes the headset, turning the game off.

Standing, since he clearly doesn't like me towering over him, he mimics my position with his arms over his chest.

"You can believe me or not," I begin, letting my arms drop so I don't look so defensive. "But if I'd known Millie was the girl you liked I would've never…" I shake my head. "You know what, I can't say for sure what I would've done, but I love her, okay? She's … she's this beautiful light that makes everything around her glow and I just want to be close to her. She makes me smile and laugh and when I hold her, I feel like I'm home." I let out a breath, not having expected to say all that.

Jonah blinks at me in surprise. "You love her?"

"I do. I really fucking do."

"You never said that to me before." He looks away, working his jaw back and forth. "Listen, it fucking hurt, okay? I thought—"

"I know what you thought." The fact that my own brother thinks I'd purposely go after the girl he liked, fucking sucks, but I guess I shouldn't be surprised with my reputation.

"Yeah, well." He runs his fingers through his hair. "I'm upset, but I'm okay. I mean, I went on one date with her, and she was up front that she was interested in someone else. I just didn't know it was you."

I sigh, looking away. "Yeah, me."

Jonah sighs, rubbing his jaw. "I shouldn't have gotten so mad at you, but finding out like I did sucks. In hindsight, I know you didn't have a way of knowing she was the girl. I'm sorry for being shitty to you."

"I'm sorry, too."

He chuckles, smiling. "Can we just agree we're both sorry and move on?"

"That's what I want."

He picks up the headset but hesitates. "You guys aren't together, right? Is it because of me?"

I shake my head. "No, we're not. Her brother—"

"What's worth losing the girl you love, Jude? Even I have to acknowledge that the way you looked at her that night says everything."

"Cree's my friend, but he's never going to think I'm good enough for his sister. And I think I'm okay with that now, because what I feel for her is worth him hating me, but I don't know if she'll take me back."

Jonah presses a hand to my shoulder. "If she feels anywhere near what you feel for her, she'll understand."

I shake my head. "I hope so."

FRIDAY, the day after Thanksgiving, I send a text I should have a long time ago.

Me: Are you at home for the holiday or with Keaton's family?

Macy replies back faster than I expected.

Macy: I'm at my parents.

I stare at her text, swallowing past the lump in my throat. Do I really want to do this? I need to, even if I don't want to. I know now I'm over Macy, but we never got proper closure, at least I didn't.

Me: Could we get together today? Lunch, maybe? I just want to talk.

Her text is slower this time, and I hold my breath waiting.

Macy: Yeah, we can do that. Just send me the time and place.

I tell her to meet me at a local café at noon. I'm nervous to see her again in this capacity, but I know it's what I need to do. I've been ignoring our past for so long instead of moving on from it. If I want this thing with Millie to work, and I do, then I need to put my demons behind me.

I ARRIVE at the café early, order a drink, and grab a table that's in sight of the door.

When I spot Macy walking toward the shop from the parking lot, I feel no sense of longing, or hate, but I do feel confusion.

She enters, smiling at the girl behind the counter. I lift my hand in a wave. She points that she's going to order first, mouthing that she'll be right there.

I wait, practically holding my breath until she slides into the seat across from me with some kind of green-colored drink.

"Hi," she says softly, hanging her purse on the side of her chair. "I was really surprised you wanted to meet."

I sigh, looking out the window to my right. "Yeah, me too."

She tucks a strand of hair behind her ear, watching me curiously. "Are you going to tell me why?"

"Did Keaton tell you he kidnapped me and took me to dinner?"

She laughs, stirring her drink. "Yes." She takes a sip, still eyeing me in a way that says she's amused and slightly baffled. "We don't have secrets."

I rub my jaw, stalling for time as I sort through my chaotic thoughts. "I want you to know I'm over you." I don't want her thinking I asked to meet up out of some weird desire to try to win her back. "But I just ... I guess I need the closure I never got. I was too pissed and hurt at the time to talk shit out with you."

She scoots back, crossing her legs. "I figured that's why you texted me. It's been a long time, Jude, but sometimes it also feels like just yesterday."

I nod, memories flashing through my mind of us as teens. "There's this girl, and I've fallen hard for her, but I realize now that when we broke up I just ... I don't know why, but I think it made me feel like I wasn't good enough and I've let that mindset plague me and my choices."

She sighs sadly. "I've hated seeing you go down the path you did. I've felt guilty for it too. Keaton tells me I'm not responsible for your actions, but indirectly, I am." She gives a small shrug.

"Don't feel guilty. There's a time I would've wanted you to." I hate admitting that, but it's true. For too long I haven't wanted to accept responsibility for my own actions. "Not anymore though."

She sips her drink, watching me with a small smile. "So, what changed?"

"I met someone, and she changed how I see things. I didn't realize it at first. Not until I fucked things up." I shake my head, angry at my own stupidity. Cree and anyone else be damned—I shouldn't have let fear of their opinions sway me from the girl I love. I'm worthy of her regardless of what anyone else thinks. "She opened my eyes to the fact that I've let the past dictate my future. That's why I wanted to see you. I wanted to say that I'm sorry."

She shakes her head. "You don't have to apologize, Jude. You have nothing to be sorry for. We both ... we were young and in love and stupid and reckless and—" She lets out a sigh. "Sorry, that was a lot of 'ands'. I should've told you how I was feeling. You were all I knew and when we got to college, I..."

"There was a whole world outside of me?" I offer and she nods weakly.

"I never cheated on you, I promise. I know you believed I did, but that's not what happened."

"I know." She looks surprised, so I elaborate. "I think I

convinced myself you did, because it was easier to deal with that—easier to blame you for everything."

She laughs softly, tracing a whorl in the table. "You hated me."

"I did," I confirm.

"But not anymore?"

I shake my head. "No. I do ... I want to know, the baby ... would it have been so bad to have a baby with me?"

She smiles sadly. "No, God no, Jude. It wasn't about *you*. I know you would've stepped up to the plate, married me in a heartbeat—"

"I would have," I confirm.

"*I* wasn't ready to be a mom. We were both so young, and I ... I wanted a *life*. I didn't want to be a parent yet, someone else's caregiver when I still felt like a kid myself. I couldn't do it and I don't regret it. I wouldn't have been a good mom back then, I just wouldn't have, and a child is a life-long commitment. It wouldn't have been fair. And all of that, it just reaffirmed thoughts I'd already been having of feeling trapped. Not that you ever made me feel trapped," she rushes to add, "but that we'd been together for so long that more often than not we felt like one person rather than individuals. I thought I'd be single for a while, but when I met Keaton it was like—"

"When you know, you know?"

"Exactly. Is that how it was for you with...?" She trails off, waiting for me to fill in the blank.

"Millie," I supply. "And yeah, it was. I didn't even realize it at first, but I should have."

"She's the girl who was waiting for you after the away game, right?" I nod, feeling choked up, because I fucking miss her so much. Even when we're under the same roof I miss her. I hope to God I can make things right when I get back to campus. "She's beautiful."

"She is. Congratulations, by the way." I nod at the engagement ring on her finger.

She lights up with happiness and excitement. "Thank you. And ... I'm glad we did this. Talked. It was long overdue."

"It was," I agree. "Thanks for coming." God knows Macy probably should've said no. I haven't been outright mean to her, but I've sent enough glares her way to probably make her hate me.

"Always." She reaches across the table and squeezes my hand. "Be happy, Jude. It's all I want for you. You deserve it."

I nod at her in thanks, words failing me.

With one last small smile, she releases my hand and grabs her drink as she stands. "I'll see you around, Jude."

I watch her go and when she's gone from my sight, I let my eyes close.

All I feel is peace.

thirty-seven

Millie

I THOUGHT I'D DREAD GETTING BACK TO CAMPUS and the house we all share after the holiday break, but I'm more than glad to get some space from my head-over-heels-in-love brother. Of course, we still live under the same roof, but Ophelia doesn't, which means he'll be out more. Since she came with us for Thanksgiving, it's been impossible to ignore the two lovebirds since they made up not too long ago.

They're in the honeymoon stage, rightfully so, while I'm

heartbroken and don't want to be around them. It's no fault of their own, but they're so happy and in love and I'm...hurting.

Cree parks his Bronco in the driveway after dropping off Ophelia at her dorm.

"What's up with you?" he asks before I can reach for the door.

"Nothing," I snap, a dead giveaway that there's definitely something going on.

His expression softens, growing contemplative. "Mills, you can talk to me, you know?"

I hesitate, because no, I can't talk to him. Not about this. What's the point? He's already inadvertently ended my relationship.

"I know," I say softly instead of all of that.

He looks like he wants to say more on the matter but doesn't.

I take the opportunity to slip out of the car, grabbing my bag from the back. Jude's truck isn't back yet, which I'm thankful for. After a few days away from him, I'm afraid I'm so weak that I'll swoon at his feet the moment I see him.

Trudging inside and up the stairs, I set my bag onto my bed. Normally I would put off unpacking, but right now I want the distraction. I didn't take much with me since we were only back home a few days and I had most everything I would need there anyway.

I hear Cree moving about in his room.

Daire moved out a week before Thanksgiving break to

live with his wife. I'm biting my tongue for now, but I'm super curious as to how that is going to turn out. Those two seem to hate each other. The whole thing is so weird to me, but it's not my business so I'm not going to pry.

Down below, I hear the garage door go up and I freeze. Since I still hear Cree in his room, that means Jude's here.

My heart begins to beat harder and faster.

I hate that I ache in desperation to see him. I want my feelings to go away, but that's not how it works. I didn't fall for him in one moment, so I can't expect it to go away in one either.

Heavy footsteps carry up the stairs and then he's in his room, mere feet away from me.

I close my eyes, fisting my hands at my sides in an effort to keep from running to him through the connecting bathroom.

But I don't have to, because when I open my eyes, he's there. He stands in the doorway, hands in his jean's pockets, a navy long-sleeve shirt clinging to him like a second skin with the sleeves rolled up his corded forearms. My eyes scan him from head to toe, like it's been a year since I've seen him and not days. His favorite boots are on his feet, his hair messy and adorable, the scruff on his cheeks heavier than normal. His eyes smile at me.

"Hey, Little Madison."

I wet my lips, inhaling a breath that I blow out long and slow. "Jude."

He takes a few steps closer, raising his hand. He hesitates, waiting for my reaction. When he can tell I'm not going to move away, he presses his palm to my cheek. I can't help myself when I sigh and lean into his touch. His hand is warm and calloused, absolutely perfect.

"Millie, I—" he begins, wincing like he's struggling for words, for the right thing to say. "I missed you."

I sigh heavily. As much as I love hearing that he missed me, those three words don't fix us, if he even wants that.

"What are you doing, Jude?" I take a step back and he lets his hand fall to his side, fingers flexing.

He rolls his tongue against his cheek. "I've been doing a lot of thinking lately, and soul-searching. Making up with my brother, with myself, honestly." He laughs humorlessly, shoving his fingers through his hair. I don't miss the slight tremble to them. The great Jude Cartwright is *nervous*. That should make me deliriously happy, but it doesn't for some reason. "I met up with Macy while I was back home."

My eyes widen with surprise. That was the last thing I expected him to say or even do. I've long thought he needs closure with her, but I figured he would never take the steps toward getting it.

"You did?"

He nods. "We met up for coffee and talked ... it was good. It's what I needed, to understand things and not feel undeserving."

My brows furrow and I take a step closer to him. It's an unconscious move on my part, the need to be near him is overwhelming. I place a gentle hand on his chest, reminding him that I'm here and he can say whatever he needs to.

"Undeserving? Of what?"

"Of love," he admits, a muscle in his jaw twitching with nerves. "Of a relationship, a future that includes a wife and kids. I started to realize that I had convinced myself that Macy ended things because I wasn't good enough. I understand now that's not the case. I'm not perfect, Millie. Not by a long shot." He cups my cheek again, his thumb moving in small circles. "And your brother definitely won't think I'm good enough for you, not now, not ever. But I'm not afraid of that anymore, because I don't give a flying fuck what he thinks. It's you, you're the one who matters, what you think of me matters." His forehead presses to mine, our lips close enough that we share the same oxygen. "I love you, Millie. I know I fucked things up with you, and I guess I'm asking for the chance at forgiveness. I'm not perfect and I'm going to mess up a lot, but this thing with you? It's the real deal and I don't want to walk away again."

My breath is held captive in my lungs. This is exactly what I've wanted to hear from him for *weeks*. Honestly, what he's said is better than anything I could have dreamed up. But...

"You hurt me. You broke my heart." My lips tremble with the threat of tears. "That pain isn't going to go away in the blink of an eye, just because you changed your mind."

He nods, his Adam's apple bobbing. "I know, and I swear to you, that I'm going to work at this—at us—to make it right, even if it takes me every day of the rest of our lives. I'll do it."

I don't know who moves first, but his lips are on mine and it's like my body is melting into his.

"Hey, Mills—"

It's like it happens in slow motion, the knock and my door opening. Jude and I jolt apart in surprise at the intrusion.

Whatever Cree's holding falls to the floor, his mouth dropping open in surprise.

"What. The. Fuck." His eyes dart back and forth between us, his brain taking the time to process what's in front of his very own eyes. "No," he says, slashing his hands through the air. "No. No. No. No. *No*." His pointer finger swishes between the two of us with each iteration of that single word, like if he says it enough, he can make the decree stick.

Jude takes a step toward my brother, hands raised in surrender. "Cree, just listen, man. Your sister and I—" The punch happens so fast that Jude doesn't see it coming. I gasp, my hands flying to my face when Cree's fist connects with Jude's face. Jude stumbles back, almost falling but manages to right himself. "I deserved that."

"No, you didn't," I defend, stepping between him and my brother that's ready to Hulk-out. I've never seen him so worked up that there were literal veins bulging in his neck, but I guess there's a first time for anything. "Cree." I try to block my brother with my body when he tries to get by me for Jude. "Stop." I shove his shoulders, but his eyes are still locked on Jude. "Can you listen for five-seconds?"

Cree glares at me. "What the fuck is this? You're ... you two are...?"

Jude steps in front of me, but I'm not having that, so I move beside him and take his hand. "We're working things out."

"Working things out? What the fuck does that even mean? Did you hurt my sister? I swear to God if you did something to her, I'll fuck you up."

"Cree!" I scream, horrified at my brother. "Jesus, where is your head at?"

"Where is yours?" He yells, his face red. "You're what? Screwing this fuck-up?" Out of the corner of my eye it's impossible not to miss the way Jude flinches at that comment. "Who are you, Millicent? This guy is the completely wrong one for you."

"How would you fucking know?" I shout back at him. If he thinks I'm going to roll over and give into his dickish behavior, he's got another thing coming for him. "He's your so-called friend, but do you even really know him? Have you ever bothered to try to see beyond the surface?" The way his jaw ticks, I know he hasn't. I laugh humorlessly. "You're my brother, and I love you, but for some fucking reason you tend to think you're better than everyone else. Newsflash, you're not. Like everyone else, you make mistakes, and you're not perfect. You're simply human like the rest of us. And you certainly have no right to judge me, or try to tell me who I can and cannot love."

It's silent for a long moment, save for the sound of my brother's deep breaths.

Jude's the one who breaks the silence. "I love your sister, and I know that's hard for you to believe, because the guy you know doesn't really love anyone, not even himself. I never meant to fall for her, and I stupidly broke things off with her because of this," he sways a hand at Cree, "because I knew how you'd react and that it would hurt her, because you're her brother and she loves you. I know I'm not good enough for her, and I don't expect you to accept this overnight, but I broke us both when I ended things, and I won't make that same mistake again, because Millie is the best thing that has *ever* happened to me. I'll be damned if I let you stand in the way of that."

Hands on his hips, Cree looks down at the ground, forming his thoughts. When he lifts his gaze, it's me he zeroes in on. I stiffen, preparing myself for a scathing remark.

"He treats you right?" I nod. "He's never forced you to do anything?"

"God, no."

"He takes care of you?"

I look up at Jude with a soft smile. "Yes."

"He loves you?" I nod, tears burning my eyes. "You love him?"

"Yes."

Cree nods to himself. "I … I can't say I'm *happy* about this, but I guess I'll get there. But remember," he speaks to Jude, "actions speak louder than words. You want me to support you guys, then you have to prove to me that she's different." Cree meets my eyes, and he looks like he might cry too. It has to be hard as an older brother, the boy who's always looked out and taken care of me, to accept that I'm not that little girl anymore who needs his protection. I'm a smart, strong, independent woman who makes her own choices. "I'm sorry, Millie. For this—my behavior. It's just…" He tugs at his hair. "I've always taken care of you and that's not my place anymore."

"I'll always need you," I tell him, because it's true. "You're my big brother."

He cracks a smile. "I love you, Mills. I want you to be happy."

"I am," I promise him. My heart isn't fully healed, it's going to take time for that, and for me to fully regain trust in Jude after he ended things, but I feel better now than I have in weeks and I think that's a start.

Cree nods and slips out of my room, closing my door behind him.

We don't always choose who we fall in love with.

Sometimes it happens in an instant. Sometimes it takes time. Sometimes it's with someone from the wrong side of the tracks, or it's with the person who's always been right there.

Jude kisses me, and as my eyes close, sinking into his kiss, I think about how sometimes you fall for your brother's friend, the guy who's all wrong on paper, but is perfectly right in your heart.

thirty-eight

Jude

It's been a week since Millie and I reconciled. I don't think I've been able to wipe the ridiculous smile off my face since. I'm not the least bit ashamed either. My love for this girl isn't something I want to hide. I want the whole world to know that I'm taken.

I open the passenger door of my truck and offer Millie my hand to help her out. She's in a tight-fitting pair of jeans, some kind of flannel shirt that she's tied up to expose her bellybutton, and a pair of cowboy boots on her feet.

It's safe to say she's ready for Harvey's.

This is sort of our official coming out, so to speak. Not that people haven't already been talking on campus since I try to meet up with her whenever I can throughout the day.

"Is my lipstick, okay?" She pouts her lips at me to check for any smearing since I kissed her as soon as she got her sweet ass in my truck. I had to scrub my own mouth free of the red color with a tissue. She looks damn hot in that color lipstick though, so I don't mind if she smears it all over me.

"You're gorgeous."

She rolls her eyes playfully at me. "I know that, but my lipstick isn't still smeared is it?"

"You got it fixed, babe."

Someone nearby gags. "You guys are fucking gross."

Cree.

I'll give the guy credit, he's been handling this impossibly well. He didn't even bitch at us earlier this week when he found us making out in the kitchen like two teenagers.

Millie sticks her tongue out at her brother. "Like you and Ophelia aren't equally as gross."

Ophelia giggles, wrapping her arm around Cree's bicep. "She's right."

Cree grumbles something, the two of them heading into Harvey's ahead of us.

"Are you sure about this?" I ask Millie as we follow behind the other two.

Her brows furrow in confusion. "About what?"

"Me," I tease.

"I think the better question is, are you sure about me?"

She bats her eyes up at me in a playful gesture, but I see the genuine worry in her gaze.

I tug on her hand, urging her to stop moving. Her brother and Ophelia head inside, leaving us alone—well as alone as you can be in a busy bar's parking lot. People are watching us, nosy fucks, but I ignore it.

"Millie, baby, I'm more certain about you than I've ever been of anything in my entire life."

She doesn't ask if I'm being serious, she knows I am. "I love you."

"I love you too, Little Madison." Since I know she'll fuss at me if I kiss her, I press one on her cheek as close as I can get to her lips. "Let's go. Everyone's already inside."

I wrap an arm around Millie's waist, keeping her snug against my body inside Harvey's since the place is crowded.

"Where are we going?" she asks as I navigate us through the crowd.

"To our table. The guys always grab this big one in the back."

When we approach the table, I blurt out, "No one told me you guys were coming."

Teddy and Vanessa are both here, but so is Mascen with Rory, and even Cole who I haven't seen since he graduated last spring. Cole sits with his girlfriend Zoey who's still attending Aldridge.

Teddy grins, putting his arm around Vanessa as Millie and I slide into the massive booth. "Cree invited us. Said there was just something we had to see if we could make the trip. I must say, I'm not surprised." He raises his eyebrows at us.

Cree's jaw drops and he glares at Teddy. "You knew and you didn't tell me?"

Teddy rolls his eyes, picking up a bottle of his favorite beer; Zombie Dust. "It's not my fault you're an idiot who can't see the signs when they're right in front of him. I don't know what you want me to do about it, dude."

Mascen shakes his head, whispering something in Rory's ear that makes her smile.

Cole reaches out a fist for me to bump mine. "I'm happy for you, dude. It's about time you settled down. It's nice to meet you, Millie. I'm Cole." He holds a hand out to her and I can tell she's instantly mesmerized by the guy.

"Hey, remember, you love me," I joke, giving her a light tap with my elbow.

She laughs, taking Cole's hand. "Sorry. It's nice to meet you, too."

"Look at us," Teddy spreads his arms wide, nearly whacking Vanessa in the head to which she glares at him, "who would've thought we'd be all coupled up. I wonder who the next sucker is?"

I raise a brow, pointing at the dancefloor. "We don't have to look far."

Everyone follows my finger to where Daire and Rosie are on the dancefloor. They're pressed tightly together, moving to the music, but it's obvious they're arguing about something.

Daire says something and Rosie looks like she might slap him, but instead pulls sharply away from him and storms off. He throws his hands up and follows after her.

Teddy throws his head back and starts laughing. "Oh, this is going to be fun. Someone get popcorn."

"Does anyone know why they got married?" Cole voices the question, so someone has been filling him in on all the Aldridge drama he's missed.

"I'm assuming it's to do with the kid." Mascen picks up his bottle of beer, taking a swig. "That's the only thing that makes sense."

Teddy points a finger in warning at me and Cree. "You fuckers better keep me updated in the group chat. I want to know all the drama."

Cree and I exchange a look, both shaking our heads. "Sure, man," Cree agrees, knowing that neither of us will.

"Good." Teddy's satisfied, for now at least.

Grabbing Millie's hand, I whisper in her ear, "What do you say, Little Madison? Why don't we show these losers a little something on the dancefloor?"

She grins, brightening. "Are you going to bust out some of those signature ballet moves on me?"

I groan, hurriedly tugging her away from the table just as Teddy says, "Jude knows ballet? Why did no one update me in the group chat? That's what it's there for!"

Millie's smile is wicked when we make it onto the dancefloor. "You know I'm never going to live that down with them now, don't you?"

She stands on her tiptoes to reach me better, tapping her finger against my nose. "That's the point."

"You're evil, babe. Pure evil."

"But you love me."

I smile down at this beautiful, tenacious girl, who stole my heart before I even realized she had. The little thief. "I do."

Lipstick be damned, I kiss her, smiling against her mouth when cheers break out. I know it's from our rowdy group of friends, so I give them the finger, and go on kissing my girl.

If there's one thing I've learned, it's that I'm not going to let anyone else's opinion stand in the way of what I want, and this girl? She's the only thing I need.

epilogue

Millie—Springtime

THE END OF MY FRESHMAN YEAR OF COLLEGE IS FAST approaching, only weeks away. It's like I blinked, and this school year blew right by me.

I've done a lot of growing in this time, learning so much about myself and what I want in the future.

And Jude?

He's done the most growing of anyone I want to know. He's still himself, but somehow better. Moving on from his past has made him a happier, more carefree person.

Even though my brother was angry at first, and doubted

Jude's intentions, they've moved past it and are closer than ever. Both will be graduating in a few weeks. Next year will look a lot different without them under the same roof. Zara will be moving in with me, which means there are still two more rooms to fill, and I have no idea who's going to use them yet. That's a problem for future Millie to figure out.

As for Jude, he's planning to stay in the area while he figures out his next steps for his future. I'm glad he won't be going far, but I'll support him even if his dreams take him away from me for a time. That's what you do for the person you love, it's not a sacrifice so much as it is having care and respect for the other person. It's kind of a good reminder to me, that no matter what your age or where you are with life, you don't have to know the next steps. Sometimes, you have to take it a day at a time and see where it leads you.

It's almost showtime for my little ballet kiddos for their spring showcase. They've been working hard for this recital, and I'm so proud of them. I love teaching ballet, and still getting to dance while not having the pressure to perform.

Peeking behind the curtain I spot, my brother and Ophelia, my parents, Daire and Rosie, and of course, Jude. I wave at them all, smiling with nerves and excitement. They wave back, but Jude tacks on a wink, mouthing, "Good luck."

I give him a thumb's up. Disappearing back behind the curtain, I face my first group of kids.

"All right, guys, gather in." I motion for them to come closer. "I want you to go out there and give it your all, but most importantly, have fun." One of the youngest raises her hand. "Yes, Nora?"

"Um, Miss Millie, what do we do if we're really nervous and forget the dance?"

I place my hands gently on her arms. "Then you wing it. All I care about is that you have fun."

She nods, satisfied with this answer. "Okay."

They take their places on the stage and I hold my breath as they begin. I don't care about perfection, I just want them to enjoy themselves and keep loving to dance.

Aleksander steps up beside me, his arm brushing mine. "You're good with them, Millie."

I smile up at him. "Thank you."

His hands are in the pockets of his slacks. "I do hope you'll return to the studio in the fall after your summer break. We want you back."

My smile grows. "You do?"

"You have a real talent for teaching and the children love you, of course we want you to come back."

"Thank you!" I hug him, taking us both by surprise. He chuckles, letting me go. "I'll absolutely be back."

"Good, good." He peers at the crowd, well what we can see of it from our tucked away corner. "And do tell that boyfriend of yours that he has nothing to worry about. I'm far more likely to be interested in *him* than you."

He eyes Jude in the front of the crowd where he glares at Aleksander.

"Oh," I laugh, shaking my head. "I ... um ... yeah, I'll tell him."

Aleksander chuckles as well, patting my shoulder. "Our little studio is lucky you walked in that day."

"I'm the lucky one."

I mean it too. This year has been full of blessings. I never expected Aldridge to feel so much like home, but I've made a family here between my friends like Zara and Jonah —who I swear have some kind of insane chemistry and won't be surprised if something happens there—and Jude too. A lot of people don't find the love of their life at our age, but I'm glad we did. I have the rest of my days to love him.

When the recital is over, and after I've received bouquets of flowers from my parents and brother, I finally walk out of the building hand in hand with Jude.

"It's raining," he remarks before opening the door, "I brought my truck around."

I bite my lip with excitement. "I love the rain."

He grins, brown eyes bright with happiness. "I know, baby."

We make a mad dash for his truck, but it doesn't matter, we're both pretty wet by the time we clamber into the truck.

"Want to go home?" He cranks the engine.

I shake my head, smoothing damp hair back from my face. "Not yet. Let's go for a drive."

Jude obliges. Like always, there's no destination, just the way I like it. I shuffle my playlist and watch him, the way he drives one-handed, his body relaxed. He's no longer running from his past, from himself.

We've been driving around twenty minutes when he pulls off the road. There are no other cars around, just us and the farms on either side of the road.

"What are you doing?"

He unbuckles his seatbelt, leaning over to me. "Get out."

"What?" I ask, flabbergasted. "Jude, I—"

"Get out and dance in the rain with me."

I stare at him open-mouthed, and then I smile. "You're going to dance with me in the rain?"

He chuckles. "Don't tell anyone. I've got to keep my street cred, but yeah, I want to dance with my girl in the rain."

I scramble out of the truck, meeting him in the front. Before I got out, he turned up the music and cracked the windows. The song that was playing ends, and as he takes me in his arms '18' by One Direction begins to play.

It's perfect.

I might be nineteen now, but I was still eighteen when I fell for him.

We dance in the rain, glowing from the headlights of his truck. It only takes a minute for us to be completely soaked, but I don't care.

He spins me around, my laughter mingling with the sound of rain hitting the pavement, and then pulls me into his arms. My left-hand settles against his chest, his heart-beat pounding a rhythm against my hand.

I blink water from my lashes. My makeup is no doubt smeared over my face, but I don't care, because with the way he's looking at me I can't feel anything but beautiful.

"Thank you, Little Madison," he murmurs.

I look at him in confusion. He rubs rain from my face, but it's a pointless, albeit sweet, gesture since the rain hasn't let up yet. "What are you thanking me for?"

"For loving me and all my storms."

I stroke his cheek gently. "That's not something you ever have to thank me for."

Lowering his head, his lips close over mine as we continue to sway to the song.

Jude thinks he's hard to love, but the truth is, loving him is like breathing. It's instinctual.

Thunder booms and we jump apart as lightning brightens the sky. Running back to the truck, we dive inside, and he cranks up the heat before he pulls back onto the road.

It feels symbolic somehow, like we're driving straight toward our future. I know, without a doubt, our life together is going to be beautiful, and we'll continue to dance through the storms.

UP NEXT IN THE BOYS SERIES

RULE BREAKERS FALL HARDEST (DAIRE AND ROSIE'S STORY)

Once upon a time, Daire Hendricks was my childhood crush. He was always there, saving me from his annoying brothers. He was my rock, my safe place from my overbearing family.

Until he wasn't.

Imagine my annoyance when we end up at the same university and I have to see his smug, too-handsome-for-his-own-good face all over campus.

Every time we cross paths, we spew hateful words at each other, so imagine my surprise when he seeks me out and utters the most surprising question.

"Marry me?"

He needs my help, and his solution is marriage. It's a pretty big ask, but somehow, I find myself saying yes. We might hate each other now, but the benefits of this arrangement are worth it.

But what neither of us expects, is when playing house starts to feel a little too real.

Falling for each other was never part of the plan, but you know what they say about the best laid plans?

They often go awry.

acknowledgments

We've come to the end of yet another book and I'm having trouble wrapping my head around the fact that this is the third book I've written this year. I also can't believe this is book five in The Boys Series. Wow. I originally thought this series would be two, maybe three, books max but here we are and I don't have any plans to stop any time soon. I can't thank you all enough for loving this series as much as I do. It brings me so much happiness to know that this series is as much a happy place for you all as it is for me.

A big thank you goes out to Emily Wittig, for not only being one of my best friends (I mean, basically family at this point if we're being real) but for creating three perfect book covers for this one book. Emily, you continue to astound me not only with your talent but with the kind of person you are. I'm so lucky to have you in my life, and I know I'm a better person for knowing you.

My sweet doggies who never leave my side, Ollie and Remy, no book is complete without you two keeping me company. Whether it's dragging your cushion over beside me, or lying at my feet, you're both always there. All I ever wanted growing up was a dog and now I have two of the best.

To my family for your endless love and support. Thanks for dealing with my craziness. I can't believe it's been a decade since I started this crazy venture and that it's ended up here. Thank you for believing me, especially in the moments where I didn't believe in myself.